BRAKE CHECK

GITTE TAMAR
BTW LLC

BTW LLC

Copyright © 2024 by Gitte Tamar

All rights reserved.

No part of this publication may be reproduced, distributed, or transmitted in any form or by any means, including photocopying, recording, or other electronic or mechanical methods, without the prior written permission of the publisher, except as permitted by U.S. copyright law. For permission requests, contact BTW LLC.

ISBN 978-1-958201-33-6 (paperback)

ISBN 978-1-958201-31-2 (hardback)

ISBN 978-1-958201-30-5 (ebook)

The story, all names, characters, and incidents portrayed in this production are fictitious. No identification with actual persons (living or deceased), places, buildings, and products is intended or should be inferred.

Book Cover by BTW LLC

To those obsessed with money and fame.

※

Remember,

The public, whom you allow to dictate your breath,
will be the last of your worries when you're facing death.

※

Haunted by choices driven by ego and fear,
what people think and how you appear.

※

It is a sad way to be when your soul is not free,
when you cast aside love and joy so frivolously.

Hello to all,

Thank you to every last of you, whether your part was big or small.

Thank you to each of my family and friends; you already know who you are, so I will refrain from listing each of your specific names. Just know I will forever be thankful for each of you who gave me never-ending love and emotional support.

Thank you to all my readers for continuing this journey with me. I am forever indebted to you.

Sincerely,

WARNING: This story includes situations of violence, gore, death, abuse, suicidal thoughts, suicide, implied assault, and swear or curse words.

Contents

1. ON THE RUN　　　　　　　　　3
2. IN A RUT　　　　　　　　　　13
3. DON'T TOUCH HIM　　　　　　21
4. CAN I HELP YOU?　　　　　　27
5. THE MORNING AFTER　　　　　41
6. FAME　　　　　　　　　　　　51
7. UNDER MY SKIN　　　　　　　65
8. DEVILISH GAMES　　　　　　　81
9. SOME NEVER LEAVE　　　　　　93
10. MENTAL GAMES　　　　　　　103
11. RACE DAY　　　　　　　　　119
12. MELTING　　　　　　　　　　137
13. ARE YOU A WINNER?　　　　　151
14. MATERIAL WORLD　　　　　　171

15.	GAS FUMES	185
16.	DON'T TELL	197
17.	BEAUTIFUL DAY FOR A FUNERAL	211
18.	THINK FAST	219
19.	BURIED SECRETS	227
20.	LEFT BEHIND	243
21.	NO SLEEP	263
22.	GET WELL SOON	271
23.	PULL THE TRIGGER	281
24.	DON'T SPILL	293
25.	DON'T DREAM	301
26.	WINNER'S PARADISE	309
27.	SMILE, CAMERA, DELUSION	321
28.	NO TIME	329
29.	WHERE THE DEVIL HIDES	341
30.	TAKE A SPIN	349
	ABOUT AUTHOR	359

1

ON THE RUN

1972, North Carolina

Beyond the therapeutic noise of chirping crickets, a subtle vibration lingers; it's coming from a grouping of tiny hummingbirds' wings. They are flying home for the night to take their rest. Fluttering to a stop, they land on the main power line of the small town of Dillweed, which leads to a trailer park community.

As the tiny birds' beady eyes shut, a faint sound of plucking strings floats through the heavy, humid air. The tune has a hint of both folk and rock.

Each bird relaxes, puffing out their feathered chests as they drift to sleep; something about the atmosphere of the aluminum-sided housing community soothes them.

Like them, everything else is winding down for the evening, including the sky above, where the sun has already begun to set. Amid the two long rows of single-wide mobile homes, various shades of warm lighting accent the overgrown patches of lawn that surround the metal kick-out steps leading to each home's front door.

The community is fashioned from a broad array of trailers, from Thomson Caravans and Streamlines to campers and Airstreams. The retro ambiance and neglected landscape don't reflect the pristine image of a traditional neighborhood found in magazines; every structure appears as if it has been around for decades.

Inside the trailer park called the Last Stop, there is no vacancy. But don't let that fool you. The fully booked status in the small community doesn't imply tenant loyalty. When most people rent a space, they intend to stay just long enough to get back on their feet.

One can estimate how long the resident has lived there by observing the number of windmill decorations, strings of lights, lawn gnomes, and wind chimes hanging from their home's gutters. Some trailers are adorned with strands of partially burned-out Christmas lights left up from the first holiday season of their stay. In contrast, others display weathered jelly chairs discolored by the buildup of tanning lotion, their once-vibrant hues now faded after years of basking in the summer sun.

One home, only a few houses into the lineup, is encircled by a large assortment of dilapidated birthday signs poking up from the ground on wooden stakes. It is clear by the themes and printed ages they span years of birthdays. The remnants of disintegrating streamers and deflated balloons barely hang on to the sides of the home with the flaking adhesive tape. The weather-worn signs cluster the front like an unkempt bulletin board.

That is where the country music is blaring. A worn-out radio inside the cramped mobile home produces a static-laden melody that seeps through the brittle seals of the windowsills and emits a muted howl.

Loretta Richardson and her son, Rich, have owned the modest residence for eighteen years.

Shortly after it was discovered that Loretta had been knocked up at sixteen, she was ousted from her family home. She bounced from one dysfunctional situation to another in the small town, crashing on couches until finally settling in the old single-wide with her twenty-two-year-old boyfriend, Rut, the father of her child.

However, like many things at the Last Stop, it didn't last long.

The day it all went downhill is engrained in her head, the imagery still plaguing her mind like it was yesterday.

It was a muggy day in June, just a week before her due date. The sun shone extra brightly. It was at the beginning of summer when flowers were in full bloom and pollen filled the air. Rut had already left for work at the mechanic shop, so Loretta was home alone, like usual.

She started her morning just like the rest. Eager to lie out and perfect her tan, she swiftly pulls on one of the few clothing items that still fit her: a red-and-white gingham bikini. With her hands pressed against her lower back, she fights the ache in her lumbar region as she mills her way to the small kitchen to make a pitcher of lemonade.

In the back of the freezer, an old tin soup can filled with pulp from some salvaged lemons hides behind a stack of metal ice cube trays. She feels a kick in her stomach while reaching in to retrieve it from the chilly compartment. Immediately, a smirk forms on her face. "Why, hello," she says, touching the bulge housing the baby. It kicks once more, stirring within her.

Giggling, she removes the can from the freezer, then happily whistles while making her way to the plastic pitcher on the counter. She grabs its handle and heads to the kitchen sink to fill the container with tap water.

Birds chirp outside a small, fogged half-circle window above the sink. She turns on the faucet and, mid-filling the plastic cylinder, a slight sound catches her attention outside. Thinking she hears a muffled version of Rut's voice, she smiles. "Awe, would you look at that, little Rich? It looks like your daddy came home early to surprise us," she says, peering through the glass.

Her eyes widen. He is lingering near the entrance of the neighbor's home. Then she hears a woman's voice echoing from the head protruding through the partially open front door.

Her eyes immediately shift to their makeshift carport. His beat-up green truck with a dented bed and chipped paint still sits underneath the rusted tin open-sided shelter.

Seeing his car incites a rage within her she's never felt before. She thinks of all the late nights and early mornings he has been away at "work" and wonders how often his car never left the driveway without her noticing. "Patsy ... that little tramp. Oh, I'm going to kill her," she says, gritting her teeth, her skin blazing. Swiftly, she uses her hand to wipe the condensation from the glass, her attention darting back to the smeared image of Rut smiling and conversing with the woman next door.

Since they moved in, Patsy has been their young, single, not-pregnant neighbor, sharing a property line with their humble abode. Sometimes, people refer to the two women as sisters; they look very similar. Both have petite, slender builds with dirty blond shoulder-length hair.

Loretta has had suspicions after noticing subtle glances and playful banter between Rut and Patsy at the spring potluck. She confronted him about it months ago, but he insisted they were only friends.

As she questions everything, a wave of humiliation washes over her, further fueling her rage. Infuriated, her hands trembling with anger, she throws down the pitcher, causing it to crash into the sink and splash water over the countertop.

The can of lemons drops to the floor, and its frozen contents explode across the vinyl tile.

Loretta stands on her toes for a better look and feels a heavy wetness trickle down her thighs. "Shit," she says, glancing at the pool of liquid near her feet. "Shit."

Trying to ignore her broken water, she stubbornly clenches her fists and releases a grunt. "This will not be my memory of you coming into this world."

The two voices gradually go silent.

Loretta feels a contraction and tightens her jaw. Baring her teeth and flooded with determination, she makes her way to the door. Each of her stomping footsteps echoes between the walls of the cramped trailer. As she grabs the door's handle, she senses the wall of her stomach tightening and trudging through the pain; she flings the door open and screams, "Rut, you piece of shit!"

Now standing beside the cab of his truck, he hears his name and nervously turns to face her. "Um ... yes... yes, sweet thing," he says, stammering.

Loretta walks outside onto the aluminum steps, wincing as she clutches her back.

Patsy hurls open her front door, resulting in a loud crash as it collides with the trailer's metal siding. "Is everything okay over there?" she asks, hiding her upper body; she is half-dressed.

Without the time or patience to confront her about what she witnessed; Loretta settles for shooting glares at the local diner waitress's smudged hot-pink lipstick. "Get back inside before I come over there to kick your ass," she yells while doubling over with another contraction.

Patsy scurries back into her house and closes the door behind her.

"That's what I thought!" Loretta moans.

Rut's white tank top is soaked with sweat beneath his Carhart jacket. Letting out a gulp, he glances from Patsy's door to his home. "Jesus Christ, Loretta, what the hell's gotten into you, woman?" Angered, he continues, "She was only trying to be neighborly."

She laughs sarcastically. "What the hell's gotten into me? I'm having your baby, you sack of shit," she says, spitting.

He finally comprehends that she is in labor, and he rushes across the overgrown lawn to help her down the last aluminum step. "You just need to calm yourself down. Whatever you saw wasn't what it looked like," he says, grabbing her arm. "I was just... picking up some cookies she made for you."

In pain, Loretta leans more of her weight into him. "Just take me to the hospital before I have this baby on the lawn," she says.

Ghostly pale and overwhelmed by the unfamiliarity of the situation, as this is his first child, as far as he knows, Rut helps her in the truck and shuts the door.

"The bag! Grab the bag with the baby stuff," she shouts out the window. "Now!" Her moan loudly echoes.

Rut's chestnut-brown hair blows in the wind as he takes off in a dead sprint toward the trailer. Upon entering, in his mad rush to the bedroom, he encounters a treacherous layer of lemon pulp that sends him skidding across the kitchen. Unable to maintain his balance, he tumbles, hitting his head on the counter on the way to the floor.

Loretta breathes deeply to ease her pain. The contractions worsen, becoming closer together, and finding that her method of controlling the ache no longer helps, she loses her patience. Digging her nails into the truck seat's cloth upholstery, she winces as one of her acrylic French tips pops off her finger. "Rut!" she yells.

The scream echoes through the open trailer door and into his unconscious ears. His eyes slowly open, but his vision is hazy. He struggles to find his balance. The room is spinning around him as he rolls to his knees and rises unsteadily to his feet before staggering toward the front door.

Loretta watches him make his way outside empty-handed. "The bag!" she yells.

He stares at her with confusion, his mouth agape.

"Do I have to do everything myself?" she asks as she tightens her grip around the car door's handle, yanks it open, and steps out onto the ground. Upon standing, she feels a heavy pressure press against her pelvic floor and falls back into the truck seat. She knows it is too late.

In the distance, Rut is still trying to orient himself. "What? What did you need?"

Rolling her eyes, Loretta pivots around, braces her back against the truck console, and, slipping off the swim bottoms, pushes. "Come on, Loretta, if you can do this, you can do anything. Remember that. Just get through this. You got to get through this," she wails.

As her screams echo through the park, the tenants emerge from their trailers to see what the commotion is about. A few doors down, an older woman with a head full of giant pink plastic curlers rushes inside to call an ambulance.

Stumbling across the lawn, Rut glances at the row of open doors and, making fists, swings them in front of his body, ready to fight. "What y'all looking at?" he asks. "Huh?"

With one final determined push, Loretta delivers her baby boy. Taking him into her hands, she holds him against her chest and exhales a heavy sigh.

An ambulance siren echoes in the distance.

Unable to take her eyes off the child, Loretta looks into his tiny blue eyes; they match hers. "I will tell you a secret that no one told me: You're meant for something way bigger than this, Rich. Do you hear me? I'm giving you that name because I know you're gonna be somebody someday. You aren't gonna be nothin' like your loser father, and I'll make damn sure of that," she whispers in the newborn's ear.

The tiny baby's nostrils nuzzle into the top of her bikini, instinctually clearing the mucus from his nose. Taking a quick breath, he cries.

Smiling, Loretta hushes him and lightly rubs the bare skin of his back to calm him. "From now on, it's only gonna be me and you. Your mama's love is all you need," she says, tapping his tiny button nose.

With its siren blaring, the ambulance barrels into the trailer park community. Loretta lifts her head and watches it come to a screeching halt in front of their home. "We're over here," she shouts. "In the truck!"

The neighbors watch as the ambulance attendants drape a sheet over her lower half and lift her onto the gurney. They swiftly collect her things, which consist only of her bikini bottoms, and place them in a transparent plastic bag at her feet.

As they place the baby back in her arms, she glances at Rut sprinting toward them. "Is that my baby boy?" he asks, excitement flooding his eyes.

A medic with a thick brown mustache looks at Rut, then shifts his attention back to Loretta and the child. With a hard shove, he continues wheeling them to the vehicle as he leans over the bed to speak to her. "Ma'am, is that the father? Would you like him to ride with you?"

Her eyes stay glued on the newborn's head of brown hair. "No, that man belongs to a cute young waitress at The Crock Pot—the place with the good peach cobbler. She lives right next door," she says, nodding in the other home's direction, "You see? Just over there."

The man's mustache curls as he smiles. "I do love their pies," he says, finishing wheeling the stretcher to the back of the vehicle.

Rut can't figure out why everyone seems to be ignoring him. Still slightly concussed, he scratches his head and plants his feet; he doesn't want to appear weak. As he watches them load the mother and baby into the ambulance, he smiles to cover his confusion and shouts to cheer them on. "I'll just wait for you right here," he says, pointing over his shoulder toward their house.

"Rich Richardson," Loretta says, "with my last name, you'll have the name of a star and one day, we will live in Charlotte."

2

IN A RUT

Loretta is sure things will take a turn for the better after that day, but fate seems to have another plan for her.

The longer she lies in the hospital bed with her child, contemplating their future, the more she tries to delay her discharge. Once she denied Rut as the father, her decision became fixed in her eyes. She dreads what awaits her back home and the confrontation that may ensue as she gathers her things to make her permanent departure.

Financially, she doesn't have a plan. Ideas of how she can make money or hitchhike to the next town flood her mind. There's no time to revel in the bliss of her newborn son; she must think of a way to escape her lackluster reality without suffering repercussions for her actions.

In the end, none of it matters. Since she's underage, she doesn't have a choice.

As she lies there contemplating, a commotion stirs outside the closed hospital door.

Suddenly, a faint knock sounds against the wood.

Expecting that it must be her next meal, she pushes her day-old hairdo from her face and clears her throat to answer. "Yes ... come in," she says. Turning her attention to the entrance, she straightens the sheet across her nightgown.

Slowly, the metal knob rotates.

"What's for break—"

Cutting her off mid-sentence, the door forcefully swings open, slamming against the wall. A woman barges into the room, her steps heavy with the overpowering scents of nicotine and cheap floral perfume.

Loretta gasps. "Dear God," she says.

Even though she hasn't seen the woman in almost nine months, the scent of her mother is engrained in her mind.

The woman's graying blond locks are fried from years of bleach treatments, and her skin is wrinkled from long days in the sun. Her heavy black eyeliner and red lipstick have stained her skin over time, making her resemble a frightened raccoon. As her bony fingers adorned with long red acrylic nails wrap around the bars of the hospital bed, her tied flamingo-print top shows the lax skin of her emaciated midriff.

Since Loretta's a minor in a small town, the staff has called her mother to come to pick her up.

Neither says a word, and they stare with hatred into one another's matching eyes.

BRAKE CHECK

Her mother breaks the silence by slowly clapping.

Loretta watches the baby sleeping in the tiny cart beside her bed from the corner of her eye, and feeling mocked; she furrows her brow. "I see you haven't changed a wink, Genie girl. I'm surprised they let you in smelling like a truck stop," she says.

Immediately, her mother ceases her condescending applause and lunges forward, backhanding her daughter. "You ungrateful little slut," she says, clenching her jaw and staggering.

Loretta clutches the reddened portion of her face. "How many beers did you down? Oh, wait, or is this a whiskey type of occasion?" Tears well in her eyes.

Regaining her balance, Genie points to a single finger housing a thick gold ring. "You're lucky I even bothered to show up," she says.

Flooded with irritation, Loretta rolls her eyes and directs her attention to the sound of footsteps near the door. It's the mustache ambulance attendant who had hauled her the day prior.

Genie and Loretta wipe the disdain from their faces and look at him with a smile. "Yes?" they say.

He waves a small stack of papers. "Just wanted to let you know that the discharge paperwork is all done, so you are more than welcome to take that bundle of joy home," he says.

Genie's smile grows. "That is too kind. Thank you so, so much. I will get her out of your hair," she says.

Having another room to attend to, he purses his lips and nodding, waves to Loretta. "It was nice to meet you, and good luck with that little boy of yours. Try to stay out of trouble," he says.

"Oh, I will," she says. Before she can respond fully, he's already darted down the hallway.

Genie's smile washes from her face, and she redirects her attention to her daughter. "All right, now, get your ass out of bed. I got other places to be," she says, her speech taking on a more inebriated tone.

The slurring of her mother's words triggers Loretta. "I'm not going anywhere with you," she says.

Already walking toward the exit, Genie shrugs. "I'm the only ride you got, so take it or leave it," she says.

Knowing what her mother says is true, Loretta quickly gets up from bed and, remembering she doesn't have her clothes, finds the bikini in which she came to the hospital. Weak, she struggles to get it on over the little flab she has around her hips and puts the hospital gown on backward like a robe.

As she rushes to grab the swaddled boy from the cart, her bare-footed steps slap against the floor tiling. Asleep and oblivious to the commotion, his perfect little face remains peaceful. "Mommy's little angel," she says, scooping him up. His tiny body flinches, and his nose wiggles. "Cute-as-a-button."

Noticing her mother is gone, she rushes out of the room with the child in her arms to catch up.

Outside the hospital's front door in the parking lot, her mother's car rumbles as it prepares to depart. Loretta clutches her baby boy tighter and, setting her gaze on the beat-up burgundy Chevy truck, races across the hot pavement to the revving vehicle. As she closes in, the passenger side window rolls down. "Atta girl," the woman utters with a grating, raspy voice.

Fighting her irritation, Loretta flings the door open, and hopping inside, scans the bench seat. "Did you bring something for the baby to ride in?" she asks.

Her mother lights a fresh cigarette and laughs. "Why? I'm not the one with the bastard child," she says. With an inhale of smoke, she reverses the car and chuckles. "Just put him on your lap. That's what I did with you, and you survived."

Loretta nervously wraps her arms tighter around her son's tiny body and scans the garbage on the truck's floor.

They're not too far from the trailer park, so their drive only lasts ten minutes and two cigarettes. Thoughts of what will happen next run through Loretta's mind, and her heart races as the sight of the single-wide mobile home approaches.

"Well, there you be," Genie says, followed by a fit of coughing.

Genie has already tipped off Rut about their arrival, and he is waiting outside for them, smoking a cigarette on the fold-out steps. "He's cute. I'd try to keep him if I were you," she says, motioning for Loretta to get out of the car.

Unbuckling her seatbelt, Loretta shudders. The thought of being dropped off where she began at the trailer park makes her feel like she's regressing. She forces her fingers around the door handle and opens it. Even though she doesn't want to get out, she knows it is the only place she and the baby have shelter. "This is only temporary," she says. Trying to remain optimistic, she forces a smile.

As Rut makes eye contact with her, he drops the cigarette butt beneath his boot and waves to Genie. "Thanks for handling her for me," he says, anger brewing beneath his sarcasm.

Loretta looks down at her bare toes as she gets out of the truck and, holding the baby, squirms to cover more of her body with the hospital gown. Rut rushes toward her, tightens his hand around her arm, and shuts the truck door behind her.

"You two remind me of her dad and me at that age," Genie says while adjusting the mirror. Then she lays her foot down and, gassing the car, peels out.

Rut's twitching lips ache from forcing a smile, and, seeing the truck is out of sight, he angrily releases his grip. "Don't you ever embarrass me like that again, woman," he says through his gritted teeth.

Loretta cowers over the child to shield him.

Rut chuckles at her reaction and spanks her. "If you're planning on keepin' my attention, you better go on inside and change into something more appealing to the eyes," he says.

The sensation of her slapped glute makes her cringe, and fighting her disgust, she heads for the trailer's front door. As she bounces the swaddled baby, she whispers in his ear, "Don't worry, little Rich. He will never touch you. I won't let him."

"I made sure to leave it just like you never left," Rut shouts from behind her.

She notices the mess on the kitchen floor as she steps inside the trailer. Carefully stepping over the lemony mixture, she heads to the back bedroom and uses her trembling hands to close the door.

3

DON'T TOUCH HIM

Loretta fumbles to lock the door, takes a deep breath, and looks around the room to think. Her eyes land on the unmade bed.

The tiny child yawns.

She rushes to the bed and rearranges the pillows to make a fluffy prison for the child to lie inside. Trying not to disturb his peaceful state, she sets his tiny body down with gentle hands. "There you go, little Rich. Safe and cozy," she says with a soft smile.

After making his way inside, Rut slams the trailer's front door behind him. The impact causes the floor to shake beneath Loretta's feet, and she clenches her muscles to stabilize herself. She looks to the closet and, fighting her exhaustion, pushes through her fatigue to flip through the hanging garments. In a frenzy, she pulls anything that is hers off the rack, tossing it into a pile on the floor. She plans to escape.

Rut's heavy boots stomp toward the bedroom and rattle the walls. "Now, don't make me come in there, Loretta," he says, reaching the door; he tries to open it and, wiggling it harder, notices a piece of paper near his feet.

Swiftly, Loretta collects her few baby items as she finishes grabbing her things. Meanwhile, Rut, distracted, picks up the paper and starts reading.

It's the birth certificate.

"Rich Richardson?" he reads under his breath. "What kind of bullshit is that?" His face turns red, and his hand crumples the paper. With it wedged between his fingers, he firmly knocks on the door.

Petrified, Loretta stops what she is doing. "Yes, Hun?" she asks, her voice cracking.

"What's Richardson doing under the kid's last name?"

"Shit," she says to herself. Noticing the anger in his voice, she tries to calm the situation. "Huh? Is that what they put on there? The hospital must have messed up. You know, they were so darn busy when I was...."

"Are you trying to take my son from me, you scheming cunt?" he says, cutting her off.

Her heartbeat grows louder in her chest. "No. Why in the world would I do that?" she asks.

The thought of the boy not belonging to him makes Rut's flesh burn. Filled with rage, he beats on the door. "You better open this goddamned door, Loretta, before I break this flimsy piece of shit down myself," he says.

Loretta works faster to gather her things. "You know, I don't enjoy talkin' to you when you are in a mood," she says.

Determined to gain entry, Rut unleashes a barrage of kicks and punches on the door. The heavy thuds cause the baby to cry.

Loretta's overwhelmed by the stress, and each piercing scream from the child intensifies the situation, sending a sharp ringing sensation through her ears. Desperately trying to regain her focus, her eyes dart back to the closet. Panicking, she scurries on all fours into the small space and begins rummaging.

Behind her, the force of each strike causes the wood of the bedroom door to crack and splinter.

In the back of the closet, she grabs ahold of something wrapped in a dirty handkerchief. "We are going to be all right, Rich. Mama is gonna make sure everything is all right," she says, unraveling the material. She is face-to-face with a loaded revolver.

"You've done it this time. Wait till I get my hands on you, Loretta. You'll regret all the wrong things you did. I'll drag your sorry ass by the hair back to the hospital to fix this bullshit!"

Loretta crawls until she reaches the bed, then positions herself against the wall, trembling as she faces the door. He continues his rant.

"I'm gonna snatch that kid away from you and keep him away for good. Do you hear me, Loretta? You can't take a man's son from him. I'll have you thrown in jail for lying," Rut says, punching a hole in the door. His fists bleed from the impact.

She grabs a fallen pillow and tightly grips the gun handle. "You got this, Loretta," she says. Letting out a deep exhale, she sniffles.

"That boy's gonna be nothin' like you! I'll see to it. I should have left your ass sitting at the bus stop that day. You're just like your deadbeat folks," she yells as Rut keeps kicking the door, trying to knock it down. "I ... I was only fifteen, and you were twenty-one. I was a child," she says, her voice quivering. The thought of his predatory ways makes her vision darken, and, placing the pillow in front of the revolver, she aims the gun barrel for the door. She takes a deep breath and steadies her hands by fixing her elbows to her sides. "You took advantage of me."

His condescending laugh echoes into the room. "Sugar, anyone who wears short skirts like you is asking for it. All you were after was a meal ticket out of your fucked-up home," he says, getting impatient. The accusation angers him. Ready to get his hands on her, he peeks through the chunk of missing wood bashed in by his fist.

The baby screams louder on the bed.

Sitting on the floor and terrified of what's coming, Loretta braces herself with the revolver pointed at the door; her teeth chatter and tears flood her cheeks.

"Oh, I'm so scared," Rut says hysterically, laughing. "What are you going to do? Huh? Bludgeon me with that pillow between your legs?"

Loretta clenches her jaw so severely that a tension headache forms and her complexion turns red. Then, as if a switch is flipped, she squints, her body relaxes, and she takes control. "Go to hell, you child-porking prick," she says, pulling the trigger. A deafening bang reverberates through the air.

Rut is struck between the eyes. His body goes limp, and he hits the trailer floor with a heavy thud. The single-wide quakes.

Immediately, the baby stops crying.

Loretta feels like she is having an out-of-body experience and is in shock. Never having hurt a fly before, she looks at the smoke coming from the tiny barrel of the gun and charred bits of the pillow. "Oh, no ... what did you do?" she says. "What did I do?" She glances at the punched hole in the door, sure she will glimpse Rut on the other side, but there is no sign of him.

The smell of burned cotton and smoking gunpowder lingers in the air.

Still looking toward the door, Loretta's pupils dilate. "Rich ... Rich," she says, noticing he's not crying; she scrambles to put down the gun, and fighting her emotional roller coaster, she stands on her shaking legs as the reality of her actions sets in. Terrified that the bullet may have ricocheted, she cries as she inches closer to the newborn.

The baby boy, still swaddled, softly smiles and returns to sleep.

Using a corner of the sheet, Loretta wipes away the dampness from his cheeks. "My little angel," she says. Reluctantly, she walks toward the bedroom door and, choosing to leave it locked, peeks through the damaged wood.

Rut's lifeless body lies on the ground, his head surrounded by a pool of blood.

In disbelief, she notices the placement of the bullet hole, and her face turns pale. "We'll figure this out, Rich, don't worry. Mama's gonna take care of it," she says as she continues to peer through the hole at him.

The growing pool of blood creeps closer, inching toward the crumpled paper in Rut's hand. Realizing it's the baby's birth certificate, Loretta fumbles to unlock the door faster. "Shit ... shit, shit," she says. With a click, the door unlocks, and she rushes out, snatching the document from Rut's outstretched hand, deliberately avoiding eye contact with the lifeless body. She frantically rolls the paper out against the doorframe, smoothing it with her hands to straighten the wrinkles. With most of the creases minimized, she carefully places it next to the child on the bed.

A thunderous knock pounds against the trailer's front door.

Loretta cringes as she looks down at the hospital gown and swimsuit clinging to her body. "Nobody's gonna know," she says.

4

CAN I HELP YOU?

The knocking intensifies. As each bang infiltrates the trailer, it resonates like a backfiring exhaust, filling the space with a new form of chaos.

Everything about the situation feeds Loretta's panic. What if someone heard the gunshot?

She knows she must pull herself together. Quickly patting the sides of her cheeks, she draws on bits of her youthful skin to bring herself back to the moment.

Another round of pounding reflects off the walls more aggressively; whoever is outside is relentless in their effort to get her attention. Loretta shuts her eyes and takes a deep breath, but rather than calming her, the oxygen feels sparse, and the noise agitates her patience. Even though she dislikes being rushed, she abandons her stubbornness, and her eyes suddenly open. As she scans the chaotic pile of clothes on the floor, her heart races as she frantically searches for an outfit, shouting, "Be right there!" Her overexerted tone creates pressure behind her vocal cords, causing a crack.

The quietness of the room makes the knocking seem even more exaggerated. Her focus falls on the rhythm, and her ears ring; trying to force herself to move, her legs lock out, and her body shakes with frustration. Attempting to center her wave of emotions, she slowly blinks and shouts again toward the door, "Coming, sugar! I'll be right there."

Ignoring her, the individual at the front door continues. Again and again, the banging persists, each lingering knock building on the next.

Its deafening presence overwhelms Loretta's mind, jarring her vision. Her knees grow weak beneath her, and the combination of physical and mental exhaustion prompts the room to spin. As she takes a staggering step forward, she grabs the first two pieces of clothing atop the pile.

Sweat drips from her lip as the stifling humidity from the summer air outside amplifies the lack of an air conditioner in the trailer.

As the thick, warm aroma of iron emanates from Rut's corpse, Loretta gets a strong whiff of death and flinches. Knowing she doesn't have much time before the body becomes stiff and the odor worsens in the summer heat, she quickly pulls on the pair of jean shorts and tattered denim button-up shirt over her swimsuit.

As she steps closer to the open bedroom doorway, she observes a difference in the body on the ground. The lifeless flesh is growing pale, and the veins are bulging with a purple hue as the heat in the enclosed metal box speeds up the skin's decomposition like a pressure cooker.

Her eye twitches nervously at the thought of who may be at the front door. "Just ignore the bastard, Loretta. Stay focused." She says, looking straight ahead, "You got bigger fish to fry."

Behind her, the tiny baby falls into a deeper sleep. His subtle snores help diminish the annoyance of the knocks.

Swept up in her emotional rollercoaster, Loretta had almost forgotten the child's presence. "You're such a good baby boy," she says. It fills her with warmth as she listens to the little purr-like chirps. His soft murmurs bring her calm, and gathering her determination, she skillfully avoids the blood pool, steps over the body, and continues toward the door. "Almost there!" she shouts.

This time, the individual outside hears her yell, and the battering falls silent.

She focuses on her path as she continues forward. As she dodges the mess across the kitchen floor, something catches her attention from the corner of her eye—a red checkered apron is hanging from the oven's handle. "Perfect," she says, snatching up the worn-out fabric.

Tying it around her waist, she walks toward the entrance, crafting an alibi. It loosely hangs off her midriff, swaying with every step. She looks down and straightens the material. "That's better ... got to look busy. Like Mama always said, no one ever questions a woman on a mission," she says with sarcasm.

Smoothing her hair with her palms, she is ready to face whoever is waiting outside, and releasing a sigh forces a smile. She cracks the door open just enough to peek.

At the base of the steps, there stands an older woman, cane in hand, leaning on her walker with her scraggly white hair pinned behind her ears—not the visitor she had in mind.

Tipping her chin for a better look, Loretta finds the woman's frazzled appearance startling. Slowly, she follows the pattern of her wrinkled skin to the pastel-yellow shirt she is wearing. A picture of a dandelion is embroidered on the front pocket, and its fluorescent color matches the yellow plastic flowers secured to her metal walker and the frames of her coke bottle glasses.

Loretta recognizes the woman as the nosy next-door neighbor. Unsure of where the conversation may go, she takes a moment to craft her words. "Geez, Louise, Mrs. Hill. You're gonna give a new mother a heart attack with all the pounding from that cane of yours," she says, placing her hand across her chest. "Not to mention, you nearly woke the baby with the noise."

Staring at her, the woman refrains from blinking. She exudes an air of skepticism and a relentless pursuit of answers.

The awkward pause makes Loretta uncomfortable. Quickly, she speaks to fill the space. "I hope whatever has your panties in a bunch is worth all this fuss." Nervously laughing, she clears her throat, pointing to her frizzed hair. "Something happen to you? You look as frazzled as ole farmer Joe when he got zapped by lightning at last year's county fair."

Mrs. Hill's face droops, and her mouth gapes open to speak, not wanting to listen to any more offensive remarks. "I think I should be the one doin' the asking. There was a mighty loud noise a little while ago. It sounded like an explosion or something. It woke me from my nap," she says. Her hand lifts from her walker for dramatic effect, and her breathing becomes heavy. "It nearly scared me right out of my dentures."

Loretta's heart pounds in her chest. The realization that the earlier gunshot may have attracted attention sends a shiver of panic down her spine. Trying to explain, she stammers, "Uh ... you..." Her voice gets higher and faster as she continues, "You must be talking about my darn fridge. It's been acting up an awful lot lately. It keeps making a weird clanking noise that sometimes sounds like..." Her hands recreate the woman's dramatics. "Kaboom! It's almost like a firecracker or a gunshot or something."

The older woman's eyes spring open; she finds camaraderie in the hand gestures. "Yes! That's it!" she says. "That's the noise I heard."

Loretta sighs. "You should've led with that right off the bat. I could've spared you from baking in the heat for so long," she says, pointing at her apron. "That's why I'm stuck wearing this old thing. Rut and I are in there working to fix it."

Mrs. Hill quickly chimes in. "Oh, how is that sweet boy doing?" she asks with a flirtatious glimmer in her eye. "Do tell him I say hello."

Wanting the conversation to be over, Loretta pretends not to hear her and, while shutting the door, talks louder, "All right, well, I better get back to the baby now."

Left outside and speechless, Mrs. Hill pauses and gives an indifferent shrug. "Well, that's that," she says. Having achieved her goal, she repositions her walker to face the opposite direction. "Time to go home," she says.

Loretta tries to remain calm, but her concern overwhelms her, and she rushes to the nearest window to peer outside. Pushing the thick crème curtains back just enough to provide a slit to peek through, she glimpses the older woman slowly making her way home. "Everything's gonna be fine. You know what? That went even better than expected," she says, sweat dripping down her back. With a nervous chuckle, she backs away and shakes her head. "That woman is like a mockingbird. It won't be long until everyone in this dump knows what caused the noise."

A slippery mixture of liquid and lemons creates a glistening puddle on the floor, infiltrating the seams of the cheap linoleum.

Loretta stares at the mess, placing her hands on her hips. "Well, I guess that's my cue to get to cleaning," she says, walking toward the kitchen.

She reaches for a tall, narrow cabinet containing housekeeping supplies. Inside the minimally shelved space are unlabeled jugs filled with different colored liquids, stained rags, a straw broom, and thick yellow rubber gloves. "Time to wash away my sins," she says. As she puts on the gloves, she revels in the feeling of control. The sensation of the rubber against her forearms is exhilarating as she pulls the oversized ends past her elbows. She stares for a moment at a repurposed plastic jug containing citrus-scented bleach.

Thoughts of a plan to cover the murder flood her. It's all she can think about. She quickly fills the kitchen bucket halfway with warm water and pours in a generous cup of the chemical. The water fizzes upon contact, sending harsh fumes into the air.

To her, the potent aroma symbolizes a new beginning. Taking in a deeper inhale, her eyes and nostrils burn, producing a trickle of tears down her cheeks.

Without hesitation, she grabs a handful of rags, drops them into the mixture, hurries to the crime scene, and begins scrubbing in circles around Rut's body. After sitting in the heat, the blood from the decaying corpse has become darker, like an aged Merlot. The idea of the gory secretions and bits of brain matter lying stagnant another moment longer makes Loretta tremble; she doesn't want it to stain the linoleum.

Her mind drifts. Losing track of time and reality, she finds the familiarity of cleaning therapeutic and uses the activity to numb her emotions.

With each new thought, she shifts her scrubbing course, compulsively scouring the floor, re-cleaning every nook and cranny. Slowly but surely, the mess disappears, along with the years of wax buildup. Her fixation is bliss. It's not until the harsh chemical eats away at one fingertip of the glove's rubber that she realizes the kitchen floor is clean.

In the distance, the baby's snores cut through the silence, pulling at her attention. The child's innocent noises give her the courage to keep going and bring her a sense of comfort. With a grin, she stands and looks at the open bedroom door. "This is for you, little Rich," she says. Carrying the bucket to the sink, she rinses and refills it with another batch of cleaning solution.

With a tiny snort, the child gives a gummy giggle. It sounds muffled from the other room.

She stops and smiles. "That's Mama's boy," she says. With a bucket in hand, she returns to the corpse. Getting down on her hands and knees, she crawls toward the body, determined to get a closer look at the head wound.

Rut's eyes are wide open, staring in her direction as if expecting her. Making eye contact with his dilated pupils, Loretta finds their dullness irks her, and she tries to avoid looking at them by glancing at his wound.

A crusty layer has formed around the bullet's entry point, creating a mound in the middle of his forehead, reminiscent of a dormant volcano. The gore element makes her hysterical, and her hyperventilating turns into giggles. "If you'd looked like this from the beginning, you know, I would've never hopped in the car that day, and we wouldn't be here in this mess," she says, leaning in to poke his shoulder.

With a snort, her voice trails off, and her rollercoaster of emotion shifts; horror sweeps over her face. Her eyes are stricken with grief. She feels numb regarding the harm she has caused.

The longer she sits in silence, staring in disbelief, the more passing time feeds the stench. Suddenly, the smell jolts her out of her complacency. "Think," she says, turning her upper body to scan the kitchen behind her.

Met with frustration, she uses the cranny of her elbow to wipe the sweat from her forehead and, grunting sarcastically, rolls her eyes. "If I had money, we could just leave him here and have a fresh start," she says. "Life would be so much easier, Rich." Again, she inappropriately laughs.

Loretta continues her one-sided conversation, expressively waving her hands as she speaks. "You know, I never liked the way he looked at me. It always creeped me out," she says; the memory makes her skin flush and clammy. "It's like he always wanted something."

Compulsively itching, she turns to face Rut.

His tongue, pale purple and blue, protrudes from his mouth while his eyes remain fixed in a stare. "Yuck," she says, her fingers sweeping his eyes to close them. "Much better."

The baby coos in the other room.

Releasing a sigh, she continues to vent. "He was trash, but he did pay for the food." As her eyes drift back to the kitchen, she looks at the refrigerator. Thinking of the can of lemons on the empty shelf, she shakes her head and grimaces, envisioning the sourness of her makeshift lemonade infiltrating her taste buds.

Some months, she would have to plead for him to make time in his day to get the groceries she needed. He always used his work schedule as an excuse, but now that she knew about his extracurricular activities, she couldn't help but question if he was truly busy or if it was just another means to show how little he valued her.

Suddenly, it hits her; she's over it. "To hell with him. He's not worth another second of my time!"

Squinching her eyes shut, she recenters her thoughts, determined to find solutions to her current predicament. "I got it!" she says, her face lighting up with excitement. "I'll just shove him in one of those big-ass trash bags under the sink, and then, when it gets dark, I'll chuck him out like the trash he is next to the cans. Then, when the trash man comes tomorrow, he'll toss him in the truck with the rest of the garbage and get rid of him for me." Her eyes pop open. "Piece of cake."

Responding to the exhilaration in her voice, the baby, mid-sleep, giggles. She giggles back. To her, it's a sign. "Bingo ... Mama's got it handled," she says.

Jumping to her feet, she runs to the kitchen and grabs a one-hundred-gallon XXL garbage bag from under the sink. Ironically, the box of bags is one that Rut recently plucked from a construction site located nearby. Despite Loretta's request for a kitchen-sized box, he insisted she use the ones he found, which were twenty times too big. She finally recognizes the value of the discovery. "I already know he's gonna be a heavy son of a bitch," she says. Leaving on the gloves, she races back to his corpse.

His bloated stomach challenges the elasticity of his tight clothes. She leans forward and, starting at his feet, begins stuffing him inside the bag. "Come on," she says, grunting while rocking him back and forth, shimmying him into the plastic. The exertion of energy is more than she expected, causing her to sweat and her muscles to tremble. Even though she wants to take a break, her stubbornness takes over, and upon finishing the task, she ties the bag shut.

Loretta douses the rags with more cleaning solution, turns the bagged body to its side to remove smudges from the plastic surface, and cleans up any remaining residue on the floor. On a mission, she drags the heavy black garbage bag toward the front door. After thoroughly inspecting the area one last time and finding no traces of blood or bits, she rinses the bucket, wipes down the counter and sink, and stuffs the tainted rags into the bag before sealing it shut. She puts the bucket and bleach away and, with a big sigh, sets the gloves next to the bag for use later.

The baby boy, who has been waiting on the bed, is done with his long nap and fusses as he wakes up.

Loretta redirects her energy, rushing to care for the child while multitasking by rehanging the clothes and tidying the room. As she picks up the tiny shards of wood, her eyes are drawn to the hole Rut made in the door; no matter how she tries to forget, everything reminds her of what she has done. She uses feeding and changing her new baby as a distraction, but she can't ignore the mixed emotions of grief and anger when she puts him back to bed in the pillow fort.

After watching him drift to sleep, she heads back to the kitchen, aware of her remaining tasks. The lumpy black bag is the elephant in the room; each time she looks at it, she envisions Rut saying, "Boy or boy, you've really done it this time, Loretta.".

Its presence is unsettling.

Lost in frustration, she perches on the kitchen counter, fixated on the moonlight streaming through the window and bouncing off the garbage sack. "Even when you're dead, you still manage to ruin my happiness," she says.

She shifts her attention to the window as the wind whistles against the glass pane. The small gap in the curtains allows a view of the pitch-black darkness and partially burned-out strand of Christmas lights.

There is a sound of laughter coming from outside.

Hurrying to the window, Loretta opens the curtain a bit wider and spots her neighbor Patsy, the waitress, getting out of her car. "I didn't know the diner was open that late." She shrugs. As she dismisses her skepticism, she hears another, much more resounding voice.

Exiting from the passenger's side is a man.

Loretta's focus snaps back to the window to spy.

Both laugh flirtatiously as they stagger to the front door and go inside.

Loretta's pupils dilate, and her fists clench. Seeing the woman playfully interacting with another man besides Rut fills her with anger. "That little slut," she says. For some unknown reason, the thought of the waitress having a full-fledged relationship with her baby's father was more tolerable than the idea of him putting everything on the line for a casual hookup. "Oh, boy, you'll be sorry for being a tramp and playing around with other women's men like that. You go on and have your little drunk party, and we'll see who's laughing in the morning," she says.

As the neighbor's door slams shut, the lights turn off. Stepping away from the window, Loretta glares at the bag and her brow furrows. "I swear, that angel sleeping in the bedroom will be nothing like you," she says. "Nothing!"

Loretta pulls the thick yellow rubber gloves back on and, flipping a switch, turns off the strand of Christmas lights outside. Carefully propping open the front door, she musters up all her strength to drag Rut's body down the trailer's steps. She mutters with every heave, "It's gonna be okay. That boy is gonna make it big and take care of me."

Apart from the gentle chirping of crickets, the trailer park is eerily silent. As the cool breeze tousles her hair and sends a wave of goosebumps down her arms, she continues dragging the heavy bag across the small yard, her gaze unwaveringly fixed toward Patsy's trailer.

The metal top of her tin can shimmers underneath the night sky. Loretta crouches, trying to remain unseen while heaving the bag toward the neighbor's bin; she is more determined than ever. Unable to lift the contents, she leaves the lumpy sack beside the can and casts a satisfied glare toward Patsy's house before heading home. "You messed with the wrong woman," she says.

Scurrying back inside, she locks the door, puts her gloves away, and, taking a hot shower, smirks as the suds clean away the memory of the day. The idea of waking up to a fresh start fills her with a newfound excitement that she has never felt before.

As she climbs into the bed next to her child, she cuddles his tiny body and kisses the top of his head. "You better never let me down," she says, yawning.

Giving a slight fidget, the small boy readjusts his body, and his gums smack as his nose wiggles. His soft babble fills her heart with warmth. "That's Mama's little angel," she murmurs.

She falls into a deep sleep.

5

THE MORNING AFTER

In the early morning, the distant wail of police sirens disrupts the peacefulness of the sunrise outside the trailer.

The howl slowly infiltrates Loretta's dormant ears. Everything from the prior day feels like a dream. As her eyes create small slits, she fights her grogginess and lightly pats the pillows beside her. She slides her fingers into the makeshift fort, searching for her child, and panics when she only feels shapeless cotton. "Rich?" she asks. Then, wiggling her palm further, her fingers finally tap the sleeping newborns cocooned body, "There you are, my baby boy."

As her touch tickles him awake, he giggles. Smiling, she stares at the water-stained popcorn-textured ceiling and listens to the familiar sound of sirens. "What do you reckon it is today? I bet Missy down the way burned her morning grits again." She giggles.

The sirens shut off right outside, replaced by the murmur of a walkie-talkie radio, growing louder as someone talks on it while pacing the yard.

Startled, Loretta sits up in her bed to listen. "What on earth?" she says, her eyes wide.

The sound of a man's commanding voice reverberates among the metal-sided trailers. "Requesting backup for a homicide. We got a suspect handcuffed, and she is ready to be taken into custody. A young female in her twenties..." It sounds robotic as shrill beeps follow the rushed voice.

Loretta's eyes double in size; immediately, she thinks of the body she left by the trash bin. "Oh crap," she says, scooping up the swaddled child. Her heart races. "Let's go, Rich."

Her tight squeeze causes the baby boy to sense something is wrong, and he squirms. Worried he may cry and give them away; she softly bounces him to provide comfort. "Hush, now. It's going to be okay. No one's gonna hurt you," she says.

Feeling his heart rate settle, she springs out of bed and rushes in her frazzled state to the closet. With the child in one hand, she flips through the clothing on the rack. "If we wanna get outta here before they spot us, we gotta pack light and get going."

Abruptly, a thunderous knock reverberates through the home.

She tries to ignore it but finds it impossible.

The banging repeats, louder this time, in a series of three.

Knowing her escape attempt is futile, Loretta retracts her hand from gathering clothes and places it on the baby's back. As she hugs him, she clears her throat and, fighting her nerves, yells to the front door, "Yes? Who's there?"

Sterner than expected, the voice quickly responds, and more rapid knocks ensue. "This is the police, ma'am. We need to ask you a few questions."

Her stomach drops. "Just remain calm," she says, reassuring herself.

Rich's cheek nuzzles into the crease of her armpit. Overcome with nausea, she takes a deep breath and rubs the baby's back to divert her attention. She pulls a bathrobe over her mismatched clothes, and a shiver rolls over her. "Okay, let's see what they want," she says.

The room's air smells crisp, clearing her mind and sharpening her thoughts. She tries to keep her wits about her as she rushes out of the bedroom, focusing on the front door, determined not to let her gaze wander to where the crime scene once was. "Just breathe and smile," she says.

Sunlight shines through the gap in the curtain draping the front window; it accentuates the silhouettes of the two police officers standing outside. She refrains from looking, and her lips quiver as her hand reaches the metal doorknob. Ready to get the interaction over with, she slowly pulls it open.

Two men are standing at the base of the steps. One is a sheriff, an older man with salt and pepper sideburns and crow's feet at the corners of his eyes. The other is a younger deputy with slicked-back light-brown hair. They are both staring at her.

Holding the baby tight to her body, she looks at the badges on the tan shirt and dark navy uniform before her attention drifts back to make eye contact. "What's going on, officers?" she asks.

Upon noticing the baby's tiny size, the sheriff's demeanor shifts to a softer tone. "Sorry for disturbing you, ma'am. We'll try to speak a little quieter so as not to wake the child ... I know how hard it is to get them back to sleep. I have a few of my own," he says. Then, taking a pause, he looks past her into the trailer. "Does anyone live here with you?"

Loretta thinks quickly and, reading their expressions, responds. "The baby boy's father, Rut, does," she says. Then she stammers and talks faster, asking, "Is—is something wrong?"

The deputy adjusts the shirt collar around his neck. "The news we gotta give you is pretty distressing, and if we'd known you were a new mama, we would've picked a better time to talk," he says.

While listening to him speak, the sheriff, feeling uneasy, wearily rests his hand on his chin and strokes his facial hair. "Since you're holding a child, you might wanna sit down for this," he says.

Her body stiffens. "I think whatever you gotta to say, you can just say it right here," she says.

The two men exchange glances. The sheriff continues, "This morning, when the trash man was doing his rounds, he stopped in front of your neighbor's home. He had a tough time lifting one of the bags because it was too heavy, and as he struggled to get it in the truck, it suddenly burst open. He found a body inside, and it's Rut."

Thinking of what a grieving woman would do in her position, she clenches her jaw and squints to produce tears. "It ... it can't be," she says. "Is he okay?"

"I am afraid not. Rut is dead," the sheriff says.

Loretta scans the yard area behind them and tightens her grip around her baby. "But I don't understand. How did he get there? Who could have done such a thing?" she asks, becoming nervous—her leg fidgets.

"I know this is a lot to take in," he says, putting his hand on her shoulder to calm her.

As she ramps up, her breathing becomes shallow, and she swiftly continues talking faster. "But Everyone liked him. He was such a good man."

"Sometimes, these things just don't make sense," the sheriff says, then takes a moment of silence. He glances back at the police car. "Now, what I am about to tell you may be hard to hear, but I hope this helps relieve some of your nerves. We think we've got the culprit in the back of the car right now," he says. "I know it can be a touchy subject, but we believe it might've been an affair gone wrong."

Loretta's face looks shocked, then purses with anger.

The sheriff sees she may not have known about her husband's infidelity. Not wanting to upset her further, he nervously scrambles to say, "Now, ma'am, I wasn't trying to make you distressed in any way ... This whole scenario is more common than you think."

Watching his partner's train wreck of an attempt to comfort the woman, the deputy quickly chimes in. "Yeah, it sure is. Are you familiar with the Davidson family in town?"

Loretta holds her tongue. Fearing they might suspect her knowledge of the fling between her baby daddy and neighbor, she maintains her naive act. They watch her eyebrows above her doe eyes cautiously raise. "The pastor's family?" she asks.

The deputy nods. "Yep, that's the one," he says, lifting his hand in reverence. "That man, God rest his soul, was bludgeoned to death by his hideaway gal about a week ago."

Loretta has always heard rumors of the man's disgusting behavior but had not known it to be true. "Huh," she says, fighting back a chuckle. "Well, isn't that something?"

Both men silently watch her.

Suddenly, her situation doesn't seem that bad. She shakes her head, somberly looking at the floor. "May the good Lord have mercy on his soul and watch over his family. I heard something had happened to him but didn't know any details or that a woman was involved. That sure is a tragedy."

The deputy clears his throat, preparing to speak. "You'd be surprised how often that happens. It gets real messy when the other woman becomes obsessed with a man. Usually, all it takes is for them not to get what they want, and then," he says, lifting his hand and giving a quick karate chop to the air, "bam! They snap, and you got a homicide on your hands."

Startled, she jumps at his quick movement.

Oblivious to her reaction, he proudly shrugs. "We barely need more than a body to connect the dots. Cases such as this are straightforward."

Noticing his partner getting off track, the sheriff interjects, leaning closer and quieting his voice. "Based on everything we've learned, we're confident your neighbor is to blame," he says. "Just between us, she's known around town for hooking on the side, so it's not surprising that she's wrapped up in this mess."

The image of the man she saw while taking out the body to the trashcans the night before floods Loretta's thoughts.

"I realize that may be hard to hear," the sheriff says, allowing her to let it sink in.

Loretta is baffled that she has not figured it out herself. Contrary to what they may think, nothing about the news is rattling; her opinion that her husband was a piece of shit is the same. She doesn't care if the woman he was seeing on the side is a sex worker, but she's confused about how she missed the signs of the occupation.

Continuing to fixate on the ground, she thinks about the sheepish look of the man last night. "Huh..." she says. Her mind wanders, assuming he must have been a client, and shaking her head stops her mental query. Quickly raising her gaze, she returns to the conversation and continues, "You mean that little innocent, cute-as-a-button gal living next door? The same one that works for that place in town that makes the angelic peach cobbler?"

The sheriff sighs with disappointment. "Unfortunately, yes. It looks like she was there for more than the dessert. Gotta admit that cobbler is damn good, but after what we've seen today, it seems like she's been serving more than just peaches in every bite," he says.

Lost for words and unsure what to say next, Loretta feels the child in her arms, and her glance travels back to the ground. "I guess so ... um... there's still something gnawing at my nerves. You know how you mentioned the pastor's family?" she says.

"The Davidsons?" he asks.

Without hesitation, she stammers, "Yes, that's the one. Now, if you don't mind me poking ... I have a question... about her bein' a widowed single mother. How did she go on with life and support the kids without having him around? I know it may be too soon to ask, but with the father of my child being gone and all, I have more than myself to worry about. I ... I have my sweet baby boy."

Noticing her troubled speech, the sheriff touches her shoulder. The feeling of his fingers startles her, and she recoils. His concern leads his expression to take on a somber tone. "It's okay—no need to apologize. I know you're just thinking about that cute little baby," he says. "I'm pretty sure she got money from the insurance company after the man died—you know, to help her take care of the kids and stuff."

This is news to her. Having only heard about that happening in movies, she had thought it was just a Hollywood thing. The idea sends a burst of excitement through her. She struggles to fight back her happy emotions and maintain her look of innocence. "Well ... that is God's work right there. It's good to know that her children were looked after in this sad world," she says.

Abruptly, a static noise pierces the air, silencing them. Worried it might wake the baby, Loretta pulls him closer to her chest while the deputy fumbles around his waistline, eventually locating the walkie-talkie on his hip. As he brings it to his mouth, he swiftly wraps up the conversation. "Again, I am sorry for your loss, ma'am, but as you can see, we have police business to attend to," he says.

Without saying a word, she watches them turn around and walk away. Unable to fend off her emotion, her lips quiver, and the idea of having money given to her makes her eyes water with joy. "I understand, and thank you boys for taking the time out of your busy day to gab with a grieving mother. Just want you to know, I appreciate how dedicated you are to keeping our little town safe," she says. Shifting the baby's weight to free her hand, she waves goodbye.

They approach their car in unison, barely lifting a hand to acknowledge her.

Distracted by their day's next assignment, the sheriff shouts over his shoulder, "You take care of that sweet little boy of yours, miss. We promise that senseless woman will be put behind bars, and justice will be served for his father."

Balancing the child in her arms, she hugs him tighter and widens her smile. "Praise God," she says as she retreats into the trailer. Surrounded by the familiar musty smell of home, she takes a deep breath and shuts the door.

Everything inside is eerily quiet. Even though it should bring peace, Loretta can't calm her racing heart. "Damn, that was close," she says, gasping. Each rapid heartbeat makes the child anxious, and his little limbs squirm.

Giggling nervously, she glances over at the worn-out brown corduroy couch in the corner of the small living room. As she rushes toward it, the motion provokes the child, and he cries.

Quickly taking a seat, Loretta rocks him, and even though she is new to mothering, she'd know that hungry wail from anywhere.

As she continues to sway back and forth, she nurses him and, noticing him drifting off, looks into his sleepy eyes. His peaceful state makes all her sacrifices worth it. "Don't you worry. Everything will be just fine. We are gonna get that money and be taken care of," she says with a timid smirk—the tiny baby answers with a hiccup.

Her focus moves to the small television across the room, where their reflections, perfectly framed on the dark screen, stare back at her. Visions of dollar signs fill her head as she fixates on their images. The moment feels perfect, and her smirk morphs into an enormous grin. Careful not to disrupt Rich, she brings her lips closer to his ear, and a tear tumbles down her cheek. "Look, little man," she whispers. "That will be us someday. All rich and famous."

The child's plump lips pucker, and with a muffled hiccup, his chest slightly rises. Seeing how content he is warms her heart.

His perception differs. As his eyelids twitch and his fingers fidget into a clenched fist, he is experiencing a nightmare.

Gently shifting his tiny body, she places him over her shoulder and rubs his back with a loving touch. Taking in a deep inhale of his scent, she closes her eyes. "That's our destiny. I can feel it in my bones."

6

FAME

As they sit together on the couch, Loretta counts his tiny heartbeats against her breast while the warmth of the sunlight cascades in from the window, grazing her cheek. Everything is perfect; there is a sense of peace looming that she hasn't felt since early childhood. "You're gonna make something of the both of us," she says.

Little Rich is fast asleep in her arms.

Despite not wanting their moment to end, the stillness of the day brings an overwhelming wave of exhaustion into the living room, shifting the energy. As it slowly creeps over her, the heaviness sweeps across her body like a blanket. No matter how hard she tries, she cannot stay awake. Her thoughts fly, and the irises beneath her lids drift into the back of her head.

As the euphoric high of her ambitions seizes her dreams, nothing else seems to matter. Her mind enters an unprecedented meditative state, like an out-of-body experience. She feels weightless, like she's floating on a cloud, as she momentarily resides in her perfect world.

As the diminutive noises of the room meld into a low-grade mumble, a distinct sound emerges, steadily growing louder in the background. She listens to it slowly build to a whine—an irritable static.

Each high-pitched hum disrupts the peace, draining life from the air as if trying to suffocate the room. The nuisance mocks her, pecking away at her patience, and drags her out of her loopy state.

Partially coherent, she listens with her eyes closed. The thud of a car door slamming outside shakes the home's flimsy structure, and soon after, a man's voice pierces through the white noise. Something about it is dark yet soothing. "Loretta," he says. The devilish voice has the raspy tone of a chain-smoking man.

Hearing her name irks her, abruptly snapping her out of the illusionary world of fame and fortune. Despite her curiosity, annoyance prevents her from opening her eyes to uncover the source of the voice. Thinking the officer may have returned, she answers, "Who's there?"

Once again, the voice calls out, "Loretta!" Its booming coarseness shakes the floor beneath the couch.

Late to react, she gasps, and her lids spring open. She scans the room. Each hair on her arms stands on end, wiry to the touch. It's no longer morning; no glimmer of sunlight is coming through the window. Everything is dark.

As her eyes acclimate, she takes a deep breath to calm her racing heart. "I must have been awful tired. I never oversleep like that," she says, trying to make sense of it. She stretches her arms, and the motion makes her feel free, like an obligation has been lifted, and her overextended elbows make a harsh reality set in: Her arms are empty. Her child is missing.

Immediate panic, different from before, floods her veins, spiked with adrenaline, making her sweat. The thought of her baby boy being gone sends her into a state of frenzy. As she pats around her to search for him, she is met with the emptiness of her lap and the desolation of the surrounding couch cushions. "Rich?" she asks. "Rich? Where are you?"

She hears a thud from across the room. She freezes in place. "Rich, is that you?" she asks, trembling.

No one answers.

Unable to see through the darkness, she hums a child's tune, hoping to get a reaction. "Mary had a little lamb, little lamb, little lamb, Mary..." she says. Stopping, she hears something.

It's the electric buzz from earlier. The room smells of charred wires as it simmers and releases an abrupt sizzle.

Crossing her arms, she pretends to hold her child as she stands to her feet. Her knees shake, causing their bony, over-tanned caps to knock into one another. "Hello? Who's there? I'm just a helpless new mama, and I don't have much, but take whatever you need. I'm gonna go now and leave you to it," she says, shrugging.

As she takes her first step, an invisible force hits the front of her body, knocking her back down. The worn-out couch cushion doesn't bring her the same comfort as before. Instead, she sits on the foam and fabric filled with fear. The room smells musty, reminiscent of exhumed wooden coffins. She gasps for breath, still winded by the powerful impact to her chest.

A sharp popping noise and a burst of bright sparks erupt near the television, causing the room to fill with the acrid smell of burning electronics.

She looks toward the short-circuit flame, focusing on the wall outlet where the television is plugged in. A pulsating surge of electricity slowly makes its way up the chord. Its movement creates a neon blue glow, lighting its direction of travel. Each powerful wave gives the television life and triggers the screen to glitch with fuzzy bits of white-washed gray. Her attention darts around the room, wondering who has turned it on.

A baby's cry resonates from the bedroom. "Rich?" she calls, rising to her feet. But as she stands, an unseen force pushes her back down.

Her eyes shift to the television as the newborn's cries persist.

Determined to protect her child, she clenches her jaw, tightens her grip on the cushion, and makes another attempt to get up. "Mama's coming, baby boy," she says, finally managing to stand.

A gust of wind travels from the back room, blowing through the trailer and carrying with it a discordant tune. "Hush now, baby, don't say a word; Papa's gonna buy you a mockingbird..." a man's voice sings, sending shivers down her spine.

Her heart pounds. "Don't you dare touch my baby boy!" she shouts.

Suddenly, the TV makes a noise that sounds like the roar of an engine.

As she turns to look, another gust barrels through the room, catching her off-guard and forcefully knocking her back down. Upon landing, she looks straight at the television screen, and rather than seeing her reflection, she spots someone glaring back at her.

The eyeless figure with a masculine silhouette has jagged shoulders and a set of spiked horns protruding from his forehead.

Unsure if her mind is playing tricks on her, she squints to get a better look; its presence terrifies her. "Hello?" she asks. "Who's there?"

Met with silence, her eyes fill with tears.

The spotty connection causes the channels to glitch, and the excerpts of different networks erratically flip across the television screen. Every flash of light is disorienting, making it hard for her to focus.

The figure's image flickers between the bits of news, old westerns, sitcoms, and car racing.

Horrified, her entire body trembles. "What have you done with Rich?" she asks, crying. "Where is my baby?"

Inside the television frame, the demonic presence appears uncontained and bigger than life. As it leans forward, its horns tilt out from the screen, and with a harsh cackle, it tears a hole through the fifth dimension.

Digging her feet into the floor, Loretta pushes herself back in her seat to escape.

"I can give you whatever you want," the demonic being says as a spindly arm covered in sinewy muscle extends toward her. "It's right at the tip of my fingers. All you must do is ask."

"I ... I want my baby boy," she says. "I want Rich. What'd you do with him?"

Her attention is caught by a faint cry coming from the backroom, prompting her to turn her head and look.

"For now, the child is safe and sound, sleeping in the bed where you left him," he says, retracting his hand. The creature's eyes observe her through the glass; their yellow glow resembles the eyes of a cat hunting its prey in the dark.

Her jaw clenches, and her muscles quiver with tension. "But he was right here in my arms. He was just with me," she says.

Disregarding her distress, the figure continues to speak in a captivating way. "I can make you rich," he declares. "I will make you famous."

The thought distracts her from worrying about her baby. She's always dreamed of being in the spotlight, and she can imagine how jealous her neighbors will be. "I'll be famous, and everyone will know who I am?" she asks, saliva forming at the corner of her mouth.

His presence fills her with warmth, almost as if he's touching her body. "Yes, yes. All we must do is make a deal, and your worries will disappear. You can start over. Have a brand-new beginning," he says.

The opportunity entices her. "How ... but how?" she asks. "What do I have to do?"

The figure controls the television with a grin, and wanting to keep her attention, he slows the hypnotic flipping of the channels. As he watches her eyes dilate, he continues to speak. "It requires a sacrifice."

Becoming nervous, she clears her throat. "Well ... um, wasn't killing Rut enough? Can that count as a sacrifice?" she asks.

Laughter resonates from the television, echoing between the walls of the trailer. The voice reverberates with such intensity that it sends a painful jolt through the front of her skull.

The creature becomes stern. "I want something fresh. I want the child," he says.

His request slowly sets in. Her face turns pale, her eyes widen, and her breathing shallows. "No. No, you can't take him," she says, preparing to make a run for her baby.

"Sit!" he says, sending a gusting force exiting the television.

It pushes her back onto the couch, and she finds herself unable to move.

She trembles as panic takes over.

"You can't take him! He's all I have!" she says, her eyes scanning the screen.

Abruptly, the TV turns off.

The silence is unnerving.

"Rich," she says, "please cry to let Mama know you are okay ... please."

"C'mon, anything," she says.

A small cry sounds in reply.

With a bit of relief, she can think again. As she sits in silence, surrounded by darkness, she is consumed by regret over the missed opportunity. She fixates on what that fame would look like for her and her son. Immediately, desperate ambition overtakes her common sense. "Wait," she says. "I'm sure we can come to some sort of deal."

In response, the air fills with the sound of heavy footsteps drawing near.

Hearing them quicken terrifies her. Her eyes dart around the room, unsure of where to look, and in the moment of her panic, something grabs her wrist. One by one, the invisible force pries her fingers from their clenched positions around the cushions.

She resists the energy while devising a plan. "What about me?" she asks. "Just take me."

It releases her, and she continues. "Just think about it. I've had my fair share of life, and that little boy sleeping there has a whole lifetime ahead of him. I'm out of my prime, but he can be something great ... like one of those racecar drivers I see on TV."

The man chimes in, "I will need you both."

Abruptly, the room grows quiet and oppressive.

Her clammy skin and the discomfort of the silence make her squirm. She keeps talking, pleading for a deal, her words filled with determination and hope.

After several minutes of not seeing any progress, she adds, "As his Mama, I'm sure we can work something out?"

The man's devilish lips curl. "I'm always intrigued by a great deal; go on," he says.

Her eyes light up. "Perfect!" she says, nervously fidgeting. "With this plan, I gotta be honest: there is one little catch. Boys need their mamas until they're eighteen, sometimes longer, depending on when they become men. So I see it as more of a long-term thing."

Before she can say any more, the dark voice stops her. Each of its words lingers, gliding through the air. "Are you willing to strike a deal with the Devil?" he asks.

A hardened lump forms in her throat. "The Dev-Devil?"

"Yes, some call me that," he says with a sly smile, his voice oozing self-assurance. "However, that's not the name I prefer," he adds. "Let me formally introduce myself. I am Lucifer. Wouldn't you agree it has a much better ring to it?"

She frantically scans the room, looking for any movement through the darkness. Even though she can't see him, she can feel his eyes on her. "I'm Loretta," she stammers. "It—it's nice to meet you."

His presence intensifies, permeating the room. "If you promise me your soul and your son's, I will grant you what you seek," he says.

"Do you consent to surrender both of your souls to me?" he asks. A hiss lingers.

His tone sends shivers down her spine. Quickly shaking her shoulders, she tries to rid herself of her nerves. "Yes ... fine. If that means we get out of this shitty town and become something, we will do it," she says.

Abruptly, the television flips on.

Expecting to see the figure, she is startled by the flash of light and the empty room in front of her. As she catches her breath, she strains to hear the hushed voices of two familiar women emanating from the television. She squints to get a better look.

The normally friendly faces of the local news anchors don't greet her; instead, she notices something disturbing about both women - their appearance is shocking. Their attire is black rather than their usual bright floral tones. Drooping robes with inset red velvet hoods hang over their bodies. The fabric shrouds the clownish makeup on the sagging skin of their faces.

The devilish voice whispers, "What you see is their true selves shining through. Those who are most successful sell their souls for what they desire. It is the secret to achieving your goals in this lifetime. The more successful, the more they must sacrifice, which includes being forced to see what reminds them of their dark past. Their skin hides the secrets that no one else will ever know."

Seeing the newswoman in a different light terrifies Loretta, and wishing to look no longer, she glances at the floor. "I was always told people just work for what they got," she says.

The dark entity laughs. "Those are simply lies that are told to keep others from discovering their secret. If everyone knew how simple success could be, they would willingly seek their low point of desperation to barter themselves for something greater. Fame isn't meant for everyone. Like you, a person must be resilient and determined to fight for what they desire. You have proven that you will do whatever it takes to get ahead."

His timbre sends a rush of emotion through her. "But ... but I'm not a killer. I didn't mean to kill Rut; I had no choice. He was a dangerous man. It's different," she says.

In the darkness, the demon smirks from ear to ear. "Say what you wish, but your determination and desperation for something more are what called to me," he says.

She hesitantly shifts her attention to the television, focusing on the repulsive women. "So ... what you're saying is, these TV people are famous because of you? Talk show hosts, sports players, game show people? All of them are just like me?" she asks in disbelief.

"Not all, but most of them," he says.

"Even those soap stars?"

"Yes, even the actors on daytime TV," he replies.

"Holy cow. I'm practically famous, then," she says.

"Sure," he replies.

The news anchors' faces appear almost demonic, with pointed chins and raised cheekbones. Each of their eyebrows is arched and fixed in place; the perfectly combed strands of hair look plastic.

Loretta sneers in disgust. "I mean, will I end up looking like that to everyone?" she asks. A fit of pressure sweeps over her chest, taking the air from her lungs.

Slowly, Lucifer steps into the light cast by the television, revealing his lean stature, black-wash jeans, cowboy boots, and collared shirt. He resembles more of an ordinary man than a beast. "Only those who have sold their souls will see you the way you see yourself," he says and, getting closer, blows warmth onto the lobe of her ear. "Now, tell me what you desire."

Her mind becomes overwhelmed with thoughts, and the image of Rut in his greasy mechanic's uniform pops into her head. She's promised herself that her son will be something far greater than his father, and she knows exactly what would put that man to shame.

Her baby boy must become a professional racecar driver.

The idea of him standing on a winner's podium makes Loretta grin. "I tell you what, mister: My baby boy was born to drive fast and be a champion. He will be like those race car drivers on TV, living in big houses and driving fancy cars. Rich Richardson will be unstoppable. That little boy is gonna be the fastest man in the world," she says, excitedly pointing toward the bedroom.

The figure's eyebrow lifts. "Is that so?" he asks with a grin that expands from ear to ear. "And what about you?"

She pauses to think. Her smile grows, and a twinkle forms in her eye. "Well, that's easy. I'm his mother. I want to be there for him until the day I die," she says and, with a laugh, glances at the ground. "Of course, that comes with riding that wave of success with him."

Abruptly, the man disappears, and the television shuts off.

The darkness engulfs Loretta, pressing against her body and stealing the air from her lungs. Her gasp for air fills the room, and as the breath enters her body, it is mingled with the scent of ink and paper, finalizing the contract, and sealing the deal.

The man whispers, "Wake up." Drifting away into the distance, he utters again, "Wake up."

Her eyes snap open at the sudden noise of a revving engine outside and tv blaring, leaving her disoriented and unable to remember drifting off to sleep. Still positioned on the couch, she looks at the clock across the room and finds relief in the time; it's before noon. Directing her gaze to the heaviness in her arms, she sees her son and smiles. He stares back at her with a gummy grin. "There's my precious little racecar boy," she says, tapping his nose.

As the child coos, she notices an image on the television screen from the corner of her eye.

It's the Devil winking at her.

Feeling anxious, she nods to acknowledge him and, shaking off her nerves, reaches for the dial changer and quickly shuts it off. "Don't worry, Rich," she says. "Everything's gonna be fine ... Mama's got it handled."

7

UNDER MY SKIN

After Loretta had signed her pact, waking up in the morning felt exciting; the fresh start she had always hoped for had been dropped in her lap.

Glancing in the mirror to brush her teeth, she finds the woman staring back at her unrecognizable; she exudes the strength she has been pretending to embody. "Look at you. That is what beauty looks like," she says nervously, smiling. As she slowly analyzes every feature of her face, she notices something: Everything is quiet, so much so that the only sound she can hear is the hissing cockroaches in the walls.

The jarring ambiance makes her wince. She places her hands on the sink bowl to stabilize herself and closes her eyes to concentrate. "Loretta, girl, you got to keep your shit together," she says.

She tightens her grip around the porcelain, clenching her jaw, and cracks her neck. "Lord, help me now," she says.

The sound of deep, shallow breaths resonates through the tiny space.

Aware that they are not her own, she holds her breath and listens. Without looking, she can pinpoint that it is somewhere behind her, and her knees tremble. Her voice cracks as she clears her throat and asks, "Is someone there?"

A mysterious figure stands concealed behind the fogged plexiglass of the walk-in shower, patiently observing as it waits.

Gulping, she tries to ease the tightness of her vocal cords as she stares in the mirror and glimpses the reflection of the dark silhouette. The sight of the muted presence makes her freeze.

It doesn't move, remaining still, observing her.

Her heartbeats pound against her chest.

A low, gravelly voice dominates the room, resonating like the melodic strums of a bass guitar, as it mirrors her fear. "Boom, boom ... boom, boom... boom, boom," it says.

Her pupils grow larger. The weariness and struggle are evident in her eyes. As she focuses on the features of her face, she is torn between the urge to look and the desire to ignore the presence.

Without skipping a beat, the mouthed pulsations pick up speed, pounding faster and louder. "Boom, boom, boom, boom, boom, boom, boom, boom."

Unconsciously, her heart synchronizes with the rhythmic sound, quickening its pace within her chest.

"The boy. Where's the child?" the man asks.

Ignoring the troubling question, she anxiously laughs. "I look like I haven't slept a wink. I wonder if he can fix these bags under my eyes. Maybe he can throw in a get-famous beauty package deal or something," she says while massaging her dark circles.

The presence moves closer to the shower door.

Her adrenaline spikes as she hears the creak of the semi-transparent door hinges slowly opening.

"I'm sure I'll wake up tomorrow, and those circles will be gone," she says, struggling to hide her terror.

Behind her, the man creeps closer. His body radiates heat; the nearer he gets, the more it burns her skin.

A pulsating headache accompanies the paralysis that envelops her limbs, and, filled with terror, she experiences her soul separating from her body. All the newfound empowerment she has just discovered is ripped from her core, and she is left feeble. Feeling trapped, she watches a teardrop fall to the sink. Its pink hue stains the porcelain.

She gasps for air, and the taste of gunpowder fills her nose and mouth.

The figure's firm grasp wraps around her, bruising her ribs. "Remember, you belong to me," he says—his breath reeking of decay.

Terrified to look up and overwhelmed by the pressure of his fingers' grip, her attention hesitantly shifts from the sink to her waist.

The revelation of his soul's character now blurs and distorts his human features. The previously recognizable pale flesh is replaced by a layer of scarred red skin that wraps around the long, slender hands that tightly grip her waist.

Abruptly, the brim of his black cowboy hat rams into the back of her neck. She flinches; it is not the same presence she remembers. Her movement causes his discolored nails to grow longer, fusing to her skin.

Extending his tongue, he tastes the corner of her ear. "You can't escape our deal," he says with a hiss. "Remember that."

Timidly, she nods.

His whisper shifts into a sadistic laugh.

Worried her response isn't enough, she stutters, trying to speak. "Yes—yes, sir," she says.

With a feral growl, his grip tightens, and grunting, he flips her around, pressing her back into the sink's basin. "You are dancing with the Devil now, little girl," he says.

His belt buckles sparkle seizes her attention, prompting her to examine the engraved silver. It depicts a racecar with a sizable checkered flag fluttering beside it.

She watches in horror as a raised letter R appears in the ornate design. "Rich ... Rich!" she says. Her mouth hangs agape as she starts to understand the impact of her choice.

Bending to her level, he stares into her eyes.

Without having to look at him, she is haunted by the image of each pointed feature of his demonic face permanently etched in her mind. As she defiantly avoids his glare, she feels his tongue slithering into her mouth. Their lips touch, and the long red appendage thrusts down her throat.

Scrambling with fear, her hands flail to grab the sink's rim behind her while she bites down on his tongue as hard as she can.

Her panic intensifies as warm blood trickles down her chin. Hyperventilating, she breaks free and spins around, ready to run.

But as she catches sight of her reflection in the mirror, she stops.

There is no one behind her; the man is gone.

The foamy residue of pink peppermint toothpaste dribbles from her bottom lip, covering her chin. As gravity takes hold, it descends into the basin. She follows the pattern of saliva dripping from her mouth. "Silly me," she says with an anxious giggle.

Wiping the spit from her face, she finds that the longer she stares at her reflection, the more the little voice inside her head feeds her delirium.

Almost like the flip of a switch, she breaks free and rushes to the bedroom to find the baby. He wakes up, still peacefully snuggled inside the bed of pillows.

The mere sight of him brings her a sense of calm. "My little star," she says, rushing to pick him up; she smiles. "Who's ready to go get some of that free money?"

His tiny nose wiggles.

Quickly, she feeds and changes him, swiftly swaddling his tiny body in a soft, clean cotton blanket. She throws on her best sundress and jelly sandals, runs a brush through her hair, puts on some lip gloss, grabs Rich, and makes her way to the front door.

They exit the trailer with optimism. Taking a momentary pause, Loretta looks at the blue sky above. Its luster exhibits a fluorescent glow.

The color reminds her of Tiffany blue, a brand of jewelry she's only dreamed of being able to afford. "See that, little Rich?" she says, squeezing her cheek against his. "You are going to shine just as bright as that someday."

A subtle breeze carries the smell of fresh-cut grass through the air. The therapeutic aroma grounds her as she gets a whiff, pulling her back to the mission. She spots Rut's truck under the carport. Glimmers of sunshine create speckles off the chrome bumper like a disco ball.

As she descends toward the driver's side, she feels lighter, and, looking inside the window, she spots something: a single key dangles from the ignition.

Eyeing it, she snickers. "Now, I'm gonna tell you something: Leaving the keys might seem handy ... but it's a bad idea. We'll make sure you know better and don't do dumb things like your daddy," she says as she opens the door.

The sound of the screeching heavy metal of the hinges makes Rich giggle. His laughter causes tiny saliva bubbles to traipse down his chin. She finds his gummy grin contagious and joins in, laughing. "I guess you are right. The noise is funny, isn't it?" she says. With one hand holding the infant, she uses the other to grab the steering wheel and pull herself into the vehicle.

Sitting in the driver's seat, she rocks the boy in her arms and reaches for the key, but something doesn't feel right; the sight of the empty bench seat beside her prompts a flashback of their car ride from the hospital.

Her mother's voice taunts her. *Just put him on your lap. That's what I always did, and you ended up fine.*

Sitting back in the seat, she makes a quick decision, and, looking down at her son, she reaches for two pairs of sunglasses from the glove compartment. "You know what?

I think it's the perfect day for a walk," she says, pushing the door back open. They get out of the car.

Upon shutting the door, she puts on her shades, and then, juggling Rich's tiny body, she unfolds the remaining pair of oversized aviators and carefully rests them on his face. Barely lined up with his eyes, the reflective black lenses take up over half the space of his head. "There. Now you look like a winner," she says with a smile.

At first, the heaviness of the frames and sepia tone startles him, but as they walk, the rhythm of the rocking movement makes his squirming calm. As she does her best to keep him level, she monitors the glasses' position to ensure they do not fall off while shifting her focus to the end of the trailer park. "I promise this is only temporary," she says.

Her attempts to smooth her movements to a glide are futile. Each step on the uneven terrain creates a bobble in her pace. She feels her stress building and sighs. "It's just a short walk away," she says. "And after today, Mama will have the cash to get that car seat so we can get out of this dump."

Amid his mother's worry, Rich naps peacefully under the tinted blinders.

Even though the walk isn't long, Loretta flips to autopilot, giving her mind the freedom to wander. As a few reservations bubble to the surface, they cycle her thoughts; she can't help wondering if her two encounters with the entity were sincere. Never having been one to believe in the paranormal or even organized religion in church, her mind flourishes with doubt. "He promised us," she says. "That's that."

The outline of a tiny strip mall becomes more distinct in the distance. "See? Not that far at all," she says, forcing a smile on her face. Despite any concerns, she believes the risks are worth it to achieve the life she desires. Stepping foot onto the asphalt, she marches forward with nothing to lose.

Amid her optimistic approach, she takes the sunglasses off the baby and, tucking them away in the blanket, stares into his eyes. "We're here," she says.

Setting her sight on the sign of the only insurance office in town, she feels invincible, so she doesn't bother rehearsing what she will say; she mindlessly carries on, expecting things to work themselves out. With every step she takes, she visualizes a choir singing "Hallelujah" as accompaniment.

An Open sign hangs in the center of the recently shined glass front door. It casts their approaching reflection. Using its mirror-like quality, Loretta stares at herself and, realizing she has yet to remove her shades, shifts the baby's weight to take them off. As she pulls them down the bridge of her nose, a wave of goosebumps covers her arms, and her feet skid to a hard stop.

Even though her reflection suggests she's wearing a Halloween mask, she feels nothing on her face. Her features have become significantly more pointed, and beneath her elongated forehead, her fluorescent yellow eyes resemble a cat's.

A wave of panic rushes through her, increasing her body temperature and making her sweat. The longer she stares, the more petrified she becomes. Her heart races as she frantically pushes the glasses back up the bridge of her nose and quickly scans the parking lot to ensure no one has witnessed her reflection.

There are a few cars scattered nearby, but all are empty.

With a sigh of relief, she cautiously gazes into the building through the glass entrance. "Good, looks like everyone's busy, so no one saw," she says. "We can't have a bad first impression."

As the sun continues to scorch the pavement, the climate becomes sweltering. "Damn, it's hotter than baking pies in a trailer kitchen in August," Loretta says, staring at the entrance.

Shoving it open, she takes her first step onto the checkered tile floor and feels the air conditioning cool her skin. The ruffles of her yellow sundress fan out, and fluorescent light reflects off her dark shades and plastic jelly sandals.

With a new lease on life, she knows nothing matters because she and her son will soon have ample wealth and fame.

Rather than a friendly greeting, she is met with snickers.

Immediately on the defensive, her hidden pupils scour the vicinity until they fixate on the front desk. She tightens her grip around the baby, trying her best to remain calm.

A woman sits behind the reception counter, waiting for something to do; her short stature makes her barely visible.

Loretta clenches her fists, waiting for the woman's heckling to fade while shooting glares in her direction.

She finds everything about her appearance meticulously thought out. The clean-cut lines of her tailored blazer align with her long brown hair. Each follicle in her slicked-back low bun is glued down with excessive gel, resulting in a plastic-like appearance. Its severity highlights her narrow oval-shaped glasses with a strand of plastic pearls connecting the wire pieces perched behind her ears.

Without opening her mouth, Loretta knows that the woman has already passed judgment on her. She can't help but assume it's because of jealousy over her appearance.

Truthfully, the reason is far more profound than her vain assumption. Her presence reminds the woman of what her life would have been had she not chosen to make more of herself and work at an insurance office. If her mother had gotten her way, she would still live in the trailer park she grew up in.

As they stare at one another, each stands their ground, not wanting to break the silence.

Only a few seconds pass before the tension becomes unbearable in the small office space, and the whirring of an electric pencil sharpener pierces the air.

Unable to take the stagnancy any longer, Loretta's impatience gets the best of her, and, wanting her money, she decides to make the first move by clearing her throat.

The woman tries to cover-up her laughter by placing her mouth in the crease of her elbow, pretending to cough. "Hillbilly trash," she says under her breath, then passively smiles.

Loretta ignores the gibberish and, reciprocating with a fabricated smile, marches full steam ahead to the counter, ready to talk business. She stops in front of the reception desk's painted plywood ledge, adjusting the baby's position and tightening his swaddled blue blanket. Then, looking down at the woman, she purses her lips and starts whacking the service bell on the counter. Its high-pitched shrill sounds louder with every demanding flick of her wrist.

Not prepared for the wrath of the bell, three additional employees scatter from their offices, covering their ears.

Unable to bear it any longer, the secretary springs into action mid-hit, placing her hand on the dinger to silence it. "I'm right here," she says, grabbing her hand to force her to stop.

Loretta fights back a smirk. "Goodness me, I did not see you sitting down there," she says, looking surprised while leaning over the top of the desk.

Quickly sitting, the secretary extends her finger and motions to the silver-domed dinger. "The sign says only to ring the bell if no one is at the counter."

A small torn printer paper is folded, sticking out from beneath the metal base. A smiley face is drawn on it next to a message reading: Please ring for help.

Disregarding the remark, Loretta avoids looking and instead forces a bigger smile, shifting her focus to a plastic oval nametag attached to the woman's lapel. "How are you doing today ... Ms. Jesse?" she asks. "Isn't the weather just lovely this afternoon?"

The other insurance agents' dull expressions slowly evaporate; not used to the drama, they stop their nonexistent tasks to eavesdrop on the conversation.

The secretary is already annoyed by the confrontation and ready for her lunch break. "What can I help you with today?" she asks.

Loretta dramatically sighs. "Well, Ms. Jesse, I'm in a bit of a pickle ... you see, my baby's daddy passed away recently." She makes the sign of the cross. "God rest his soul, but he didn't leave us any money, so we gotta fend for ourselves. With him being so young and all, the death was unexpected."

As the secretary listens, she lifts her eyebrows.

Loretta talks faster. "When the officers in town broke the news to me, I was crushed." Pausing briefly, she lets out a sigh. "Then, they mentioned how Mrs. Davidson got insurance money after her tragedy, and I saw a light of hope for us. That's why I am here … I thought it was worth coming in and talking to you to see if you can help a newly single mother out. I'm just trying to do right by my baby."

Having heard so many stories roll through the office, Jesse is apathetic and merely pretends to care. As her features transition back to a poker face, she pushes her glasses higher on her nose. "Alrighty, then, I'll spare you the talk and stop you right there," she says, pointing a finger. "As much as I sympathize with your story, I gotta ask some questions for the paperwork."

"Of course, whatever you need," Loretta says, nodding, filled with optimism.

Without hesitation, the secretary spits out questions in a monotone timbre. "Do you have a copy of the policy? What is the last name? Were you two legally married in the eyes of our Lord and Savior, Jesus Christ?"

Startled by the question, Loretta becomes defensive, and her impulsiveness kicks in. Reflecting on her image in the glass door, she readies herself to get what she wants by instilling fear in those who gaze upon her, gradually lowering her sunglasses to the tip of her nose. Then, biting her lip, she watches for the woman's reaction, waiting for her look of terror, but there is none.

As they awkwardly stare at one another, an uncomfortable silence hangs in the air.

The lack of response irritates Loretta. She is unsure of why it's not working. As she scans the woman's frumpy brown woolen dress, she coldly answers, "Why does that matter?"

Without pause, the secretary smirks, viewing her response as a win. "My next question is, do you have the child's birth certificate? Or any way of proving that the boy is the man's next of kin?" she asks.

Never did Loretta imagine her decision to withhold Rut's last name at the hospital would come back to haunt her, leaving her frustrated and feeling attacked. "Has anyone told you, Ms. Jesse, that it is way too sweltering outside to wear your fashion choice?" she asks.

Loretta's defensiveness and lack of response to her questions are enough to tell the secretary she has no credibility. Keeping eye contact, she resists the urge to gloat over the mother's humbling. "Next," she says, clearing her throat. She shouts louder, "I can help whoever is next in line!"

Loretta turns to scan the room behind her.

There are no other customers; the space is empty.

Returning her gaze to Ms. Jesse, she rolls her eyes. "That's so childish. You damn well know I'm the only one here," she says.

Without flinching, the woman glares at her and announces, "Lunch time!" She pulls a piece of paper from her desk drawer and, with a broad tip marker, writes Be back soon, then sets it by the bell. Then, looking past Loretta, she says, "I will be back in thirty if anyone needs me." Rising from her chair, she spins around and walks away.

Loretta's mouth hangs agape as she struggles to conceal her anger. "Think. You gotta think," she says quietly. "There's gotta be another way that doesn't involve her."

The rest of the staff stay silent.

As they attempt to remain inconspicuous until Loretta leaves, a member of the office staff, who suffers from restless leg syndrome, loses control and kicks the desk, producing a loud thud that fills the room.

Desperate, Loretta spins around and, grasping the baby closer, scans their faces for anyone who might lend a hand. Their gazes divert to their desks, pretending to work. Their refusal to offer help only adds to her anger. "That is no way to treat a newly widowed mother ... no way at all," she says, staring each of them down.

They continue to ignore her, pretending to be busy, shuffling paperwork that doesn't exist.

Unable to hold back any longer, Loretta snaps, and her face becomes red. "Y'all are gonna regret this day ... you don't know who you're messing with," she says, lifting her child into the air. "You see this boy right here? He is gonna be a professional racecar driver. When he wins the Victor Cup, he'll have more money than you can dream of. Yep! That's right! You heard me, and I swear that after our piss-poor treatment today, he'll never get his insurance from this place."

Thinking she's ridiculous, a wave of quiet snickers plagues the air.

"Someone from our little town ... win the Victors Cup?" one agent jokingly asks, looking at the others, barely able to keep it together. "I'll believe that when pigs fly."

As the laughter fills the room, Loretta says, "Just you wait. We'll see who's laughing."

Staring at his mother with doe eyes, Rich wiggles his nose, and his mouth blows a small bubble. Frazzled, she grunts and turns toward the door. "Don't let their stupidity bother you; we don't need them, little Rich. They'll regret this day when they see you racing cars on TV. We're gonna be laughing all the way to the bank," she whispers, giving him a tight hug. "They'll see."

The tiny baby puckers his lips and coos.

Loretta rushes toward the exit, and as she's about to open the door, she spins around to take one last look at the office and sneers. "Go to hell!" she shouts.

Her icy expression leaves an eerie energy in the room, and all fall silent as they watch the door shut behind her.

8

DEVILISH GAMES

The blistering heat makes the walk back to the trailer park feel like an eternity. With no clouds for protection, they are left vulnerable to the scorching rays. The warmth penetrates the ground, causing each small pebble of the gravel road to radiate heat like a furnace.

Already frustrated, Loretta channels her irritation through her steps and stomps. The extra energy spent in the theatrics exhausts her, making her wearily drag her feet as the hot pebbles and dirt cling to the toes of her jelly sandals. Squinting and wiping away a bead of sweat with her shoulder, she strains to see the trailer park in the distance.

Tall grass covers the empty field, with no trees in view to provide shade or escape. It makes the gap between the road and the trailer park seem more significant than remembered. "Not too much further," she says, trying to remain optimistic.

The lack of breeze makes the trek unbearable. Even though she is doing everything she can to remain positive, she is emotionally and physically exhausted.

As little Rich attempts to get comfortable, he wiggles his legs. The exposed parts of his skin are turning a shade of pink. Worried, Loretta glances down to check on him and, forgetting she had placed the oversized sunglasses back on his face, becomes startled by her reflection. The pointed peak of her chin makes her feel like she is staring at a stranger. Quick to react, she nervously tilts her son's body toward her to hide his face. "You know what always cheers me up?" she says with an anxious giggle. "A story. Do you want to hear a story, Rich?"

The eyelet lace on the cuff of the puffed sleeve of her sundress brushes against his nose, causing him to sneeze. Already on edge, she skittishly jumps. "All right. Let me think," she says.

She's only heard stories from others and struggles to tell one herself. Regardless of her skills, she takes a deep breath and begins, "Once upon a time, there was this little boy who grew up to be a man everyone knew."

The child is lulled to sleep by the rhythm of her steps, unaware she is telling a tale. His snoring provides her with a sense of relief, as she no longer feels pressured to create the perfect fairytale. As she ponders, she kicks rocks with each step. "Um ... well, when he was little, he lived a simple life in a single-wide trailer far, far away," she says.

A flock of crows flies overhead and loudly caws, interrupting her. Startled by the racket, she grunts with frustration. "What kind of story is that?" she asks herself. "Shouldn't it rhyme? It's all because of those stupid birds. How's a new mama supposed to concentrate with all that noise?" She grunts.

Little by little, the nuisance of squawking dissipates, triggering a spark of creativity. Unable to contain it, the words spew from her lips; she feels like something is possessing her. "His mother cared for him the best she could. Then, one day, a man arrived to save the day and made her a deal, and she accepted. Some might think he's strange, but she invited him to stay. He fought dragons and evil people. All he asked was that she complete a few quick whacks, and they could finally experience the life they had always dreamed of."

Chills race down her spine, and an eerie feeling washes over her as she tries to change the subject. "Almost there. Home, sweet home," she says, picking up the pace.

They are only a few steps from reaching the trailer park entrance. The scent of freshly cut grass instantly brings her a sense of security. "The trailer park saved the day." She chuckles. "Your Mama's not the best at telling stories, huh? We need to leave the fairytales to the pros."

As they make their way down the dirt road, a gust of wind pushes against their back. It carries the sound of emergency vehicles heading in the opposite direction, toward town.

Still jumpy from earlier, the noise startles her, and she walks faster. "The closer it gets to dark, the more all the crazies come out," she whispers, trying not to wake the baby.

While she's unlocking the door, another wave of sirens fills the air as more emergency vehicles rush toward town. Swiftly entering, she shuts the door. "Good thing we came back when we did, because that doesn't sound good," she says, locking it.

She carefully removes the child's sunglasses and sets them on the kitchen counter. "How about we take off some of those layers?" she says, taking him to the bedroom.

His lips expand to a slight smirk.

Unwrapping the blanket from his body, she cleans him with a dampened cloth and changes him into a fresh onesie. "Much better," she says. Feeling free, he wiggles his toes.

Loretta holds him close and nurses him until he falls asleep. After gently rocking him, she lays him on the bed for a nap. "Night, night, my little prince," she says. Exiting the room, she slowly shuts the door.

Walking to the kitchen, she hears another wave of emergency vehicles. "Jesus Christ. Its gotta be a full moon or something," she says, kicking off her jelly sandals.

A flock of goldfinches happily chirps outside. "Glad to hear that some of us had a good day," she says. She strips down to her bra and underwear and lays her sweaty dress across the kitchen counter to dry. Then, grabbing a handful of ice cubes from the freezer, she rubs them on the back of her neck.

Scuffling noises emanate from just outside the trailer's entrance. Immediately, she recognizes the familiar sound; it's the mailman. "Can't believe it's already that late," she says.

A single envelope momentarily gets caught on the metal flap of the mail slot before tumbling to the floor. She swirls past it and cracks open the window to help cool the place down. "Gotta love that good old Texas air conditioning," she says.

Her focus returns to the letter on the floor. Even though she assumes it's junk, she picks it up. The sound of the sirens still lingers in the distance.

Shaking her head, she tucks the envelope under her arm and grabs a cup of water. "With all that racket, you'd think there is some kind of disaster or something," she says, pondering what's causing the fuss.

A gleam of light reflects off the television, catching her attention. As more sirens join the chaos, her curiosity takes over, and she grabs the remote. "I gotta know what is going on out there," she says.

Flopping onto the couch, she tosses the letter onto the nearby cushion before pressing the power button. The in-pouring electricity makes the television hum and the screen flash; it's already set on the local channel from the night before.

With a whimsical chime, a spot advertising toothpaste pops on the screen. Growing impatient, she taps her foot; she wants to hear the news. "Come on," she mutters, irritated by the start of a commercial break. Having to sit through the annoying jingle fuels her agitation. "Hurry it up!" she says, snapping her fingers.

An announcement flashes across the screen after a brief pause and the news segment returns. Her eyes widen.

A new male anchor has replaced the females from the day before. Although she is relieved not to see the triggering images of the women, she finds him to be almost more distracting. His gelled blond hair, tan skin, and baby-blue suit take her focus. "He's definitely not from this neck of the woods," she says.

Standing outside amid the chaos of the onlookers and emergency personnel, he raises his voice to be heard. "For all of you tuning in, I am here live on the scene of what appears to be the worst tragedy this town has ever seen," he says.

As he continues to talk, Loretta squints, trying to analyze the parking lot behind him. "Wait ... isn't that..." she says, swiftly lowering herself to the floor and leaning toward the small screen.

There is something familiar about the place.

She scoots closer to the TV to get a better look. As the camera zooms in, it pushes beyond the slew of ambulances, firetrucks, and police cars to the storefront where the crime occurred. "Holy shit, it's the insurance office!" She says.

The reporter waves his hand, gesturing for someone to come closer, and states, "We have a witness on the scene."

Slowly, an older woman using a walker enters the frame. The news anchor nods for the crew to follow him as he walks to meet her halfway. With a blank expression, she stops and turns to face the camera. Her stark white complexion and frizzed hair make her look crazed on the screen.

Loretta fixates on her sunflower-patterned shirt and walker covered in yellow plastic flowers.

"You gotta be kidding me," she says. "Of course, it's Mrs. Hill. That lady is always sticking her nose in everyone's business."

With a gasp, the woman seizes the microphone from the reporter's hand. "Evil! Pure evil is lurkin' in this town!" She points behind her. "I've seen it with my own eyes!"

Panicked by losing control over the broadcast, the reporter's eyes dart to the film crew, signaling for help; he doesn't know what to do.

Mrs. Hill's face turns red, and spit flies with each of her words. "This is the work of the Devil!" she says. "We sinned, and now our maker is gonna make us suffer!"

Her words trigger the news crew to remain still. They are reluctant to engage with the erratic woman, so they keep their distance and watch her. Knowing he must take charge of the situation; the reporter playfully reaches for the microphone. "Easy, now. Let's not scare the folks out there," he says, laughing nervously.

"You think hell is funny, young man?" she asks. "You won't be laughing when your skin is on fire, I bet!"

She moves the microphone further away, keeping it just out of his reach, and, smiling at the camera, gives a wave. "For the record, as a devout Christian, I don't find the topic the least bit funny; in fact, I consider the matter damn serious," she says.

Seizing her moment of fame, she braces herself for balance and creeps closer to the camera. "I'm sure you all at home are dying to hear more about what I saw and how I ended up here to witness this awful tragedy," she says.

Intrigued, Loretta scoots a little closer to the television. "I can't believe they're still letting her blabber on," she says.

As Mrs. Hill takes a quick breath to resume the story, the camera zooms in on the wild look in her eye. She points her trembling finger to the lens. "I came in to drop off my check to pay my car insurance like I do every month, and when I walked inside, it became real clear the Devil had gotten here before me. It was a mess. Blood everywhere," she says, her eyes getting big. "It was horrifying, and did I mention the stink? The whole place smelled like chicken shit."

Quickly sprinting forward, the news anchor lunges for her and starts wrestling her for the microphone. "All right, that's enough, now," he says, struggling to take it from her.

Meanwhile, four gurneys carrying body bags roll out from the building to the ambulance behind them.

Instead of recording the news, the camera operator becomes distracted by the commotion of rolling corpses and the fight over the microphone, shifting his camera between each, resulting in a disjointed broadcast.

With one final grunt, the anchor man tears the microphone away. He glares at Mrs. Hill, then tries to save face by smiling at the camera. "Bless her heart. Everything she's gone through has made her a little delirious," he says.

Offended by his remarks, her complexion drains of color, and she clenches her fists in anger as she moves closer. "Have you ever looked into the Devil's eyes? You—you didn't see the look in his eyes as he drank their blood, but I did! He locked eyes with me, and I got a view straight into hell," she stammers.

Loretta lifts her eyebrows. "Jesus," she says. "That woman is a loose cannon. She is a total nut job."

Ignoring Mrs. Hill's approach, the reporter steps in the opposite direction to ensure she remains out of the frame and quickly continues, "As I was saying, right behind me, at that little insurance office, a tragedy occurred. People say it's the most horrific crime ever recorded in this town. The brutal killings, seemingly motivated by hatred, have claimed the lives of all four office employees. People are advised to remain indoors while the police investigate, as the perpetrator of this heinous act is still at large. I have been informed that they are scanning the security footage for an image of the culprit and hope to release it soon."

Nervously biting her nails, Loretta can't help but wonder if she'll face questioning about her recent visit to the office. "Foot-footage?" she asks, unable to look away; her heart races.

A crew member rushes into the frame and, pausing, whispers something in the reporter's ear. He nods, adjusts his earpiece, and clears his throat. "Well, folks, I have just been informed that someone has tampered with the security camera recording, leaving only a tiny portion salvageable. This suspicious activity is making them question whether this was, in fact, an inside job," he says. Shifting gears, he motions to the cameraman. "Okay, Bill, let's roll the tape."

Loretta's heart sinks to the pit of her stomach, and she feels nauseous. Her eyes remain locked on the broadcast, watching with anxiety as the screen becomes granulated. Abruptly, a wave of uncomfortable static fills the air, making her shudder. "Oh, boy, here we go," she says.

As the six-second clip plays across the screen, the view shows the entrance of the insurance shop.

Nervously, Loretta's eyes scan the time stamp at the bottom of the screen. "Thank God," she says with relief. "It must have just missed us."

A mysterious figure suddenly emerges in front of the office, opens the glass door, lowers his hat, and enters.

The visual fills her with terror. "It's him," she says, shaking.

A burst of warm air blows on her neck. It feels like a breath.

Spontaneously, the film becomes static, and a piercing noise blares from the television. She scrambles to the volume knob to turn it down. "Shit, shit, shit," she says, worried it will wake Rich.

The channel fluctuates between grainy images and footage from a professional car race that aired the previous night.

Loretta's body turns cold. She grabs the remote and flips back and forth between channels until the news reappears. The tone of the anchor's voice becomes more serious. "If anyone has information or recognizes the individual, we ask you to please call your local authorities. Any information you can provide would be helpful."

Suddenly, the television powers off, and she is greeted by a distorted reflection of herself staring back at her from the black screen. "I know it was you," she says, sensing someone behind her. "I know you did that."

The smell of cigarettes wafts through the air. "And?" he says, his voice rumbling.

Slowly turning around, she feels a lump build in her throat. His presence possesses an electrifying quality that invigorates her and draws her toward him.

He sits on the couch with his upper body slumped forward, waiting for her; his red skin glows beneath his dark clothing coated in speckles of blood.

The sight of him makes her lips twitch with a subtle grin. "Thank ... thank you," she says. "I'm not used to someone standing up for me like that."

Touching his cigarette butt on the couch, he smashes it into the cushion. He gives a nod and tips his hat.

Loretta's eyes nervously flutter as she looks toward the window, thinking she hears a noise. A diesel car rumbles outside as it slowly drives by, and as it stops, the woman driving the vehicle shouts to a neighbor.

The familiar voice triggers Loretta's memory of Mrs. Hill arriving at her doorstep after shooting Rut, reigniting her annoyance toward her. "I think she knows too much," she says. "That woman is worse than a swarm of gnats on a hot summer day."

The dark figure grins. Abruptly, the temperature of the room rises. As he stands up from the couch, he sees the mail on the cushion and flings it at Loretta. "I'll take care of it," he says, walking toward the door.

As she picks up the envelope, his heavy footsteps send a burst of adrenaline through her veins. Unable to contain her excitement, she closes her eyes. "I think I'm in love."

The door slams, bringing her back to reality.

9

SOME NEVER LEAVE

From the moment the door shuts, Loretta's world shifts.

Clutching the envelope, she remains still, feeling the weight of reality sinking in. Her eyes are fixed on the exit as she contemplates whether Mrs. Hill will be the Devil's next victim. The longer she sits alone in silence, the more her haunting thoughts and guilt escalate.

Suddenly, the rumble of a truck's engine creeps into the background as it revs outside. She can't listen to the muffled tune of spattering oil without it striking a nerve and reminding her of the woman.

Trying to escape her thoughts, she loudly hums and taps her fingers against the floor to think. Then, with a casual shrug, she clears her throat. "Worst-case scenario ... she's kind of old, anyway. Something's gonna happen to her eventually," she says. "I know it's true. It's the same as if she died later from a fall or something. How would I ever be to blame? How could anyone know I was the reason? She's at that age where anything could happen, so I shouldn't feel bad."

The truck's engine gets quieter, trailing off in the distance. Loretta momentarily holds her breath and listens. The peace seems surreal, bringing a false sense of security.

The late afternoon breeze creates a barrier, dampening the sounds of bird chirps and insect hisses. As the air settles back into its usual stagnancy, the sounds of the surroundings return. Each noise makes her cringe and provokes her anxiety to flood back. She remains sitting crisscrossed on the floor, afraid of moving. "What if I got her all wrong? I already killed someone, but I think it was in self-defense. I know Rut was a son of a bitch, but her? Does she really gotta die, or was she just being annoying?"

With a manic giggle, she shrugs. Feeling another wave of guilt, she tries to distract herself and glances at the unopened letter. "Maybe she won't kick the bucket," she says. "Maybe I'm just overthinking things."

The room becomes dark.

Having come home at the peak of daylight, she forgot to turn on the light switch when walking through the door. "Shoot," she says, glancing at the window. Night has come quicker than usual, turning the sky black. It doesn't seem like a typical summer night; there is an element of gloom.

Nervously, her knees clack together as she slowly stands. Worried about seeing something grim, she cautiously approaches the window. "I'm sure if she dies, it will be real fast, and she won't even feel a thing," she says.

Reluctant to see what's outside, she hesitantly grabs the curtain with her fingers. As her trembling hand pulls the material back, she can see the stars are gone, and a thick cloud is blocking the moon. Squinting to focus, she peers into the darkness. "Where could they be?"

The cloud coverage drifts. As the gray shields separate, the moon is revealed. It looks different; its reddish tone appears ominous, as if it is drenched in blood. The shocking hue makes her feel faint, and stumbling, she grabs the windowsill.

Her attention shifts to the neighboring trailer belonging to Mrs. Hill. All the windows glow yellow, signaling that the lights are still on.

Relieved, she places her hand with the envelope against her chest. "See? Everything is gonna be just fine," she says.

Just as she relaxes, a sudden howling wind blasts down the dirt road, causing the trailer's siding to clatter. The aggression of the bursting air mimics an oncoming tornado. She becomes paranoid and scans the terrain outside, her heart pounding in her chest.

Suddenly, she notices a peculiar, shadowy figure. With each step closer, she discerns its tall, lean, and masculine form, leaving no doubt about the individual's identity. He takes his time as he slinks down the center of the road toward Mrs. Hill's house; each of his steps kicks puffs of dirt from the steel toes of his boots.

In denial, Loretta shakes her head. "Can't be sure of anything. I mean, it looks like him, but how do you know it's him? Lots of men live here, so it doesn't have to be him. It could be any of the neighbors," she says, frantic for a better view; she strains to see through the darkness.

As she watches his every move, she notices him making a jarring turn at the older woman's walkway; his sharp pivot sends panic shooting through her.

With a whistle miming a howling wind, he elongates his steps and stops. Loretta watches him pause, and her heart races. "What's he doing?" she asks, confused.

A flower bed filled with weeds and dandelions is next to the walkway, and in its center is a wooden Welcome sign decorated with sunflowers.

Abruptly snatching the rotted wood from the dirt, he swings it beside him. Then, with a smooth movement, he spins the stick to raise the jagged end and, at the door, strikes it against the metal front. "Knock, knock," he says.

Mrs. Hill is inside, sitting in her cushioned brown recliner, watching a game show on the television. Startled, she sits up and turns down the volume to listen.

He whacks the door several more times.

Having not expected anyone, Mrs. Hill feels inconvenienced and irritated that it interrupts her evening routine. She straightens her pink flannel pajamas and slowly rises to her feet, sliding on her slippers. "I better not miss my show," she says, grabbing her walker beside the chair. She shuffles toward the door and, after clearing her throat, calls out, "Hello?"

The man's devilish grin grows as he patiently waits, swinging the sign; the closer she gets to the door, the more the ends of his lips curl.

Loretta watches the woman's shadow pass by each window, getting closer to her fate. She becomes petrified. "No," she says. "Don't open the door."

Mrs. Hill stops before the window to peek outside. "This better be worth disturbing me at this hour," she says and, not seeing anything, raises her voice. "I'm gonna give you a fair warning! If you are those pesky neighbor boys up to no good again, you better run before I whoop you myself."

The man catches her scent through the door and snarls, his narrow pupils glowing underneath the brim of the cowboy hat.

Annoyed by the lack of response, Mrs. Hill takes a deep breath and cautiously approaches the door.

Loretta's nose smashes against the window's glass; no longer able to see Mrs. Hill's shadow, she panics. Noticing the man's posture tighten, she can tell he is ready to strike. "Shit, I can't just stand here and watch. I ... I gotta do something. If I don't warn her, I'm gonna feel real guilty," she says, sprinting to the door and grabbing the handle. She pulls with all her might, but the door won't budge.

As Mrs. Hill pulls her door open, she glances back at the television and, noticing the credits rolling, releases her anger. "Goddamn it! I'm gonna give those neighbor kids a whooping that'll send them to hell and back," she says, all fired up.

The man stops swinging the object in his hand and playfully shrugs. "Not if I beat you to it," he says.

The rumbling voice puts goosebumps on Mrs. Hill's arms. Terrified of whom she has opened the door to, she reluctantly turns to face him, and her entire body trembles. "It's you ... You were at the insurance office. I ... I...was sure you were the neighbor boys playing another one of their tricks on me," she says with a stutter.

A smile more exhaustive than a jester etches onto the charred skin of his lips, and the excitement behind his thoughts makes them quiver. "You're in luck," he says with a snigger, "because I may have devoured them before they could trouble you."

What Mrs. Hill thinks is a joke is, in fact, a truth. On the way back from wreaking havoc on the office, the man stumbled across the mischievous kids riding their bikes in the street and couldn't help himself. He was famished.

With a belch, he feels a tickle in his throat and hacks, regurgitating an ear; he spits it onto the floor. "Oh, look—one of them must have heard we were talking about them," he says, placing a hand over his lips to hide his snicker.

Horrified, Mrs. Hill's complexion turns ashen. She takes a step back to get away. "Don't you dare come any closer; I'm warning you. I attend church. Get out, Devil! I banish you from this home," she says. She scans the room, looking for something to defend herself with while tightening her grip around the edges of her walker.

Taking his time, he gives her a moment to think there's a glimmer of hope, but then his smile twists into a scowl, and his face elongates, creating a terrifying sight. As his mouth unhinges, his teeth gleam menacingly.

Then he lunges toward her, thrusting the stake deep into her body. The wooden splintered stick protrudes from the wall of her chest. An immense wave of pressure plagues her torso as it punctures her lung. He watches her stunned face, glaring at the image of the bloodstained sunflower.

Delirious, she feels for the base of the sign sticking out of her, and coughing up blood, she gasps for air.

Already moving on, he chuckles. "Such a drag," he says, polishing the racecar belt buckle between his hips. "I usually enjoy a bit more foreplay." He snaps his fingers, and the door slams shut.

Still battling to escape her home, Loretta hears the bang of the woman's front door, and her heart sinks. "Why won't it open?" she says, giving the knob another hard pull.

The trailer's air thickens, slowly getting hotter.

She finds the humidity suffocating. Lightheaded, she frantically tugs at the door again with a hefty heave.

She falls backward, and as she sits on the floor, she looks at the metal knob in her hand. "Help! Someone's gotta help her!" she says, quickly dropping the item from her hands as she rushes to look out the window.

It's only gotten darker, making seeing anything outside impossible.

In a state of distress, she falls to her knees, struggling to catch her breath. While hunched over, she glimpses the white envelope on the floor next to the door handle. There is cursive writing on the outside.

Finding it odd that it has no stamps, she becomes curious and crawls toward it. She carefully takes it in her hands and reads the words aloud, "Your worst nightmare..." she says; her pupils constrict.

Abruptly, the lights in the room flicker.

She flips the envelope over and, noticing a red wax seal, traces the indentation of two crossed flags. As she opens it, she feels her surroundings become nonexistent. Immediately, her focus locks on the folded piece of crème-tone paper waiting inside. She hears a wave of whispering voices within the creases as she focuses. It feels like they are speaking to her, their words tickling her ears. The temperature in the room slowly grows hotter.

She removes the message. As she unfolds it, she feels a sharp prick beneath her knuckle. She checks to see if she is cut or bleeding, and, not seeing anything, she continues to examine the page.

The paper is blank.

Confused, she flips it over and is met with the faint sound of a chanting chorus.

In a growing panic, she swiftly scans the document, clutching it tightly as she flips it once more. A drop of blood escapes from her paper cut as she clenches her fist.

As it falls to the papyrus and absorbs, words written in cursive immediately appear one by one, highlighting the terms of their contract. She panics as she reads the document. "I ... I didn't agree to any of this," she says, scrambling to her feet. "I mean, there must be a mistake."

A blast of static travels through the air from across the room.

The noise makes her shudder; someone has turned on the television.

Irritated and wanting to take control, she crumples up the contract, throws it onto the floor, and kicks it. "You son of a bitch," she says, approaching the tv. "That's not the deal we made. It doesn't even mention me living for a long time."

A burst of deep laughter echoes throughout the room.

Unsure of where it is coming from, she spins in a circle. "I said my boy needs me. I never said I was disposable. It doesn't even mention us moving out of this shithole," she says.

The cackle grows louder. "As you said, a boy needs his mother until he's grown," he says.

"I thought there would be wiggle room. What if he needs me longer than that? Huh?" she asks. "What then?"

The Devil finds her antics entertaining. "Your role is simply to get him from point A to point B. After that, your services will no longer be required, and you will be discarded. Once he attains fame and glory, he won't have any regard for you," he says.

Having thought she could manipulate the situation, Loretta becomes flustered and allows her anger to get the best of her. "That's bullshit. It would be best if you took that back," she says. Her face becomes flushed with rage, and her trembling words are filled with hate. Spit spews from her lips as she continues, "You can't take my son away from me. He is mine; I made him."

The ominous presence grows stern. "A deal is a deal," he says, his voice fading.

Unable to pinpoint his location, she spins in circles, frantically scanning the room. Suddenly, the television screen flickers, catching her eye.

There is something on the screen. Two checkered flags are outlined in the static, symbolizing a car race, while the distant sound of a cheering crowd chanting "Rich, Rich, Rich" can be heard.

"Go, Rich Richardson!" they scream as a car passes the finish line.

The thought of their fates being sealed makes her dizzy, and she collapses to the floor. "Don't worry, Rich; Your Mama's not going anywhere. I will never leave you, my baby boy. Cross my heart," she mumbles as her vision slowly drifts to black.

"Mama will always be here ... I swear, the Devil will never take you from me."

10

MENTAL GAMES

A throbbing headache engulfs Loretta's mind, forcing her to wake.

A bright fluorescent glow projecting from the light fixture above heightens the intensity of the walls' white paint. The fogginess holding her irises captive makes the gleam unbearable, and she winces.

The room is unrecognizable. Nothing reminds her of home. Wanting to escape, she shuts her eyes.

She imagines the hue's intensity to be like the glimmer of Heaven as it filters through her lids. "We all know I'm not going there," she says with a smirk.

Rather than getting swept up in the moment, she suddenly remembers the devilish man who haunts her, and she chuckles at the contradiction of the radiant white. Trapped in her thoughts, the previous day's events appear as a blurry nightmare.

A continuous beeping fills the room, blending with the confusion and dominating the background of her reminiscence. As the shrill sound touches each wall, it bounces to the next, mirroring an analog delay.

Unable to concentrate over the tinny clamor, she coughs, trying to be louder than the noise. The friction created by the arid state of her vocal cords makes her throat feel like it is on fire. Annoyed, she opens her eyes and attempts to survey her surroundings again.

Her view, still coated with a hazy film, blends her surroundings into a single color. She's unable to tell left from right, causing her frustration to rise as she feels trapped in a disorienting world of blurred visuals and overwhelming sounds.

Her panic festers, and with each heavy breath, she can feel the dryness of her throat intensifying, leaving it raw and making it feel tighter. With her heart racing, she coughs forcefully, desperate to break free from the gripping sensation.

The beeping noise persists, growing more aggressive with each of her hacks and escalating in pace to match her nerves. Something about it oddly reminds her of the day she birthed her son.

She extends her arms to pat the space beside her. "My ... my baby..." she says, her voice filled with panic. "Where ... is my son?"

The mattress seems much firmer than what she remembers from home, and whenever she touches it, there's a distinct sound of plastic crinkling. The eerie emptiness beneath her palms triggers her deepest fear: the thought of her child going missing.

Becoming frantic, she shouts, "No, no ... no. I'm a real good mama," she asserts, patting the sweat-drenched mattress for Rich. She talks faster, shaking her head in disbelief. "There is no way I lost my son. He's gotta be around here somewhere."

The vent above starts blowing cold air. As the gust rumbles through the tin ducts, it projects toward the bed. The cold front, paired with the dampness of the sheets, makes her shiver. Everything surrounding her body is soaked.

She tries to ignore it as she shifts her hands to feel the area of her stomach. "Rich, my baby boy, where are you?" she asks.

He is nowhere to be found.

She rolls from side to side, unable to cry because of dehydration, flailing her arms helplessly.

Just as she is about to give up, she is startled by the sound of a door opening and crashing into the wall. A pair of heavy footsteps follows it; someone has entered the room.

Even though the sound should be alarming, her fixation on her lost child makes her complacent about the intruder.

The steps quicken, rushing around the space. The sinister clack of cowboy boots strikes a nerve, and with a final sniffle, Loretta stops to listen, worried that they belong to the man in black. She lies frozen in bed, her mind racing with the belief that he must have taken the child.

Abruptly, the lights go out, and she hears the curtains' rings being drawn against the metal rods, causing her eyes to widen. She nervously scans the popcorn-textured bumps in the ceiling and notices the blurriness is gone.

With a final stomp, the person stops near the doorway. Everything is quiet.

The lack of light creates a dim atmosphere except for the fluorescent glow from the hallway, which acts as backlighting for the figure. The silhouette of a grown man lingers near the entrance.

Loretta knows that if she wants her child, she must act fast. Despite her intention to jump out of bed and confront the intruder, her weakness forces her to roll onto her side, facing the doorway. "What did you do with him?" she asks, clenching her jaw.

As her attention fixates on the man, he stares at her, saying nothing. His silent presence fills her with anger. "You!" she says, shaking. "What did you do with him?"

The figure remains motionless, showing no signs of flinching.

"Don't just stand there torturing me; say something, dammit!" she says, scanning the dark figure. "I need answers. Now!"

The air conditioning unit loudly clinks, kicking out another chilling wave of air, but it carries an unexpected scent this time. Loretta sniffs and notices the aroma of cleaning supplies. "Where am I?" she asks, while trying to kick the sheets away from her feet. "Where'd you take me?"

Abruptly, the man sprints to the light switch. "It's okay. No need to panic ... it's only me," he says, adjusting the dimmer control to add more light to the room.

She watches him gradually move toward her.

He talks slower as he holds up his hands to show he is not a threat. "Mama, it's me."

His southern drawl sounds nothing like the presence that has been tormenting her. She silently scans the room to process her confusion, and with the added brightness and clearer sight, she recognizes she is in a hospital.

He stares at her in awe, unable to tear his eyes away. Startled by his gaze, she quickly hides her face under the sheets; then his words sink in. "Wait. Now, wait a minute ... did you call me Mama?" she asks, peering over the top of the covers and scanning each of his features.

The young man, who is in his late teens, is quite handsome. He is muscular and lean, with a farmer's tan and a defined jawline.

She tilts her head to get another angle; some of his attributes resemble Rut's, but with more refinement, mirroring hers. "Rich," she says under her breath.

Unsure of what she said, he straightens his posture.

Slowly, Loretta lowers the sheet from her face. "Wait ... it can't be," she says, forcing herself to blink.

He nervously adjusts his weight. He stays silent, allowing her to process everything as a smile forms on his face. Loretta shakes her head, trying to gather her thoughts, and as her mind wanders, her eyes land on his shirt. Nothing makes sense. "But ... it can't be... you. I mean, you ... you were just a little baby yesterday," she says. Unable to make complete sentences, she stops.

He glances down at what she is fixated on and notices a dark layer of grease staining his collar. "Shit, I'm sorry, Mama. I should've dressed better," he says. As he's talking, he licks his finger and tries to wipe off the oily residue. "I knew I should've kept an extra shirt in my truck, but I hurried over as soon as they told me you might be waking up."

Loretta's attention shifts to his collar. The smudge shares similarities with the stains on Rut's clothing from work. Her posture stiffens. "Is that engine grease?" she asks.

He stops what he's doing and smirks. "How'd you know?" he asks.

She immediately remembers all the time she spent scrubbing Rut's mechanic clothes by hand. Then, the image of lugging his corpse to the trash cans flashes in her mind, causing her stomach to churn. She shrugs off the thought and says, "I don't know, just a guess. When I was little, my daddy worked at a mechanic shop, fixing cars."

With excitement, Rich lowers his hands to his hips. "I didn't know Gramps worked on cars. Well, I'll be damned. Sometimes, I feel like I don't know anything about our family, especially you and my dad."

Loretta wipes the sweat from her brow while desperately trying to steady her trembling hand. "You don't know anything about your daddy?"

"Nope, not a lick," he says.

"And your Grandma and Grandpa?" she asks.

Saddened, he scans the tiles near his feet. "Oh, shit," he says, panicking. "I guess you wouldn't know."

Loretta is quick to respond. "Know what?"

He places his hand on his neck and nervously massages his skin. "Uh, well ... you know... I didn't want to tell you like this, but they died," he says.

The news doesn't shock her. "Huh," she says.

As Rich returns his gaze to her, he continues, "It wasn't too long after you ended up here. I was so young that I don't remember them, but I heard they went real fast. There was some sort of accident or something."

Not wanting to seem heartless, she forces a light smile. "I'm sure they are in a better place now," she says.

Swiftly, he nods.

Still processing the whole situation, she realizes he knows too much not to be her son, and, in disbelief, she shakes her head. "I still can't believe my eyes. Is that really you, Rich?"

A twinkle forms in his eye. "Sure, is Mama," he says, smiling. "They all said you may not remember me, but I always knew you would. That's how I know I'm a mama's boy."

The sound of being referred to as the young man's mother strikes a nerve. She knows that to be his biological mother, she must have aged. Reluctant to embrace having wrinkles, she neurotically chuckles while retracting her acceptance of the scenario. "Hold up—you can't possibly be my baby boy. That's just plain silly. You gotta be nearly eighteen, way too grown to be mine," she says, hesitantly looking him up and down. "Shoot, it was only yesterday that my child was brand new and sucking on my tit. We both know I'm not old enough to have a child your age."

Shocked, he anxiously laughs, thinking it's a joke. "Well, you better believe it ... who else would I be?" he asks. "Now I know where my sense of humor came from."

"But you have stubble on your face," she says, flailing her hand toward him. "My baby didn't have any of that."

He laughs and, taking a step closer, runs his fingers over the top of the five-clock shadow on his jaw. "It's a hit with the ladies," he says, smirking.

Loretta watches him with horror; the comment reminds her of something Rut would have said. "Nope. No chance you're my sweet baby," she says, looking disgusted.

"C'mon, now, don't look at me like that, Mama," he begs. "I know it's hard to believe, but I'm your boy, not some stranger."

As she picks apart each of his features, a slew of questions fills her mind. "But ... how?" she says, stammering. Quickly, she mimes cradling an infant. "Just yesterday, you were just a baby in my arms."

Noticing her attempting to sit up, he rushes to her side and helps her lay back down. "The doctor told me you gotta rest," he says. "You're still as weak as a baby deer. It's gonna take you a little time to get your strength back."

She realizes that in all the chaos, she has forgotten to ask the most crucial question. "How did I get here?"

The machine monitoring her vitals emits a high-pitched beeping sound that increases in speed as her anxiety rises. She glances in the direction where the noise is coming from. As she watches the waves of the rhythmic beats bouncing across the screen, she willingly allows him to fluff the pillow under her head.

The smile vanishes from his face, and he adopts a serious tone. "Now, I don't know how much you remember, but you took an awful nasty fall—"

A sudden influx of hurried footsteps enters the room. Mid-sentence, Rich shifts his attention to the nurse rushing in. "Saved by the bell," he says with an anxious chuckle.

"I got here as soon as I found out she's awake," the nurse says, gasping for air. "I sprinted from the other wing."

Rich greets him with a handshake. "Can you believe it? She's up," he says, looking back at Loretta; he nervously touches the skin on the top of her hand, and smiling, talks faster. "It just doesn't even feel real."

Frustrated and wanting answers, her patience wears thin. "How long have..." she says; the dryness of her throat triggers a coughing spell, stopping her speech.

Removing a stethoscope from around his neck, the nurse rushes to her side and places the metal piece against her chest. "That sounds reassuring," he says.

She gets her coughing under control and glares at him. "What is that supposed to mean?"

"It means you are alive," the doctor says with a chuckle.

Rolling her eyes, she takes a deep breath and tries to calm herself. "Baby, you gotta tell me this instant: How long has Mama been asleep?" she asks. Softening her focus, she glances at her son.

Unsure how to break the news, he looks to the medical professional for help. "Someone hasn't changed one bit. You are still that same feisty girl I remember," the nurse says.

Taking a moment to observe him, Loretta notices a hint of familiarity in his facial hair. "I know I've seen you somewhere before, haven't I?" she asks.

The nurse smiles. He has been secretly waiting for this very moment. "It's funny that you ask. Just last week, I had this same chat with your son," he says, nodding toward Rich. "I was the one that helped you care for that sweet boy after you delivered him in that truck. That seems so long ago. It was when I was still studying to be a nurse and worked as an ambulance attendant to pay the bills."

She awkwardly laughs. "Oh ... boy, that sure was something, wasn't it?" she says.

Without skipping a beat, his excitement builds as he continues, "I will never forget the look in your eye..."

Pretending to share his enthusiasm, she loudly cackles. "Yes!" she says, pointing at him. He stops and, with an open mouth smile, waits for her to finish. "I knew that mustache looked familiar," she says, struggling to sit up. "Never seen anything like it since."

Fearful that she may hurt herself, the nurse extends his hands to assist. "Be careful trying to sit up like that," he says. "You're weaker than you think."

Ignoring him, she waves him away. Immediately, her son steps in to help. "Yeah, Mama, you have been out for a while," he says. "I already told you that you gotta take it easy."

"I know, I know—I'm weaker than a baby deer," she says, rolling her eyes. Though reluctant, she allows them to assist her and, working to remain calm, talks slower. "So, you boys remember that question I asked earlier?"

They tentatively nod in unison.

Her smile extends from ear to ear. "Good, because I'm gonna ask it again," she says. "So, how long have I been asleep?"

Rich, trying to avoid the question, nervously picks at the brass rivets on his dark jeans, his gaze fixated on the floor. "Well ... I suppose it's been most of my life," he says.

Her smile vanishes, and her complexion turns pale. Trying to give her space, they both step back from the bed.

A slight twitch starts at the corner of her eye. "What—what year is it?" she stammers.

"It's 1989," the doctor chimes in with a smile, wanting to be helpful.

Working to contain her rage, Loretta clenches her jaw and, trying to distract herself, looks down at the tubes running fluid into her left hand's veins. A piece of her skin is puckered underneath the tape, securely holding the IV. Her lip quivers, and on the verge of screaming, she says, "I'm ... old!"

Nervously fidgeting, the doctor glances at the door.

Rich rushes to comfort her. "Mama, it's okay. There's no need to be upset. It wasn't your fault that you were asleep for so long. Don't you worry; I've been well taken care of," he says, softly touching her arm. Hyperventilating, she brushes his hand away to look again at her wrinkled skin.

The nurse, reading the room, covertly makes his way to the exit and pretends to check his watch. "Wow, would you look at the time? I'm sure you two have plenty to catch up on, and I've got other patients to tend to, so I'll let you have some alone time," he says. Glancing over his shoulder as he leaves, he adds, "I'll come back to check on you later."

Before Rich can say anything, he hears the door shut.

The noise irks Loretta, sending her into an angry spiral. Ready to explode, she shifts all her attention to the stain on her son's shirt. "So, that's what my son became for my sacrifice, a fucking mechanic? Huh?" she asks. With a condescending laugh, she continues, "Is that why I ended up being sedated like an animal? So I wouldn't get in the way of you living in your greasy paradise? Is that why my youthful years were stolen from me?"

Her hostility confuses him, and each harsh word makes him cringe. As he absorbs their sting, he slowly turns to meet her glare. Wanting to defend himself, he says, "No, I never said that. I came straight from practice. That's why I have grease on me."

Immediately, his defensiveness makes her heart sink, and she tightly closes her eyes. Not wanting to get off on the wrong foot, she tries to repair the conversation. "I'm sorry, sugar. I just thought I had agreed —" She stops mid-sentence. Then, she quickly resumes, "I mean ... I swore I would always be here to help raise you. It's a real shame that I missed so much of your life. That's why I'm acting like this, I guess."

He gives a sympathetic nod. "I know it's a lot to take in, but I hope you're proud of me, Mama," he says, fixing his pants. "I'm not a mechanic, you know. Your boy is a racecar driver."

The news leaves her speechless; she had convinced herself that she would be a key element for his success. "You're ... a driver?"

He nervously clears his throat. "Well, I'm in the minors for now, like the drag strip stuff, which doesn't make bad prize money, but things will change real soon. I just know it. I can feel it coming."

She's completely distracted by thoughts of the contract, attempting to remember its specific wording.

Thinking she is worried about his career choice leading to a dead-end, he grabs her shoulder. "Mama, who do you think paid for this hospital room?" he asks, motioning around. "I did."

As she comes to a stark realization, each of his words slowly sinks in, and her complexion turns ghostly white. "He never needed me..." she says under her breath.

Not hearing her mutter, he proudly continues, "When I hit fifteen, I didn't have many choices. We were in a heap of debt with medical bills, so I did what I had to do and went to work. I thought of you every step of the way."

She stays silent and shifts her gaze to the wall because she can't stand that she's been pushed out of her son's life. Noticing her pull away, he stops talking, worried he may have upset her. Her mind wanders to the last moments in her living room, unsure of when things went awry.

As he gives her a moment, Rich shifts his attention to the clock on the wall, notices the time, and talks faster. "I hate to do this, Mama, but I'm gonna have to go. It's a big day for us. There's a race tonight that could qualify me for the big leagues. This will put us on the map. We could be famous."

He points to the corner of the room, where an old box television rests against the wall. "They let me bring the one from home, just in case," he says, his voice full of excitement. "That way, you can watch me."

She shifts her eyes to look, but the familiarity of the appliance puts goosebumps on her arms.

"It will be just like you being in the bleachers. I promise," he says. Reaching for the nightstand near her bed, he fumbles for the remote. "I just got to find the right channel, and you will be ready to watch."

Hearing static, Loretta looks away.

With a smile, Rich settles on the sports network. "There we go. Isn't it cool, Mama?" he says, turning up the volume; he sets the remote down and, in a rush, talks faster. "Shit. It looks like the pre-show stuff has already started. I gotta get going."

Taking a deep breath to calm her nerves, Loretta reluctantly looks up to see two male announcers on the network; she is relieved to see their faces appear normal. Focusing on the colossal racetrack behind them, she sighs.

"Luckily, it's not too far from here," Rich says, glancing again at the clock on the wall.

She smiles, staring at the grass the men are standing on, which is perfectly manicured and bright green. Then, her attention shifts back to the pair.

One has sandy blond hair, clearly teased; it's swooped to one side, and his skin tone, paired with the baby-blue color of his suit, makes him appear extra tan. The other man next to him has the same hairstyle, but it's mocha brown, and even though his navy-blue suit is darker than the other one, his golden skin shines equally orange. Underneath, both wear white dress shirts with checkered ties.

Captivated by their choice of outfits, Loretta clears her throat. "What are they wearing?" she asks.

"Welcome to the eighties," Rich says, chuckling. "Believe it or not, that's what's in style."

As she attempts to hide her disgust, she shifts her attention to the stands filling up behind them. "The crowd..." she says.

"I know," he says with a smile, quickly kissing her forehead. "All right, Mama, wish me luck. Gotta go. I got a race to win."

She stares in disbelief, fixated on the screen. Complacently nodding to acknowledge him, she doesn't realize he's already left.

After a delay, the door shuts behind him.

Startled by the echo, Loretta shifts her eyes to look. "Make Mama proud," she says with a grin.

11

RACE DAY

Loretta's attention snaps back to the television. The colors of the broadcast seem brighter than before.

No longer fearful of it being a portal for demons to enter, she looks toward the glimmering screen with awe; it is her beacon of hope. "Isn't that just glorious?" she says, imagining herself at the finish line, all dressed up, cameras clamoring for her picture, as she cheers on her son's victory.

The broadcaster's banter ramps up; each word is followed by laughter. Their cheerful conversation depletes her patience. "Come on, let's get to it," she says, tapping her leg.

Short beeps echo from the heart monitor.

Closing her eyes, she focuses on their pattern; she doesn't remember them being so noticeable. The thought of it distracting her from her moment annoys her. She smiles as she snatches up the remote and turns up the volume. With each click, the banter between the male broadcasters further drowns out the pulsating sound of her vitals.

She scoots herself to elevate her head and get more comfortable. "Much better," she says.

Mid-conversation, one man uses his microphone to give a grand gesture, and at the exact moment, a gust of wind sweeps through the stadium.

Convinced that the race is about to start, Loretta gives her undivided attention and leans closer.

"All right, hang tight, everyone; we will be right back after a word from our sponsors," the man says as he holds his blond hair in place.

A commercial break takes over, and a group of kids appear on the screen. Sunlight streams through bay windows, illuminating their smiling faces as they gather around the kitchen table in a picture-perfect home. With each bite from their cereal bowls, they share what they would like to be when they grow up.

Every crunch triggers Loretta, causing her to neurotically play with the folds in her sheets. It highlights her hidden insecurities about her absent role in her child's narrative. She can't help focusing on how she wasn't needed for his development. "I'm not disposable," she says, frantically shaking her head. "I'm not."

As if on cue, the children laugh in unison.

Engulfed in a blanket of insecurity, she talks faster. "You heard him. If it weren't for me being in that damn coma, that boy wouldn't have gotten where he is today. I was his source of motivation. I was the one who inspired him. I gave him the drive to win. They owe me for that."

The children's cackles grow louder, building on one another, lingering in the air.

Loretta can't stop dwelling on thoughts of her exclusion and crazed; she starts to shake. Just as she reaches her breaking point, the giggles abruptly cease, and a wave of relief washes over her as she gazes upward at the screen.

The broadcast returns to the track, and the sportscaster with chestnut hair takes center stage. "Just in, folks. We are about thirty minutes from our start time," he says.

"Praise the Lord," she says, her thoughts returning to the finish line. Again, she pictures Rich standing on the podium, dedicating his win to her, and the visual brings with it a sense of accomplishment.

A rattling overhead brings another wave of conditioned air from the vent, creating a chill, but Loretta is rejuvenated by the frigid air, finding a renewed sense of purpose that brings a smile to her face. "Real queens don't gotta work hard. They've got people to do it for them," she says, patting the bed. "All they gotta do is sit on their thrones all day and look good."

As she basks in her royalty, watching the men banter on screen, Rich drives like a bat out of hell, trying to make the race on time and continuing to replay their encounter. Unlike his mother's notions of nobility, his version played out quite differently; the reunion was nothing he had hoped it to be. Sure, the long-awaited meeting motivated him to set his aspirations high, but he had thought she would exude more love when seeing him, and he was surprised by her lack of gratitude for his commitment to her and his sacrifice.

Making his final merge onto the freeway, he takes out his emotions by laying his foot heavily on the gas pedal; the revving of the engine is music to his ears. The faster the wheels turn, the more the view of the rural scenery through the side windows appears blurred into streaks of vibrant hues.

He smiles at the sight of the setting sun and the swirl of vivid colors. The beautiful phenomenon makes his mind quiet, allowing him to think. "Name one painter in the world that could do that justice," he says. "There is not one."

Inside the car, he knows that even if everything else crumbles around him, it's something he controls. That's why he fell in love with driving in the first place—feeling like he was good at something gave him enough confidence to stay strong and not let his depression swallow him whole.

As the signs pass by the vehicle, he sees that a few are adorned with racing flags. Following their direction, he eases off the gas pedal and takes the offramp, rolling down the window to get a better view of the track rapidly approaching.

The sounds of the crowded stadium create an ambiance of excitement. Briefly closing his eyes, he listens to the chaos and imagines the fans chanting his name; it gives him a rush of adrenaline. "Won't be long," he says, entering the parking lot.

A sign with a neon yellow arrow points to an area sectioned off for the competitors' parking.

As he gets closer, his grip on the wheel tightens, his knuckles turning white upon noticing the tall silhouette of a man he knows all too well.

Wearing a dark button-down shirt and a black cowboy hat, he waits for Rich's arrival, standing in his assigned spot. His glare casts daggers as he takes the last drag of his cigarette while Rich pulls up beside him and parks.

"Shit," he says, shutting off his car. "Doesn't he have anything better to do?"

The man steps aside, raises his eyebrows, and smiles. "How's that Mama of yours doing?" he asks, patting the hood. "Did you tell her I said hello?"

Hopping out of the car, Rich shuts the door with a sarcastic laugh. The man's eyes widen as he feeds off his disappointment.

Not wanting to think about it, Rich speeds past him toward the stadium. "Well, you were right," he says over his shoulder. "She's not the woman I imagined she'd be. She wasn't grateful at all ... Honestly, she was a bitch, and I hate to use words like that."

The slender man remains in place, and enjoying the moment, lifts his hand to his ear. "I don't think I heard you right," he says. "You may need to repeat what you said."

Rich rolls his eyes. "Uncle Roy, your hearing is way better than mine," he says. "Plus, you know I'm stubborn as an ox, so I'm not gonna repeat it."

Laughing, the man jogs ahead. "That's one quality you got from that woman," he says, snapping his fingers for Rich to follow.

He obediently walks faster. "Gotta say I should have listened when you told me about how she is. I mean, I don't know what it's like to have siblings, but you seem to know your sister better than anyone," he says, looking at the grandstand ahead.

Underneath it is a bathroom. Roy points at it. "All your stuff is laid out for you in there," he says.

"You got it, boss," Rich replies, speeding up. He opens the door and walks inside. Roy follows behind.

A solid black jumpsuit hangs from the stall. The number eight with a checkered pattern is etched into the sleeve.

Unable to contain his excitement, Rich snatches it from the hanger; his eyes fixate on a green viper embroidered on the back. "Holy smokes. This looks expensive," he says.

"Yup, that's what sponsorship gets you ... cool shit," Roy says, trying to get him to move faster.

"I know I've been doing pretty good in pre-competitions and stuff, but I didn't think sponsors would come until after winning today," Rich says, still analyzing the garment.

Above their heads, the bleachers erupt with louder cheering.

Roy taps the toe of his cowboy boot against the concrete floor, counting each second. "Don't think about it; just be grateful. Money is money, my boy. Listen to that crowd. Now, get your ass in gear and act like a winner," he says, brushing off the questions.

"Sorry, Uncle Roy, it's probably just the race nerves," Rich says while pulling on the perfectly fit jumpsuit. As he zips it up, the material seamlessly molds onto his skin.

Having finished the conversation, Roy exits and heads toward the track. Rich closely trails behind, flinging the door open and rushing to catch up.

"Your crew is already out there with your car prepared," Roy says, motioning for Rich to walk ahead; he continues, "Just wait until you get inside; its engine purrs like a wildcat in heat."

A man in checkered apparel nods, allowing them access to the pit. Just as they are about to step onto the asphalt, Roy sees a group of drivers lining up under the bleachers one gate over. "Change of plans. Looks like all the guys dressed like you are lining up for the introductions," he says, guiding his nephew in a new direction.

"Introductions?" Rich asks, confused; he glances in the direction his uncle's talking about.

The men waiting their turn are mostly older than him, ranging from roughly twenty to forty. A man dressed in the same official checkered apparel with a blue name tag that reads Matt paces the line with a clipboard. Yelling has left him hoarse and his face bright red. "Rich Richardson? Is there a Rich Richardson here?!" he shouts while consulting his clipboard. "Rich Richardson?!"

Having no clue what's happening, the sound of his name sends chills trickling down Rich's spine.

"Got him right here!" Roy says, pushing him forward and waving.

Matt squints, looking in their direction. "You gotta hurry, boy. You're near the front of the line," he says. As he removes his hat to fan himself, a patch of gray hair sticks out like wires.

Rich blankly stares at the graying man and then at his uncle.

"Don't be shy. I'll see you out there!" Roy says, giving a thumbs-up.

The man places his hat back on his head and grabs Rich's arm. Pulling him along, he glances again at his clipboard. "Okay, so you are behind..." he says, pointing to a man wearing a red jumpsuit, "Bob. Right here."

Turning around, the man gives Rich a smug look. "Bob, Rich, and Rich, this is Bob," Matt says. Then, done with the quick introduction, he leaves.

Rich awkwardly squeezes in line, avoiding eye contact. With a chuckle, Bob rolls his eyes. "Newb," he says, facing forward.

The other men join in with muffled laughter.

Feeling someone tap his shoulder, Rich turns around.

A driver wearing a forest green jumpsuit smiles at him; he has the number twelve on his sleeve. "Third in line. That's pretty good," he says.

Rich turns to count the people in front of him, but the sight of Bob glaring at him makes him turn back around.

Trying to keep his voice down, the driver in forest green continues, "Honestly, if I were you, I wouldn't be taking that shit personally. I was in your spot last year. Those guys are against any new driver, especially one that is younger than them."

"How old is he?" Rich asks with a whisper.

"That one is turning fifty this year," the driver says.

Rich, shocked by the information, struggles to keep from choking.

"This your first professional race?" the driver asks, redirecting the conversation.

Rich nervously averts his eyes. "Yeah, I've done the drag-circuit stuff, but nothing on TV," he says, trying not to stammer.

"Nice! Always refreshing to have someone closer to my age, unlike these old fuckers," the driver says with a laugh, then extends his arm. "Anyway, my name is Ben. Ben Samuels."

"I'm Rich. Rich Richardson," he says, shaking the driver's hand and smiling. "Wait ... Samuels? Are you related to Mason Samuels? The race car driver?"

"Yup, I sure am. The one and only," he says. "That's my grandad."

In disbelief, Rich stares at him, analyzing the curls in his blond hair. "That's epic," he says under his breath.

With time running out, Ben quickly whispers, "Okay, here's the deal: When they call your name, go out there and wave to the camera. Sometimes, they'll give you the mic to say something, but usually, you head to the tents in the middle of the track to find your crew."

Rich is surprised by the abundance of information. As he considers asking for a repeat, Matt's voice interrupts with an announcement.

"It's showtime, boys!" he says. Waving his clipboard above his head, he motions for the first person in line to go.

The speaker system blares with a song that blends country and rock, creating a lively ambiance—the men in line nod to the catchy beat.

Ben laughs and slaps Rich's back. "Good song choice," he says.

Then, one by one, the drivers' names are announced over the loudspeaker, each followed by raucous cheers and applause as they disappear through the curtains.

With his mind racing and sweat dripping from his forehead, Rich's nerves get the best of him. Convinced it is his turn to go, he bolts through the curtains and is met with a television camera and a series of blinding strobe lights. He lifts his hand to shield his eyes and, unable to see, awkwardly waves.

The crowd goes wild.

Unable to hear anything besides the screaming fans, Rich's attention is caught by a pair of flailing hands from below.

A man dressed in the same checkered uniform as Matt is frantically waving his arms, signaling him to move.

Taking the cue, he hurries to find the steps and, once on the ground, locates the pit crew tents in the center of the track. He winces as a microphone is shoved in his face.

"Hey there, champ! Do you have anything to say to the folks at home?" the broadcaster asks; his verbal pace mimics an auctioneer's.

Rich glances at his chestnut-brown hair and freezes, noticing the cameraman getting closer. "Uh—um—" he stammers. "I—"

As the broadcaster covers his annoyance with a giant smile, he touches up his hair in the camera's lens.

Rich responds with a shrug, saying, "Um ... Howdy out there?"

The broadcaster yanks the microphone away and sprints to catch Ben as he walks off the stage. He appears eager to talk and looks like a pro answering the questions.

"He looks so natural, just like his grandad," Rich says, feeling sentimental.

His attention shifts back to the tents. Each driver's car is in its respective spot.

Unable to locate his car in the lineup, he panics, and then someone grabs his shoulder. Turning around, he is met with a familiar face. "Thank God it's you," he says.

Rich's expression of terror makes Roy laugh. "You got to work on that," he says. "Come on. I got something to show you."

As Rich follows his uncle, he catches sight of a car with decals on the hood matching his uniform. Located midway down the pack, its stark black paint stands out from the others' bright colors. "Doesn't it look mean?" Roy asks.

The crowd's deafening cheers grow louder, causing Rich's ears to ring and pushing him to his breaking point. "Where ... what happened to my other car?" he asks, panicking.

Irritated, Roy gives him a stern nudge, forcing him to walk. "Sponsors," he says, gritting his teeth. He quiets his tone before he continues, "Now, put on a fucking smile. We are on camera."

Like clockwork, a female news anchor approaches them with a cameraman close behind; she points to the tents. "This is where the magic happens. Right now, everyone is getting ready for the biggest night of their lives..." she says, her eyes brimming with excitement.

Feeling uncomfortable, Rich nervously smiles.

"Look! There is newcomer Rich Richardson, heading to his car now," she says; with every step, her baby-blue pencil skirt makes her waddle, and her shoulder-length blond hair, sprayed in place, doesn't move in the breeze.

Roy waves and tips his hat with a wink to hide his anger.

The friendly reaction is enough, and, not wanting to walk that far in her kitten heels, she motions for the camera to follow. "There's plenty more where that came from.

Let's go see what everyone else is up to," she says, heading over to other racers to get their reactions.

With a sigh of relief, Rich makes his way to the front of his car as Roy talks faster. "This is the big leagues, son. So, if you're going to be a winner, you gotta act like one."

"But I haven't even gotten a test lap yet," Rich interjects.

Roy ignores him and gives him a push toward the vehicle. "All right, time to get in," he says.

Caught off-guard, Rich trips, stumbling forward.

"This is your time to shine!" Roy yells. Using two fingers to whistle, he calls for the pit crew.

The fans go wild in the bleachers as an announcement starts. "We are only moments away from history in the making for some of these drivers. So, let's make some noise!" Without delay, everyone screams in unison. Their enthusiasm makes the ground shake.

Rich tries to gather his bearings and, looking through the missing window of the car, squints to see inside. "Shit," he says, finding that the black netting blocks his view.

He is so distracted that he doesn't realize his uncle has vanished. With a predator's instinct, Roy seamlessly merges into the crowd, studying the boy's actions, and with a grin, he fixates on the blood contract Rich's mother made. He tilts his head side to side to crack his neck. "I don't usually deal with kids, but I'm glad I didn't eat that one. His mother was right. There's something special about him. I can tell he's gonna go places," he says to himself.

Rich's attention immediately turns to a reflection in the paint. He scans the outlines of the crew members approaching from behind; they all look unfamiliar.

"It won't be long before he learns you can't outrun the Devil," Roy says. Then, with one last snicker, he falls silent.

Wanting to get a better look, Rich spins around. He scans each crew member, who are all sporting baseball caps and matching buzz cuts. They look like clones.

A petite man shoves his way to the front of the pack. His polo shirt is embroidered with the word Chief.

"You gotta be my Crew chief," Rich says, relieved. As he prepares to ask questions, the man rushes past him, fixated on the car door and seemingly on a mission.

Rich's attention shifts to the helmet in his hands.

A green viper that coordinates with his race suit and car is painted on the top.

As he stares into its eyes, the snake's tongue flickers with a hiss. The ominous sound rattles his ears and sends his heart racing. "What the..." he says, wondering if the others heard it; he looks around.

The noise persists, growing louder, mirroring the crowd's enthusiasm.

Rich spins around, searching for his uncle, and in his dizziness, he catches sight of a crew member with peculiarly pointed features in his peripheral vision. The man looks at Rich and smiles.

Rich takes a deep breath and notices the hiss is gone. "Guess this is what they mean by race jitters," he says. He smiles back at the crew as he hears the announcer's voice over the speaker system.

"Ten minutes until showtime!" the man says, the bass echoing through the stadium.

Without warning, the crew swarms Rich, putting on his helmet and gloves. Then, they forcefully shove him into the vehicle. Their voices are muffled by the helmet and engine noise as they chat while strapping him in. Before he knows it, they are gone. "Damn," he says, feeling constricted. He moves his trembling hands to double-check the safety buckles.

A series of miscellaneous buttons on the dashboard flash bright green. Watching the pattern, he recognizes their placement and feels at ease. "Besides being a little fancier, this isn't any different from my other car," he says, smirking.

Suddenly, the car rolls, propelled by the crew pushing it out of the pit.

Rich grins as his body sways with the motion. "Oh, boy, here we go," he says.

The dashboard crackles with static, transforming into a voice. "How's my winning boy doing?"

"Jesus Christ!" Rich says, jumping.

Another static wave brings with it a sinister cackle that blasts right in his ear. He realizes the voice is coming from inside his helmet, and pushing the button, he laughs. "Ha, ha—funny, Uncle Roy. Should have known you'd try to fuck with me when I'm trying to concentrate."

As he finishes speaking, the earpiece glitches and emits an eerie, distorted, scream-like sound.

Done with the boot-up sequence, Rich pulls his hand away from the dash. "Roy? Are you good?" he asks.

A deep and gravelly voice responds with a burst of laughter. Though it sounds different from his uncle's, Rich is sure it belongs to him. "Now is not the time for pranks," he says; a row of goosebumps prickles his skin.

The voice grows serious. "How badly do you want to win?"

Rich anxiously clings to the steering wheel, gripping it tightly with both hands. "You already know the answer, Roy. More ... more than anything," he says. "Why are you asking me that right now?"

A dark abyss consumes the vehicle's passenger side as Roy continues, "Would you say it's more important than life itself?" His voice lacks static, suggesting it's originating from inside the car.

Rich stutters, unable to speak as red pupils abruptly materialize beside him, highlighted by radiant yellow tear ducts. His stomach drops, and he can feel the weight of their watchful gaze upon him as he glimpses the eyes in his peripheral vision.

The glare looks eerily familiar to the serpents etched into his helmet.

Terrified sweat pools on his brow. "What ... who... what are you?" he asks, clutching the wheel tighter.

The voice takes on a demonic tenor. "I'm the Devil, son, but you can still call me Roy or Uncle, whichever you prefer. Devil or not, I still raised you. No reason to be frightened. Just imagine that you are talking to the same guy you've been calling your uncle for all these years," he says. "Hell, the only difference is that now, we can finally be ourselves. I can show you the real me, dark parts included, and it feels damn good. Let me tell you, this moment has been a long time coming."

"Wait, are you telling me you're not my Uncle Roy? Great fucking time to find out my entire childhood was a lie! Leave it to my Mama to leave me in the hands of the Devil!" Rich says.

Roy's voice mimics a snake's and takes on a more serious tone. "Bingo! But it's not as bad as you think. She did you a favor by leaving you in my care. I can do something better than any Uncle Roy can: make your wildest dreams come true. Your mama already got the ball rolling, but now it's time you put the final touches on your destiny. What is it you want? Having fame and fortune beyond your wildest dreams?" He hisses and says, "Unless you've changed your mind and don't wanna win.... Maybe being a mechanic is more your speed."

The words strike a nerve, spiking Rich's anger. "I'm not a damn mechanic, Roy, and you know that! I'm ... I'm a racecar driver," he says, stumbling over his reply. "This is what I was born to do."

Roy has him right where he wants him. "Well, then, give me your hand," he says; his snarl causes spit to land on the shield of Rich's helmet.

As he faces the set of eyes, he notices something additionally unsettling—a set of sharp teeth has taken shape beneath the devious pupils.

Roy's running out of patience. "For us to seal the deal, we must shake on it. Oh, but before we do, I have to let you know—you may be asked to complete a few minor tasks in return, but they're so insignificant that they're hardly worth mentioning."

Visualizing his dreams, Rich lifts his trembling hand from the wheel and extends it toward his sinister companion.

With a snarl, Roy lunges from his crouched position and bites through the glove, puncturing Rich's skin and drawing blood. Staring at the pair of crazed eyes, he pulls his hand back with terror.

"Drive!" Roy shouts. "Now!" His voice blends in with the revving engines.

Through the chaos, a gunshot starts the race.

An overwhelming sensation blows through Rich like a shockwave, jolting his entire body and causing his hands to fall like a magnet to the wheel. As scorching heat infiltrates his limbs, his wounds miraculously heal, and he shifts the car into high gear.

Laying his foot on the pedal, he drives.

12

MELTING

Back at the hospital, the race plays on the television.

As Loretta fixates on the broadcast, her eyes widen. "Oh, it's starting," she says.

The cars spread out from one another, using different strategies. The roaring sound of each engine rev adds to the chaotic atmosphere as vehicles zoom by.

Unable to contain her excitement, she squeals, "That boy had better make Mama proud."

Gripping the blanket, she locks eyes on the cars as they speed across the screen. Her mind is suddenly flooded with an epiphany, causing her to panic. "He didn't tell me his number. How the hell am I supposed to know what car to watch for if I don't know which one is his?" she asks.

Nervously fiddling with her sheets, she hears the announcer's voice drowning out the howling motors. Between the raucous roar of the engines, bits of commentary piece together the scene. "Number eight, newcomer Rich Richardson, is making his way to the front," he says.

As she holds her breath to listen, her eyes light up, spotting his car. "There he is," she says with a manic laugh. "That's my boy." Her gaze shifts to the image of the snake on the car's hood.

The creature's beady eyes reflect shimmers of metallic green. The intoxicating luster captivates her, deepening her stare and loosening her grip on the covers.

A hissing sound fills the room, originating from the air vent. The unsettling sound transforms into words as her eyes remain locked on the viper.

"Loretta..." it says. Even though the voice is nondescript, the tone has a familiar warmth.

With the start of the second lap, the race intensifies, and the announcer's voice grows increasingly enthusiastic. "I can tell you one thing: From the looks of the start, this will be one that you will not want to miss," he says; the bass in his voice shakes the television. Loretta nods in agreement, consumed by the race.

She coughs to clear her throat and is annoyed by the inconvenience of feeling the scratchy lining of her esophagus. "Nurse! I'm in here, watching my boy race, and I need some water ... now!" she shouts, snapping her fingers. Leaving her eyes glued on the broadcast, she waits for a response.

The door remains closed.

Her condescending tone sends spit flying as she mutters, "Doesn't seem like anyone wants to do their job anymore?"

The race picks up pace, and the car engines rev louder. Her impatience causes her to shift her attention reluctantly toward the room's entrance. With a dramatic cough, she claps her hands. "I better not miss anything tryin' to see if you're coming," she says. There's no reply, so she screams even louder, "Whoever is out there, you better get your lazy ass in here right now and bring me some water ... or...or else!"

A blast of static noise echoes through the stale room, cutting off her train of thought.

The sight of the television glitching makes her angry. "Now there's something wrong with the damn TV!" she shouts. "Add that to your list of things to fix!"

As the pixelation worsens, it skews the images of the cars, making them look like colorful smudges. Loretta pounds her fists against the bed, frustrated she can't tell the vehicles apart. "You gotta be kidding me!" she says, furious; she returns her attention to the door. "What in God's name are you all doing out there? Is everyone on a break or something?"

The blurry screen is joined by a high-decibel squeal that pierces the air, as if screaming at her to listen. "What the hell?" she says. Covering her ears, she pats the nightstand beside the bed, feeling for the remote, and grabbing it, quickly drills her finger into the volume button.

Rather than cooperating, the sound only increases.

She frantically shifts her attention to the controls. None appear to coordinate with what they are supposed to do.

Squinching her face, she presses every key on the remote, trying to find the one that will reduce the sound. Her head pulsates with frustration.

There is only one button left.

She digs her fingernail into the power button and is relieved to find it turns down the volume. Hearing the harsh buzzing cease, she slowly shifts her weight back into the pillow, catches her breath, and, with a heavy sigh, feels a cool liquid dripping down her cheek. The sensation startles her, and she wipes the area to see what it is.

Her fingers are painted red.

It's blood.

Taken aback by the revelation, she realizes there is more emerging from her eardrum. As it grows in abundance, the liquid overflows onto the sheets, staining them crimson. Frantically, she grabs the pillow behind her and presses it against her ear, horrified by the view of the gruesome fabric surrounding her.

The lights flicker. Each bright pulsation mimics the pattern of the heart monitor beside the bed.

She winces and quiets her breath to listen. Pressing the pillow tightly against the side of her head to contain the bleeding, she shifts her attention to focus on the only consistent light source: the washed-out image projected on the television screen.

A clanking sound projects from the vent.

As she feels the room temperature climbing, her stomach becomes uneasy, and a prickling sensation floods her skin. Something about the humidity transports her back to her final moments of consciousness before falling into her coma.

The memory of her last time in the living room floods her mind, causing her complexion to pale as her eyes dart nervously around the room.

She knows what it means.

"He's coming," she says. Releasing the pillow, she stammers, "I gotta ... gotta... get out of here."

There is movement on the television screen, and, noticing something is taking form, her heart races. As the pixelation transitions to solid shapes, the electricity surges one last time before leaving her in darkness.

A creak echoes from the room's far corner.

Her eyes widen as her gaze fixates on the ceiling, too afraid to look.

Taking a moment to recover, she glances back at the glowing screen and is startled by a row of three misshapen sixes. "It's ... him," she says.

A pair of heavy footsteps enters the room.

With the click ... click...click of the cowboy boots, she steadies her hands against the bed, trying to remain calm. "What do you want?" she asks.

The uninvited visitor stops just inside the door and callously stares at her. "Is that any way to greet an old friend you haven't seen in ages?" he asks.

His voice sends a wave of emotions through her, and she seethes with anger for all the time she has missed. "Are you serious? Is that your way of saying thanks? Putting someone in a coma after they give you their child?" she asks, clenching her jaw.

He watches her, tracking each of her breaths.

She doesn't hear any movement and her heart races.

His voice deepens as he laughs. "You should have thought about that before you reacted. You know, Loretta, I held up my end of the bargain. He didn't need you around for this long, but regardless, I honored my obligation," he says.

Irritated, she quickly interjects, "A boy needs his mother."

He gives a condescending grin, his devilish smile growing in the darkness. "I think you are a little too confident. We've been doing just fine without you," he says.

Each of his words fills her with anger. "You know nothing about parenting," she says, ready to snap.

His laugh haunts her. "Oh? I guess we both have something in common there," he says, snickering. "The difference is that I am a giver, supplying him with everything he needs to become great! You, on the other hand, Loretta, are nothing but a taker, a parasite, a leech. Ha! Your sole desire is to bask in the spotlight and reap the rewards of his fame."

While listening, she starts to squirm. "But we are a package deal," she says.

With a snap of his fingers, he dismisses her concerns.

She watches the race return to the television, and her attention becomes glued to the monitor.

"You see that? The boy did that without you," he says.

Stammering, she struggles to find the right words to form a rebuttal. "That's not—" she says.

He continues, talking louder, his voice growing more intense with each word. "That means your end of the agreement has long expired. He doesn't need you, and he never did by the looks of it."

Watching Rich's car edge up to the lead, Loretta shakes her head. "That's not true," she says. "His poor mama in the hospital was his motivation. That's why that boy is going to win."

As he takes a step forward, his smirk becomes more pronounced. "Nonsense! Winning has nothing to do with you, Loretta. It is a longing that resides deep within his soul. The impact of your involvement is comparable to a persistent wad of gum clinging to the bottom of his shoe. It serves no purpose, and it is inconvenient as hell," he says, and, with a mischievous chuckle, he inches closer. "Your depressing existence will only hold him back. Think of how the sponsors will eat up the storyline of him winning the biggest race of his life after discovering his mother's tragic death."

Unable to stand it, Loretta snaps, shifting her gaze toward his. "He won't let that happen," she says. "He won't let you get rid of me."

He has been waiting for her to bring up that point. As his voice turns into an evil hiss, the floor shakes. "I talked to the boy. We both agree on your fate," he says with a hint of amusement. "In fact..." He pauses, his gaze shifting toward the door. "It shouldn't be long before he gets here to say his last goodbyes."

Opening her mouth to speak, Loretta is hit by the sharp, acrid scent of bleach, causing her throat to constrict. A guttural groan comes from the direction of the wafting odor rolling in from the hallway.

The Devil's smirk dissipates as he glances up at the screen. "Well, well, would you look at that? Right on time," he says, quickening his speech; he has other places to be.

Loretta hyperventilates, stressed and unsure of what's happening.

"You have a few visitors who are dying to see you, and I have some other loose ends to tie up, so I'm going to leave you to it," he says. His smile vanishes into the darkness.

Panicking, she scans the dark room. "What the hell does that even mean?" she asks. Without answers, she is left feeling uneasy.

The moaning becomes louder, and Loretta hears boots dragging closer to the room from the hallway. She clears her throat to speak. "Hello?" she asks. "Is someone there?"

A trickle of liquid cuts the silence short, creating an eerie drip ... drip...drip.

Slowly, she notices a lean body taking shape in the doorway.

As the male figure clenches his fists, the monitors and television in the room flash brighter, illuminating more of his identity.

Her attention shifts to his horrific head injury and his unmistakable clothes, a bloody mechanic's shirt, leaving no room for doubt that it is Rut.

The ends of his sunken lips curl, smiling at her.

She anxiously stares into the whites of his recessed eyes. "Hey, there, sugar," she says.

He stands still, grinning, as if he knows something is coming.

Working to hide her nerves, she talks faster. "There are no hard feelings between us, right? You know how I can be."

A spurt of bodily matter exits his gunshot wound, spattering the floor in front of him. He remains motionless.

"I was just being a mama bear, protecting my cub," she continues, babbling. "You were so right about hormones making women go crazy."

Clenching his jaw, his eyes bulge, and his blue-tinged sockets swell, revealing pulsating purple spider veins. The sight of him is so unsettling that she finds herself transfixed, unable to look away.

A flicker catches her attention, and she glances at his hand. Her heart races upon realizing that he is holding the gun she shot him with. With a heavy gasp, her words fall under her breath. "Where'd you get that?"

He tightens his fingers around the grip. His unyielding hold causes his knuckles to turn a deep purple.

Swiftly, Loretta rocks her body from side to side, struggling to move herself to the back corner of the bed. Her attention shifts from the trigger to the door as she plans her escape. Panic sets in, and she starts sweating and talking faster. "You know, I'm glad you are here. I've been feeling a little guilty about what happened between us, but I think if we have a chat, we can sort things out."

Rut cuts her off with a cackle. "There's no escaping this, Loretta. You can't sweet-talk your way out of this one. No matter how much you bat your eyes, you won't get what you want. You made your bed, and now, you gotta lie in it."

His words make her shudder as she stares at him in disbelief. "That can't be," she says, barely audible. Feeling the mattress sway, she shifts her attention to the chaos under the bed and clutches the sheets. "What—what is this place?" Her terror makes her stammer.

Nothing is stable; the familiar tiles are gone, molded into a tarry, quicksand-like layer.

Rut chuckles. "Welcome to the life you've always dreamed of, my dear—a world that revolves around you."

Ignoring him, Loretta fixates on the thick pool of goop swirling around her and smells the pungent aroma of burning sulfur. "You can't do this to me. I'm a good person," she states with conviction.

Rut shakes his head without uttering a word.

She watches intently as he lifts the gun, mentally preparing herself for the deadly bang when he pulls the trigger.

But it doesn't come.

Surprised by the delay, she frantically scans his hand and notices the pistol's positioning. With a cynical grin, Rut is pointing the nose of the barrel toward the floor near the side of the bed.

Looking below, Loretta notices movement from the sludge.

The static from the television casts tiny flickers off the small bubbles surrounding the emerging object. As bits of aluminum surface, they create the arches of the handrails of a walker. Then, the upper half of an older woman's head rises from the abyss, coated in black slime. The sludge stretches to the floor, making her skin appear to be melting, connecting her to the tarry tile.

Loretta fixates on the crevasses encompassing the woman's decomposing mouth and eyes. Wilted sunflowers adorn each goop-filled hole. While her mouth, full of stems, sounds a muddled howl, each of her movements brings the jagged end of a wooden garden sign to light, revealing the bloody end protruding from her chest.

As Loretta kicks her feet to wriggle further back on the bed, she watches Mrs. Hill's open mouth twist into an angry scowl. "You ... I know you. We know each other." Loretta says. "You are that neighbor who lives down the way. We are friends, remember? You don't wanna hurt me because I am sure there's something I can do to help you."

From the look on the woman's face, it's clear that she holds a deep-seated grudge; she wants revenge.

Scrambling to make a connection, Loretta's words tumble out faster, as if trying to catch up to her racing thoughts. "Hey, what happened to you is not my fault," she says. "I had nothing to do with that ... it was all him."

While Loretta's speaking in circles, a loud cracking sound disrupts the scene, causing her to shift her attention to the noise coming from the vent.

From inside the ducting, fingers emerge through the slats of the vent cover, gripping its edges tightly before forcefully removing the plate from the wall. Loretta stares at the square piece of metal as it tumbles to the floor and mixes with the sticky goo.

Suddenly, a piercing hiss shatters the quietness. "It's time to pay up. We've arrived to escort you to your new home in hell," the voices say, echoing menacingly.

The noise from the pitch-black tunnel becomes louder as disfigured bodies wearing office attire emerge from the wall and descend one by one to the ground. They plant their hands against the floor and crawl toward her, pulling up the sticky residue as they travel. With every slinking movement, their howls reveal their misery. "We are only like this because of you," they chant in unison; their beady eyes glow green, matching the viper of Rich's racecar.

"No!" she says. "It wasn't me."

"You all have the wrong person. There's no way a young mama holding her baby could've done that to you, and you damn well know it. I had nothing to do with it. It was all the doing of the Devil. He is the one you're looking for, not me," she says, nervously looking around for a way out.

With no one else to turn to, she looks to Rut for help.

Unlike before, he points the gun in her direction, and his finger tightens around the trigger. "Thanks to you, we're all dead. Now it's your turn," he says.

His unwavering voice fills her with fear, and she shuts her eyes, bracing herself for the sound of the gunshot that will bring an end to the horror. "Just get it over with!" she says. "Kill me if that's what you're gonna do!"

Instead of the crack of a bullet and the smell of gunpowder, the hospital bed trembles with Rut's boisterous laughter before gradually fading away.

Hyperventilating, Loretta opens her eyes and is immediately met with the pixelated television. Its crackling noise fills the room. Although the stench of disinfectant lingers, the lights have returned to normal, leaving her space well-lit.

She no longer sees the bright lights or smells as bothersome; instead, she finds their familiarity a source of relief. Her eyes sweep across the floor tiles, and upon seeing that they, too, have returned to normal, she shifts her gaze toward the door.

It remains closed.

Loretta chuckles, convinced it's all just figments of her coma-induced imagination. "Just some nightmares," she says, trying to slow her racing heart. "Sleeping that long must have really messed with my head."

The distinct sound of booted footsteps approaches the doorway. She shudders, remembering the Devil's words. "He's coming," she whispers.

While reflecting on his comment, she realizes she has already encountered every person who could be the subject of his vague reference. Then it hits her. What if he meant Rich?

All traces of maternal instinct, feigned or not, vanish as she plans her next move. "One thing's for damn sure: if it's between the boy and me, he's gotta go."

The hallway's fluorescent lights surge in reply.

13

ARE YOU A WINNER?

Firm in her decision, Loretta lies dormant in her hospital bed, listening to the sound of the roaring engines through the static.

Back at the track, with every turn, the blood in Rich's veins painfully boils as if he's been hard-wired to the car's engine. His eyes gloss over, and as he grows numb to the torture, his smile twitches to a twisted grin.

Over and over, the words of his "uncle" play in his head. "You'll have fame and fortune beyond your wildest dreams."

The thought of having everything he desires creates a voracious greed that gnaws at his soul. He briefly reflects on what he might have to do in return, but then bounces back to imagining what he will purchase first.

Roy shifts through the caged bars of the passenger side to get closer. "Do you trust me?" he asks with a whisper. Impatient for a response, he snaps his fingers, and the wheel abruptly pulls to the left, grabbing Rich's attention.

"Yes, yes, I trust you," Rich replies, panicking. "I trust you."

The wheel readjusts.

Rich struggles to catch his breath as he listens to his uncle's bone-chilling laugh.

"Remember when I mentioned that there would be a few minor tasks in return for my generosity? Well ... the moment has arrived for my first request."

"What is it? Just let me know what I gotta do," Rich says.

Roy smiles. "Well, first things first, we have to eliminate the dead weight, so ... your mama's gotta go," he says.

Feeling a drop of sweat heading for his eyes, Rich winces, shutting them. "Ok, well, I guess if it has to be done, then..."

The dark entity snaps his spindly fingers, and abruptly, Rich's ears are engulfed by a persistent ringing.

Panicked, his heart races. Noticing the engine's revving is gone, he opens his eyes.

Even though it is still daytime, his surroundings are pitch-black. "No!" he exclaims while searching for the wheel in the darkness.

Something substantial scurries across the floor near his feet.

He squirms in his seat. "Roy!" he shouts, throwing up his arms in frustration.

His breath becomes heavy as his stress levels rise, creating a foggy layer on the helmet's shield. "How ... how am I supposed to win if I can't see the race?" he asks. "Shit, I'm not even in the car."

He wants to say more but stops.

Something is lurking in the room.

A steady ticking sound grows louder nearby. He slows his breath to listen, directing his attention to a small light emerging from the pitch-black.

Little by little, the numbers of a clock illuminate, coming to life on the wall. Their analog appearance is identical to the dashboard of his race car.

Squinting to adjust his vision, he reads the time. "Three?" he asks. "What's that supposed to mean?"

A crisp alarm blasts through the obscurity. As it stops, the numbers change to two hours and fifty-nine minutes.

Rich's pupils dilate. "Is that a timer?" he asks, his fear growing as he wonders what it could be counting down to.

A steady hum envelops the room, muffling the ticking sounds. Its even distribution makes him frantic; he can't pinpoint the direction it's coming from.

Suddenly, a voice bursts through the buzz as if it were being broadcasted through an intercom system. "It's simple. You have the time of the race to complete the task," a deep voice says, cutting through the crackling. "If you finish before time runs out, you'll be granted what you desire most."

Rich instantly recognizes that it is Roy, and trying to hide his anxiousness, he takes on a relaxed posture, slumping in his seat. "Come on. Enough with the games, Roy," he says. "Just put me back in the race."

A twinge of laughter breaks through the thick static.

"Oh, my dear boy, that's not how a pact with the Devil works. Since we made a deal and shook on it, your soul is technically mine, and I get to call all the shots," Roy says.

Rich trembles and a chill runs down his spine. "And ... what if I refuse to do what you say?" he asks. "What if I don't do the job?"

The lights in the room spark and flash red.

Roy's playful nature goes cold, and he snaps his fingers, stopping the clock. "Do you really want to know the answer? The consequences are rather unpleasant. You will experience the pain and suffering of those who died in the name of your success and drum roll, please ... those who died at your victim's hands as well — for eternity!" he says. His words accent the harsh silence of the room.

Rich's complexion turns pale.

Snapping his fingers again, Roy chuckles. "Fun, huh? It's all in the contract."

As the timer on the wall resumes the countdown, the sound of each tick makes Rich feel like vomiting. "Fuck," he says. "I ... I didn't agree to that... you tricked me."

"What did you think would happen? Me handing you the fame?" Roy asks, stepping out of the darkness and into the clock's light; he stares into Rich's eyes.

Rich fixates on his uncle's crooked teeth as he smiles; he looks different.

"You should know by now that life isn't fair. It's the sacrifices one makes that set winners apart from losers. The key to fulfilling your desires lies in your willingness to take action."

A wave of humidity sweeps over the room, and Rich starts to sweat.

"I've got to say, you're different from your mother. She had no hesitation in sacrificing her own child's future for fame. You're way smarter than that," Roy says, smiling. "With me by your side, you'll go far, kid. Just remember that."

Rich listens in disbelief. "Wait! My Mom agreed to this shit?" he asks.

Roy's voice fades away as his image disappears, replaced by persistent static and the ticking clock.

Stricken with panic, Rich springs to his feet. "What does all that even mean? Did she make a deal with you? You can't just drop all that on me. I've got questions," he says, moving the Plexiglass shield to sit on the top of his helmet.

In response, a voice whispers, "There is only one question that demands an answer: How strong is your desire to win?"

Rich glances at the clock.

Time is running out.

"More—more than anything," Rich stammers, "but I gotta be driving to make it happen."

The counting beeps grow louder.

Unable to make out right from left, Rich spins around in circles, trying to gain his bearings. "Everything looks the same," he says. "This is impossible. I have no fucking idea where to go or what to do."

Feeling overwhelmed and ready to give up, he hears a voice again.

"Prove your trust in me ... and victory will be yours," Roy says.

Rich sprints to follow the muffled tone and collides with a wall. He can hear the voice resonating on the other side.

Pounding against the surface, he notices a hollow spot and becomes convinced it's a door, so he searches for a knob to open it. "There we go," he says, grabbing a handle.

"I'll leave you to it. You'll know what to do. Good luck," Roy says with a chuckle.

Rich quickly opens the door and is startled by the sight of the hospital hallway. The overpowering scent of disinfectant, intermingled with the unsettling smells of sickness, reminds him of death. Both the walls and floor are darker in tone than he remembered during his earlier visit; the color appears dingy, almost as if it's been abandoned for years.

Feeling nauseous, he glances at the dwindling time on the clock behind him.

Then, making his choice, he steps into the dimly lit corridor and closes the door.

Three sharp knocks and the unwelcoming words "Get out" startle him, sending a shiver down his spine. He looks in both directions to see who's there, but the hallway is empty. Still not convinced he is alone, he takes a moment to listen.

The corridor remains silent, with no hint of a whisper or knock.

With a sigh of relief, he picks a direction. "Yep, this looks right. Now let's go find Mama," he says, his racing boots squeaking against the tile floor with each step.

Every door that lines the hall has a dedicated number etched into a brass plate.

Halfway down the corridor, Rich pauses and focuses on the multiple combinations. "Shit, what room was she in?" he says.

As he turns around, he spots a nursing station. Lined up behind the dusty reception counter is a row of file cabinets. Rushing toward them, he hops over the desk and sifts through the drawers. "Gotta hurry," he says.

They are in alphabetical order. "All right, if those are the R ... s... then Richardson's gotta be here somewhere?" He moves his fingers faster and, with a smile, pulls her file and holds it toward the light to read. "Lucky number three-fourteen. Here I come."

Unprovoked, the lights flicker.

The flash of darkness catches him off-guard, and he drops the file. "Shit," he says, watching the papers scatter. As he lowers himself to retrieve them, another electrical buzz sounds. Worried a power outage will happen again, he shifts his gaze toward the end of the hallway and notices a panel of fluorescent lights is not working.

As his stare lingers on the ceiling, he feels something watching him.

The next set of lights in the line flashes briefly and then goes out, followed by the resonating clang of metal hitting the floor from within the now-lightless abyss.

In a panic, he refuses to wait and see what it is. "Nope, not today," he says, spinning back around to face the well-lit direction of the hallway.

As he moves forward, the next fluorescent panel in the line flickers behind him, and, with a spark, it bursts.

Doing his best to ignore it, Rich hears a woman giggle from the darkness. His nerves eat him alive as he walks faster, trying to find the room. The span between each echoing footstep seems like an eternity. The thought of something watching him has become all he can think about.

"Three-thirteen," he says, scanning the room numbers. "No, wait, it's three-fourteen. Three-fourteen, not three-thirteen."

"There you are," he says, spotting the number a few doors down and a faint glow emerging from the gap beneath the entrance. Simultaneously, a rattle emerges from the ventilation, accompanied by a rush of air and the scent of citrus-scented bleach.

The idea of someone being inside makes him second-guess himself, and the aroma stops him dead in his tracks. The odor evokes a sense of déjà vu, like a memory he can't quite identify.

Behind him, the darkness keeps growing while something lurking in the distance releases a squeak reminiscent of rusty bedsprings.

He spins around, his heart racing in response to the shrill sound. "Look, I don't want to cause any trouble. I didn't know anyone was working today," he says, lifting his hands in surrender.

He frantically scans the corridor, unable to pinpoint the cause of the noise in the cave-like space; his attention shifts to the next flickering fluorescent panel. Below, the light illuminates the edge of a gurney.

"Hello?" he asks. "Is someone there?"

As he waits for a reply, the wheels sound a final screech. The carriage stops directly under the strobes of light, creating a sharp shine off the metal.

"Is ... is someone there?" he asks again.

There is still no reply.

"I guess I better be on my way, then," he says and turns around, giving a nervous laugh.

The wheels of the bed release another screech as it slowly inches forward.

"What the—" he exclaims, unable to move.

A woman's scream pierces the air.

Frightened, he swiftly turns back and looks at the stretcher, his eyes firmly fixed on the darkness. The plastic-covered mattress squeaks as something shifts on the stretcher, compressing its rusted springs into tight coils.

Sweat pools at his armpits. "What ... what the fuck is that?" he asks.

Trembling, he watches as a pair of bony hands emerge from the darkness and curl around the sides of the bed. As the grip tightens, the brittle skin covering each knuckle turns stark white. The rustling sound intensifies as a woman slowly reveals herself on the bed. Each strobe from the panel above casts tiny speckles of light that hit her back, accenting her disjointed movement.

Her presence paralyzes him with fear.

As he watches her pull herself onto the mattress, her animalistic tendencies send a cold shiver down his spine, and, with a growl, she digs her palms into the stiff sheet, bracing herself on all fours. Her long over, bleached gray hair hangs over her face, swinging back and forth, sweeping the dust as she crawls to the center of the rolling bed.

Desperate for Roy's help, Rich glances toward the ceiling, trying to find a speaker. "Are you seeing this?" he asks, shifting his attention to the woman on the bed.

Not wanting to draw more attention to himself, he lowers his voice to a whisper and, clenching his jaw, talks faster. "Come on, Roy, I know you can hear me."

Her jaw unhinges, allowing dust to enter her mouth, causing her to cough and protrude her decaying tongue through the gap in her teeth.

Rich fidgets and taps his foot, preparing to run. "Roy?" he asks, staring at the gaudy attire hanging off her skeletal frame.

Rounding out her back, she locks her arms and, digging her long red fingernails into the mattress, gains a steady bounce. Abruptly, she dismounts from the bed, leaving a cloud of dust in her wake.

Rich jumps. "Shit," he says under his breath.

Remaining still on all fours, she stares at the floor, resembling a spider preparing to strike.

Rich's posture stiffens. The heaviness of his racing heart constricts his breath; a cold shiver rolls down his back.

With the slightest tilt, she lifts her head to look at him.

A slight part of her hair exposes more of her face, drawing attention to the withered blue flesh bordering her stained red lips and smeared mascara. Her mouth curls into a smirk, and the failing skin around it splits open, creating fresh lacerations that ooze a bloody green discharge that drips to the floor.

"What are you willing to do to get what you desire?" she asks; her demonic cackle rattles the nursing station's filing cabinets.

In a state of panic, Rich is willing to do whatever it takes to escape. With a split-second decision, he spins around, only to find that the corridor has transformed. The once well-lit hallway has become dark, dingy, and filled with an ominous atmosphere, making it nearly impossible to see anything. Rich frantically scans the brass plates beside the doors, desperately searching for his mother's room. Everything has shifted, and the hall has turned ominous.

The woman suddenly erupts into a deep, guttural howl of laughter that echoes throughout the hall. "Where do you think you're going?" she asks, her mouth frothing as her nails click against the tiled floor.

Further down the hall, dust and cobwebs cover the brass plaques, making them hard to read. Knowing he doesn't have time to clean them off, Rich glances at the bottom of the doorframes for any sign of occupancy.

Only one appears to have light coming from underneath.

He picks up his pace and rushes to wipe the numbers with his sleeve. "Three-fourteen ... three-fourteen," he says; seeing that they match, he frantically enters.

As Rich shuts the door, the woman launches forward, barreling down the corridor like a wild animal, crawling toward him on her hands and knees. He fumbles to push the lock on the metal handle as she crashes into the entry.

Struggling for breath, he stares at the door. As her body falls lifeless to the ground, he leans forward in relief, his helmet lightly tapping against the wooden surface. Drops of sweat tumble from the open visor onto the floor. "Shit, what did I get myself into?" he says.

A familiar sound echoes throughout the room, capturing his attention. "The TV," he says, attempting to calm his nerves with a deep breath, only to trigger a coughing fit.

The smell of bleach is overpowering.

He quickly lowers his helmet shield to protect his eyes from the fumes and ease his burning throat, clutching his pants tightly to control his trembling hands. As he turns to face what awaits him, everything appears bright, unlike in the hallway. The lighting creates a warm ambiance, free from darkness.

He looks at the heart monitor beside the bed. The rhythm remains steady, indicating a healthy cardiac pattern. The normalcy shocks him, and he shifts his attention to his mother's body while waiting for the other shoe to drop.

Loretta is tucked beneath the covers, just as he had left her. The only difference is that she seems much more peaceful than he recalls.

After a moment of gazing at her, he takes a step forward but is immediately stopped by a rush of overpowering emotions. "Damn it," he says under his breath—something about her tugs at his empathy.

She waits with her eyes closed, feigning sleep, listening for his movement.

Rich's guilt grows the longer he stares at her face. "It's like she's trying to make this harder on me," he says, second-guessing his decision and promise to his uncle.

Underneath the covers, Loretta coils her fingers into tightly clenched fists.

Trying to avoid his internal conflict, Rich glances at the television across the room. He recalls the amusing memory of nearly dropping it while carrying it up the stairs. "I wish things could be the way they were. It was so much simpler," he says, picturing when he struggled to place it on the rolling cart.

A burst of granulated pixels skews the picture.

Drawn to it, he squints to focus on what's behind the chaos, and, thinking he spots an outline of a car, he moves closer. "Is ... is that the race?" he says, his eyes wide, as more shapes become clear despite the poorly projected picture.

The discovery fills him with excitement, offering a temporary mental escape from the present moment. "It is the race! I wonder how I am doing," he says, rushing toward it.

Loretta listens to his footsteps pass the bed, and, hearing them far enough away, she cracks her eyes open to look. Her pupils follow his movement like those of a haunted portrait.

Obsessed with seeing who's winning, Rich fixates on the static skewing the picture; it's impossible to decipher the cars from one another. Remembering seeing a doctor's stool at his earlier visit, he rushes to grab it from the opposite corner, paying no heed to his mother. His gaze remains locked on the screen.

As he sets up the chair in front of the television and adjusts the antennae, Loretta quietly watches while carefully removing the IV needle from her hand. Blood spurts from the site where the needle had been, sending tiny scarlet speckles spattering the white sheets.

The television's static crackle fills Rich's ears, leaving him unaware of what's happening behind him. "Come on, old girl. I know you can do it. Just a few more tweaks," he says, observing a slight change in quality while making his adjustments.

As Loretta carefully lifts the covers from her body, the corners of her mouth raise to the bottom of her cheeks, forming a sadistic smirk. While facing her son, she slithers to the floor and yanks the plug of the heart monitor from the wall. The emaciation in her legs causes her knees to appear hyper-extended as she unpredictably rises to her feet.

"Come on ..." Rich says; grunting, he shifts his weight to his tiptoes as he fusses with the rabbit ears. The static goes from quiet to loud with each change. He remains oblivious to his mother's movements and the sudden cessation of the incessant beeping of the monitor.

The pixels finally materialize into more recognizable features. Quickly, he takes a step back to admire the screen. "Yes!" he says, spotting his car; he sees it trailing closely behind one with a racing stripe detailing the number twelve, painted in white. He frantically presses the volume button to turn it up.

The announcer's voice drowns out the car's engines. "With less than an hour remaining, Newcomer Rich Richardson is inching his way up to claim first position," he says.

"Hell yeah," Rich says, grinning.

With a flash, an abrupt burst of crackling cuts through the program, interrupting the race. "Are you f-ing kidding me?" he says, annoyed. Smacking the side of the television, he loudly grunts. Rather than improving, the fuzziness becomes worse with even brighter gray tones. "It was just getting to the good part."

As Rich begrudgingly reaches for the antennae, he notices a shape in the screen's reflection, transforming his irritation into horror.

A woman wearing a hospital nightgown is standing behind him.

His stomach churns as he clears his throat. "Mama?" he asks. "Is that you?"

She remains silent, her body gently swaying from side to side.

Taken aback by her sudden appearance, he stares at her reflection in shock before saying, "You know you're not supposed to be up. Now, let's get you back to bed."

When he turns to look at her, he's startled by what he sees.

She looks different from before; her once-soft features appear pointed and demonic.

"You're..." he says, trying to speak but is tongue-tied.

With a hiss, Loretta grabs the stool and shakes it.

The sudden movement sends Rich off-balance, and he flails his arms to find stability, grabbing the television.

His mother throws the stool aside, her eyes fixed on him as he desperately clings to the monitor. "I know you're in on it with him," she says, stepping closer.

Not wanting her to touch him, Rich frantically kicks at the air to keep her away. "'Him' who?" he asks.

Loretta's jagged-toothed snarl sends shock waves through the room, cracking the walls' sheetrock, and Rich tightens his grip on the screen. "You were mine to raise, not his," she says, getting closer.

Her unsettling movements send shivers down his spine, and as the walls continue to crack, he anxiously glances up at the ceiling. "Please ... Roy, I'm freaking out here. I'm not sure if I can handle this," he says.

The sound of his weakness repulses Loretta, causing her skin to sag into a frown. As the scowl deepens, the skin peels from the bone, revealing a peek at the mutated version of herself beneath.

When Rich is on the verge of losing his grip, a garbled command emerges from his helmet. "Kill her now!" the voice demands.

Rich knows it's his uncle. "What the fuck happened to you?" he asks.

"Why, I've been watching you," Roy replies.

Rich, too busy for his uncle's cynicism, notices something odd happening beneath the hanging skin of his mother's grimace—there's an eye peering out at him. Startled, he believes his sanity is slipping. "What ... what the hell is that thing?" he says.

The dangling flesh makes Loretta's words muffled. "You took advantage of me and then thought you could just get rid of me like trash," she says.

She reaches out to touch Rich, and he quickly scrambles back to stay out of reach. Her malevolent stare darkens, and her lips sag further, exposing more of the man trapped inside.

Horrified, Rich panics as he recognizes the bridge of the man's nose is identical to his.

Loretta talks faster, and the clump of her lower lip sways. "I know it's not just him. You both are behind this. I'm sure you had an agreement with him to cut me out."

Rich watches with terror as the man's nostrils flare behind his mother's teeth.

"Well, I have news for you, son: I brought you into this world, so it's my motherly right to take you out." She laughs. Her intent to kill him grows more serious, causing her to drool and announce, "Now I'm going to eat you alive."

Rich becomes overwhelmed by the threat, focusing on her distorted appearance. Quickly, he mumbles in defense of himself. "But I—I just learned about this today." The sight of her mouth opening wider makes his heart race.

With a demonic howl, Loretta prepares to bite. Her scream is so powerful that she loses balance and tumbles to the floor. The walls tremble as the shrill tone reverberates through the room, causing the wall cracks to deepen and the table holding the television to rattle.

Rich desperately clings to the TV, trying to save it from falling, but the monitor's gravity pulls him along. A loud crash resounds through the room as he hits the floor. After taking a moment to regain his bearings, he stands slowly, attempting to orient himself.

Specks of bloody matter spatter the plexiglass shield of his helmet. Horrified, he uses his sleeve to clean it, but the specks smear.

After quickly scanning himself for injury and finding none, Rich lowers his gaze to the floor.

Then he sees it: the horrifying sight of his mother's lifeless body, lying motionless on the floor, her skull crushed by the weight of the television.

He finds himself unable to look away from her, mesmerized by how her body juts out from the shattered screen. Blood slowly pools around her, carrying with it bone fragments from her crushed skull.

Rich's complexion goes ashen, and he winces, squeezing his eyes shut. "What ... what did I do?" he asks.

Roy's laughing voice returns inside his helmet. "Well, my boy, you won. That's what you did."

Already on edge, Rich jumps at the sound of cheering from the crowded stadium. His eyes snap open, and he is greeted by a shower of champagne droplets cascading down his visor as he's standing on a podium.

The announcer's voice loudly echoes, filling the arena. "Let's hear it for our new champion, Rich Richardson!" he says, and the crowd goes wild.

As he looks down, his eyes widen in surprise as he discovers a gold medal hanging around his neck. His hands trembling, he removes his helmet and is hit with a tidal wave of emotions as he scans the stadium.

"Rich! Rich! Rich!" the crowd chants in unison.

Grasping the gold, he redirects his attention to the audience as his name grows louder. Lights flash rapidly below. Startled, he glances in their direction and sees a line of reporters. As they take pictures, he scans the faces of the swarming crowd on the surrounding track.

His uncle seamlessly blends into the group of spectators, and upon noticing him, Rich pauses as they make eye contact. Roy winks and motions to the crowd with a mischievous smirk.

Rich smiles and proudly holds his medal high in the air. His gaze is drawn to the cheering fans in the stands, and he raises his hand above his head to acknowledge their support. Slowly, he points a single finger to the sky.

The camera operators rush in unison toward the podium to snap a photo.

Rich holds his smile and position like a statue, suppressing a tear to ensure everyone gets the perfect shot. "I'm unstoppable. You all are lookin' at number one," he says, speaking through his teeth. "Nobody's gonna take this moment from me."

14

MATERIAL WORLD

As he goes to bed the night after his win, Rich can barely sleep; all he can think about is the crowd cheering his name. Their continual chant creates a permanent melody in his mind. "Rich! Rich! Rich!" In their enthusiastic voices, he finds inspiration to visualize everything he desires for his future life.

He's sitting in the driver's seat of his brand-new truck as the chrome hydraulics smooth the ride and the scent of fresh leather lingers in the cab. He smiles as he tightly grips the wheel.

Rays of sunshine infiltrate the windows from every direction. The light draws attention to a black sign with a single green arrow on the side of the road; its dark wooden stick pierces a newly tilled dirt mound.

Watching it draw nearer, he becomes curious and follows where it's pointing. He finds that when one sign vanishes, another appears, creating a pathway.

After a mile, the arrows curve to the right, leading to a freshly paved asphalt road. Without hesitation, Rich turns down the driveway lined with a thick row of trees and a meticulously clipped lawn.

Impressed by the well-manicured landscaping, he eases off the gas pedal to admire the view through the trees: a grand white house with massive columns. He can't tear his eyes away from the home; it's everything he's ever dreamed of.

Rolling down his window to smell the dew-soaked air, he shifts the car to park and admires the backdrop of Lake Norman. "I've made it," he says. "I've made it."

Unable to believe his new reality, he squeezes his eyes shut and, rubbing his lids, reopens them to get another look.

He suddenly finds himself parked in front of the home's entrance, peering out of his truck's window at the ornate white pillars supporting the awning. "Wow," he says. "That is a sight for sore eyes." With a laugh, he continues, "Sure is rich. Get it? Rich?"

As he continues to chuckle, the bright blue-sky shifts, turning grayish-green. He shifts his attention to the windshield to get a better look.

A gentle breeze rustles through the unblemished leaves of the trees and enters through the truck's open window. He sniffs and winces; the air smells of rancid pond water and dead fish.

Suddenly, it begins to rain.

Plugging his nose, Rich rolls up the window, jumps out of the cab, and runs for the front door, leaving the keys behind in the ignition. "You better be unlocked," he says, pulling on the carved handle.

The door opens with ease.

As he moves inside, a tingling sensation rushes through his body. Becoming lightheaded and dizzy, he stumbles forward. He glances at the shined marble floor as he works to gain footing and notices his clothes morphing.

With a loud thud, the door slams behind him. The harsh tone signals the end of his transition into his racing outfit. Panic fuels his racing heart; on the plexiglass shield are speckles of blood. "What's happening?" he asks, sliding the visor of his helmet up.

A large crystal chandelier overhead gives a subtle flicker, making the double staircases in the foyer sparkle. Staring at their glory, Rich wonders if the adjacent staircases are for decorative reasons or hold a purpose, leading to separate sets of rooms. He imagines growing up in the house and how his childhood would have been different with all the grandeur and extra space.

A child's laughter echoes in the distance, accompanied by the sound of a needle scratching a record. He is not alone.

The tinny tone of a vaudeville tune begins to play, causing the hair on his arms to stand on end. "Hello?" he calls.

But there is no reply.

Looking past the majestic entrance, a pit forms in his stomach. No one is there. Everything is eerily silent except for the haunting tune from the record player. Suddenly, a wave of thunder rolls over the sky, rattling the house's structure.

Pausing briefly, Rich glances toward the grand archway leading into a spacious living room. "Huh," he mutters quietly. Each piece of furniture has cream-colored blankets covering the top; it appears someone is moving. Even though it's subtle, he finds the detail unwelcoming, and fearful of trespassing, he feels the urge to leave.

As he turns to go, lightning strikes outside, casting a blinding flash through the large bay windows facing the lake, startling him. The weather's rumble gives rise to the laughter of a young child. Their footsteps echo up the stairs in perfect harmony.

With a gulp, Rich stops, sweat forming under the padding of his helmet's visor. "I'm getting the hell out of here," he says, turning toward the doorway.

Suddenly, the chandelier goes out.

Left in complete darkness, he extends his arms. "Come on," he says, feeling his surroundings as he searches for the exit.

Footsteps approach behind him, reminding him again that he is not alone. The instant he starts to ask, "Who—" a pair of powerful hands forcefully pushes him. As he stumbles backward, a chair conveniently catches his fall.

Rich struggles to orient himself to his surroundings. With another eerie scratch of the record needle, the trumpet's shrill sound dissipates, and the ambiance quiets.

A man's deep voice replaces the music. "I know the old classics are an acquired taste, but it just seemed so fitting for the house."

Taking a moment, Rich tries to place the familiar sound of the voice.

"How's that favorite nephew of mine doing?" Roy interjects.

Unable to see his uncle, Rich is skeptical about the circumstances. "Uncle Roy?" he asks. "What are you doing in my dream?"

Roy churns with excitement; he's been waiting for Rich's arrival. Skipping across the floor, he pounds on the walls; his commotion sends a thrill through the room's stagnancy. "Ding, ding, ding!" he says. "I have news for you: this is not a dream!"

The exaggerated rhythm of his dancing footsteps brings to mind the ticking clock. As Rich sits in the darkness, he perceives everything with a slight sense of familiarity, and it triggers unsettling memories of his first encounter in the hospital. "Wait a minute. I just dozed off, so I know it's not a race day," he says, trying not to overthink it.

With a shrug, Roy laughs. "Or so you thought." Clicking his heels together, he grins from ear to ear.

As denial overtakes Rich, he is ready to leave and springs to his feet. "No. I just finished my last race. I know that I just fell asleep," he says, trying to make sense of it.

Snapping his fingers, Roy sends a wave of force through the room. "Not so fast," he says.

The burst of energy hits Rich's chest, knocking the wind out of him and pushing him back into his seat. He tries to get up, but gravity restricts his movement from every direction. "Let me go!" he says. The pressure holds him down, imprisoning him. "I did what you asked. You can't do this to me!"

Abruptly, everything falls silent.

Thinking his uncle has disappeared, Rich squirms to escape.

In a flash of light, Roy materializes behind him. "Here's the deal: Originally, I had wanted all of this to be a surprise, but I seem to have run into a slight snag," he says.

The thought of what that could mean makes Rich gulp. "'A ... slight snag?'"

Roy wastes no time saying, "Let me tell you what's going on in my head. That way, we're all on the same page."

Remaining quiet, Rich listens to him.

"Anyway ... to speed things up, I inhabited your body, which sent your soul into a slumber. While you were stuck in limbo, I took it upon myself to win a few more races and make enough dough to buy a place," Roy says.

Rich is stunned and doesn't know what to say. "Wait ... so—"

"You didn't actually think we could buy a place with only winning one race, did you?" Roy chuckles.

In a state of horror, Rich frantically pats his body, seeking reassurance of his existence while trying to process the news. "Hold on—you're saying you possessed me?"

His uncle ponders the question, pacing the room. "If that's what you wanna call it, go ahead. But for me, I view it as teamwork," Roy says, ignoring his concern. "My plan was for you to wake up in your new home. Do you like it?"

With a surprised look, Rich nods and says, "Yeah, it's exactly what I dreamed of."

Roy stops; his eyes glow, feeding off his nephew's energy. "See? I know you pretty damn well," he says.

Remembering his earlier comment, Rich stammers, "But—but what's the catch?"

Roy springs forward in front of the chair and grins. The sudden movement makes Rich flinch. Roy continues, "Every night, when you thought you were dreaming, I put up signs for you to follow, leading you to different homes—some for sale, and some not—so you could decide where you wanted to live. Picture it like a fun game with an incredible first prize."

Rich, getting annoyed with his uncle's evasiveness, asks once more. "Roy, for the last time, what's the catch?" he asks.

"Correct me if I'm wrong, but you said you want this house, right?" With a casual shrug, Roy chuckles.

An abundance of sweat drips down Rich's forehead. "I mean ... yeah. It's like everything I ever wanted. It's on Lake Norman, it's huge, and it has property,"

His uncle smiles and snickers. "Before getting too excited about the prize, there's one little thing I should have mentioned earlier about the rules of this exciting game: if you are to choose a home not for sale, which you did, you must kill whoever inhabits it."

The smile leaves Rich's face, and his complexion turns stark white as the childlike giggles replay in his mind.

With drool dripping from his lip to his chin, Roy envisions the imminent bloodbath. "I would do it myself, but rules are rules, and I have a race to tend to," he says.

Then, with a snap of his fingers, a clock mirroring the analog display of Rich's racecar's dashboard appears on the adjacent wall. With the countdown initiated, each jarring tick grows louder, reverberating through the room.

Seeing the large numbers sends an excruciating jolt through Rich's nervous system. He winces, his mind plagued by the haunting imagery of his mother's smashed skull, causing him to break into a cold sweat as he reads the time. "Two hours and thirty minutes? But that's even less time than before."

Ignoring his nephew's panic, Roy nonchalantly hums to the rhythm of the countdown. "I won't bore you by going over the rules again. They are the same as before. You have until we reach the finish line to complete your task, and if you don't, well, I will not spoil the moment by revisiting that topic. So, chop-chop, boy. You better hurry because I'm determined to win in record time."

As Roy's voice fades, only his grinning teeth remain. "You know the consequences,"

The sound of his uncle's words dissipating sends Rich's mind into a state of chaos. He is not ready to be left alone and nervously scans the room.

A slight white luminosity still lingers where his uncle's smile had been, and an eerie green glow from the clock numbers illuminates a path to the door.

Rich springs to his feet and finds that the gravitational force has been lifted from his body. Certain that Roy may be lurking in the shadows, he sprints toward the toothy impression, adrenaline surging through his veins, and tries to grab his uncle, but each attempt is only met with frustration; he is nowhere to be found.

Left empty-handed, Rich bends forward to catch his breath and notices the green light reflecting from the clock's numbers onto the floor. Every small glimmer provides a glimpse of the room.

His heart races. "Shit," he says. Following the glowing trail, he sees the outline of scattered pieces of furniture. Each is covered by dust clothes, like the downstairs, except for one item: a rocking horse.

He slowly shifts his gaze to the mare's dirty blond mane and worn eyes. Goosebumps form on his arms.

A dingy substance that looks like a tiny cloud is near his foot. Cautiously giving it a nudge, he realizes it's a poof of cotton stuffing.

As he turns in a full circle, his chest cavity constricts.

Around him are other miscellaneous toys painted with dust.

With his back to the rocking horse, he stands in the middle of a child's playroom, frozen in fear. Even though the furniture is neglected, he can't help but visualize small children playing and laughing as they hold each item in their hands.

The rocking horse subtly moves as if someone is climbing onto it.

Rich focuses on the remaining scattered playthings. The room's temperature is rising. "Would you look at that?" he says, the ends of his mouth twitching.

A worn-out tin racecar sits alone, covered in patches of rust and chipped paint, its decals worn beyond recognition.

As he lowers himself to the floor, he fans his neck to cool off and, picking the racecar up, holds it close to his face for a better look. There is something familiar about the body style; he remembers playing with a similar one as a kid. Utterly oblivious to his surroundings, he stands up and remains fixated on the car while the rocking horse continues to rock steadily, unnoticed.

With each fluid, unhurried movement, the rockers remain silent as it sways back and forth ... back and forth...back and forth.

"What are the odds?" Rich says, grinning nostalgically. "The only difference is that mine was red to match my favorite driver." Even though it's battered, he is thrilled that the black paint matches his racecar.

While preparing to give it another spin, he stops and inspects the blemishes. There's a small worn-through area on the hood, and beneath the thin layer of black paint is a hint of red.

He nervously laughs. "I'm sure it's just a coincidence." Without overthinking it, he shifts his focus to the idea of someone idolizing him enough to repaint their toy car to match his own, which excites him. Quickly, he opens the tiny, hinged door to peer inside at the driver.

Unlike the vehicle's exterior, the driver has been freshly painted with vibrant hues that mirror Rich's race suit. Thinking the similarity odd, he extends his finger to touch the black and green colors.

The rocking horse emits a sudden sharp creak. Rich is startled, causing his fingertip to slip. The movement smears the small number eight painted on the figurine's shoulder. His heart races as he feels something watching him from behind. "Is ... is someone there?" he asks.

A young boy responds with laughter.

Conflicted with what to do, Rich slowly turns to check the clock's time, the weight of his decision exacerbated by its loud ticks.

Suddenly, he is taken by surprise as the sound of tiny running feet fills the air, and the toy is ripped from his grasp.

"Don't touch it!" a boy shouts in a voice transitioning from prepubescence to a guttural growl.

Rich tries to remain calm as he scans the clock once more. "A little over two hours," he murmurs. He glances at the rocking horse, which is noisily swaying on its own. Nervously coiling his fingers into fists, he turns around to face the child. "Are you the boy that lives here?" he asks.

The pitter-pat of the child's feet echoes again through the darkness. "No!" he screams in reply.

Rich flinches as the sharp sound causes his muscles to tense up.

The scurrying continues, filling the air with the sound of tiny footsteps dashing across the floor and up the walls.

Rich stays motionless, his eyes darting to trace every sound and monitor the child's movements. "I saw you liked my toy," he says nervously, waiting for a reply.

The child makes a heavy thud as he lands on the floor. "It's mine. You stole from me!" he says.

Becoming anxious about the time, Rich attempts to change the subject. "Do you know who owns this house?"

The rocking horse comes to a dead stop as the boy responds. "I was riding my bike home from a friend's one night when a man stopped me to ask for directions. But he lied! He didn't want to find his way to town. He wanted to eat me, and he did, bones and all."

Rich watches the tiny car emerge from the darkness. As it approaches him, the clock's glow reflects off the hood, illuminating a deep set of scratches etched into the tin in the shape of three sixes.

"It's your fault I am dead!" The boy's scream rattles the walls.

The car collides with Rich's foot, coming to a stop. "The Devil's right hand!" the boy shrieks.

His accusation makes Rich defensive, and the gruesome images of his estranged mother again pop into his mind. "It wasn't me! Goddammit! I didn't do what you think," he shouts, matching the child's tone.

The heckling intensifies as two more young boys add their voices to the mix, chanting, "The Devil's right hand ... the Devil's right hand... the Devil's right hand."

Unable to take the discord any longer, Rich rushes to the door and clutches the knob.

The ting-a-ling of a bell makes him pause as it cuts through the chaos.

It reminds him of the one on the handlebars of the bike his uncle gave him as a kid. The positive memory compels him to turn, but instead of his beloved bike, he sees three children standing in a row.

Despite the limited light, he can oddly distinguish their torn, gory clothes and missing chunks of flesh as if a beast savagely attacked them.

"We were having fun, and then the Devil showed up and ruined everything, tearing us apart and eating us alive," they say. "He wouldn't have been at the trailer park if it wasn't for you. He even swiped our toys and bikes. It's all your fault we're dead!" They lift their hands, pointing at him.

Terrified, Rich shakes his head, and seeing them move closer, fumbles with the doorknob. "Stay away!"

Their faces contort into grins, making the green glow of the countdown clock reflect off their sharp teeth.

With a swift motion, Rich yanks the door open, rushes out of the room, and slams it closed behind him.

While catching his breath, he turns to face the long hallway but finds it difficult to focus; the image of the toy car haunts his mind. Then, he thinks again of the mutilated boys. "Who were they?" he whispers.

15

GAS FUMES

Once again, lightning strikes, causing the thunder to boom and the building to shake.

Flinching, Rich tries to ignore the sting from sweat rolling into his eyes, but the dull bite of the salty drops makes him irritable.

A shadow sweeps across the hallway's earth-toned wallpaper, contradicting the calming effect of the dim lighting. Broad golden accents spackle the walls.

Rich's heart skips a beat as he hears children's racing footsteps. Startled by the breeze caused by someone running past, he immediately focuses straight ahead. He quickly scans from left to right; he's alone. Sighing, he shakes his head. "You can't let every little noise distract you. You gotta focus."

Both ends of the hallway look to be an equal distance from where he stands.

Frustration sets in as he struggles to choose a direction. "You can out-drive anyone out there but can't make a simple decision when your life is on the line? Seriously?"

Falling silent, he listens for a clue, and his ears are met with the sound of a high-performance engine idling in the distance. Taking a deep breath, he says, "I've gotta race to win!"

He proceeds down the hallway until he reaches a flight of stairs and swiftly descends to the bottom. Each strike of thunder rumbles louder outside, blending with the howl of the motor. As the unforgiving marble floor repels each engine echo, the sounds mush together, creating a deafening roar in the darkness.

Unable to tell where it is coming from, Rich nervously clenches his fists and shifts his attention to any hint of light.

Across the way is a dingy white door. Even though it is partially hidden behind the opposing stairwell, he can see a stream of warm lighting coming from beneath it.

He finds something about it unsettling as he analyzes its rundown nature and the surrounding discolored walls. It reminds him of his last visit to his mother's hospital room.

Clearing his throat to stop his emotions, he sighs. "Boy, I sure hope that's the garage."

As the scent of gasoline wafts through the air, he hears a wave of children's laughter coming from the top of the stairs and skittishly jumps. Giving an anxious laugh, he diverts his attention to the aroma. The familiar stench brings him an odd comfort. "This place smells like a mechanic's shop," he says. "Just like home."

Swiftly following the odor, he finds himself standing in front of the door. The pungent stench of fuel wafts from the other side as he looks down, drawn in by the captivating warmth of the light.

"Rich," a deep voice whispers. "I'm in here..."

Before he can process the call, another wave of thunder rattles the home, making him jump. He grabs the handle and aggressively rips it away from the door—the intense aroma of gasoline leaks from the gaping hole, along with a loud engine rattle.

Clutching the metal in his hand, he lowers himself to the ground for a better view. Blinding lights pierce through the hole, making it impossible to see.

His irritation gets the best of him, and he grunts. "You gotta be kidding me. I can't see a damn thing," he says. Refusing to give up, he strains his eyes, trying to see past the glare.

The staircase steps creak behind him; it sounds like someone is descending.

He springs to his feet; the sound triggers his memory of the children's playroom and the dwindling clock on the wall. As the image haunts his mind, he stares at the door. "The time," he says. "Shit, I'm running out of time."

Overwhelmed by the sudden revelation, he desperately pounds his fists against the door, relentlessly trying to break the deadbolts' grip. With each strike, light from inside infiltrates through the splintering cracks, reflecting off the shield of his helmet. The act causes his adrenaline to surge and his heart to race. "I'm a winner, dammit!" he says, quickening his pace. "I'm number one."

He uses all his energy to give a final whack. Immediately, a section of the door breaks away, and bright light floods the entry, followed by a wave of bold gas fumes.

Ignoring the pungent odor, Rich stares at the gap. "That should do," he says, contorting his body sideways to fit.

As he leads with his torso, he is greeted by two beams of light pointed directly toward the door. Their harsh glare reflects off the plastic shield of his helmet. Swiftly, he uses the crease of his elbow to shield his eyes and steps inside.

Fumes thickly lace the air, and the monstrous rattle of the engine is deafening. He takes a deep breath to calm himself, and his throat burns. Feeling himself choking, he frantically rushes to the hole in the door and, sticking his head back through, loudly gasps for air. "Fuck!" he says.

Taking a deep breath, he fills his lungs with oxygen and, with his cheeks puffed under his helmet, turns around. Avoiding the glare, he redirects his gaze to the center of the room.

Sitting there alone is a bright red sports car; the loud color stands out from the white walls and white-speckled marble floor surrounding it.

While admiring the flawless vintage 1970s body, Rich spots a hood mount that gives it the feel of a genuine professional racecar. As the engine revs, he wonders if someone is inside the vehicle.

From a distance, he can't see through the windows, so his attention shifts to a set of big white block numbers outlined in black on the door. They read sixty-six. Then he looks at the matching black-and-white racing stripe filled with sponsorship emblems running down the middle of the hood.

Growing up, there was one racer he admired most, and ironically, in his first race, he met his grandson, Ben. The memory makes him smirk. Even if the vehicle is only a collector's replica of Mason Samuel's car, he hopes it will come with the house so he can live his fantasy of driving it.

Caught in a daydream, he closes his eyes. As his memories linger, they mix with the alluring sound of the engine. "Rich," a voice whispers, "come closer."

It snaps his attention away from his trance; he glances at the car's headlights. The bright light reminds him of the photographers' flashes at the end of the race, and he envisions Mason's grandson standing on the step below him on the podium. All he can think about is winning. The desire consumes him.

"Rich! Rich! Rich!" The voice grows louder, shifting to a gurgling shriek. Each word stands out from the engine's rattle.

Hearing the call, his heart races, and he pans the room. The reflection of the headlights against the floor grabs his attention. There is something different about the section of marble; it has grown in luminosity.

As he stares at the bright-white reflection, he steps forward to investigate, and his legs turn to jelly; he needs air. Feeling flush, he rushes to the door and, gasping, sticks his head through the hole. The red hue of his face slowly dissipates, and he shifts his eyes to look around.

Everything is much quieter than back in the garage. The darkness is pleasant; he finds the shadowed colors are less straining on the eyes. As he enjoys the peace, he takes a moment of solitude to gather his thoughts.

While he focuses, a soft hum becomes audible nearby, eventually transforming into distinct words. "Rich ... Rich, Rich, Rich," the voice says. The sound of his name puts prickles on his skin.

The tone takes on a feminine quality, and with a hiss, it whispers, "Was it worth it?"

He panics and, unsure of his response, scans the dark. "Um..."

Suddenly, the woman's voice transforms into a piercing scream. "Was it worth killing your mother?!"

The severity of her question drains the color from Rich's face. Struggling to speak, his throat tightens with anxiety, causing him to stammer, "Uh ... I dunno... I..."

He halts his speech upon seeing the outline of a dark figure swaying back and forth, watching him from a lightless nook in the far corner of the room.

He gazes at her legs protruding from a blood-soaked and torn hospital gown as she takes her initial step into the light. Red droplets trickle down her ankles and onto her feet, and a smashed television with a static-filled luminosity rests on her shoulders.

He moves his gaze to look at the glow, his heart pounding in his chest. The dangling shards of glass reveal a gruesome sight—glimpses of her mangled head hiding inside. Her disturbing movements are stressed by the tinges of static that highlight her severely disfigured jawline. The fractured bone dangles, causing the skin to stretch, resulting in a distorted grin.

"Damn," he says. "I thought I was finished with you." Swiftly, he releases the doorknob, placing his hands against the back of what's left of the wooden door, pushing on it to open it and make his escape.

The sound of her stomping feet fills the room as she moves toward him. With a sudden jolt, she thrusts her hands through the breach and seizes him by his helmet while the television flickers and the screen eerily portrays the moment of her death. "You're never done," she says.

Pushing harder against the backside of the door for leverage, he fights to free himself. "Let go!" he says, grunting. "I'm running out of time!"

As she latches on tighter, Loretta's anger projects through the influx of static, creating sparks on the broken screen. "Every kill is gonna haunt you till the day you die. You're gonna regret what you did," she spits, gasping for air. "Just wait and see."

Ignoring her, Rich squirms, trying to get unstuck. "Get off me!"

She wiggles his head back and forth. "Tick, tock, tick, tock. Thirty minutes says the clock!" she says.

Being reminded of the time makes him frantic. Thinking fast, he desperately grabs the strap around his chin. "Thirty ... thirty minutes?" he asks, scrambling for the buckle. With bated breath, he pushes the latch harder, hears the safety click, and slips out of the helmet, freeing him from her clutches.

As he falls backward onto the floor, he hears the ticking clock between the booming rumbles of the engine. He spins around to face the car. The gas fumes make his eyes burn and water. Tears roll down his cheeks, and he quickly brushes them away with his sleeves.

The motor's echo off the marble grows louder, escalating the chaos. Staying low, he fights his cloudy vision and follows the noise by crawling on his hands and knees. Waves of snot dislodge from his nose as he feels for the car and, pulling himself up, looks into the open window.

A man is sitting in the driver's seat, fully strapped in.

Rich stares at the blurred outline of his red racing suit and helmet. Running out of breath, he pulls himself partially through the window of the door, fumbling to remove the keys from the ignition.

As the sound of the engine cuts out, the ticking clock becomes the focal point.

Rich's pupils, bright red from the carbon monoxide in the air, scan the key ring to find a small remote. He falls back out the window and lands on the marble floor. In a frenzy, he pushes every button until he finally activates the garage door; as it lifts, he turns to face the rush of fresh air. The wind blows forcefully, driving rain sideways into the room.

Rich lies on his back to catch his breath and, staring at the ceiling, wants to succumb to exhaustion, but the harsh ticks grow louder, matching the thunderous roars outside. Rising to his feet, he runs his fingers through his wet hair and looks at the car; he knows deep down that if the clock is still running, he's not done.

Staring at the windowless door, he clenches his fists and thinks about everything he's just endured. "You tried to kill me ... but now, we're gonna see who's tough," he says, gritting his teeth.

As he slowly gets closer, lightning flashes from the opening behind him, reflecting off something metal on the floor.

Seeing the doorknob he dropped earlier reminds Rich he might need to finish the man in the car. Swiftly placing the keys in his pocket, he races to pick it up, and, tightly clutching the weapon, he feels a wave of confidence. "This is my house now, and neither you nor anyone else can stop me!"

As he lunges at the vehicle, he notices that the man's body is no longer blurred. He remains seated in the driver's seat, buckled up and not moving.

"You think you're a pro or something?" Rich asks, laughing as he looks at the red racing suit and helmet.

The man doesn't respond.

Ready to finish him, Rich slows his approach and raises his voice. "Did you hear me?"

The room resonates with the eerie sound of the clock ticking, resembling the fading pulse of a dying heart.

Annoyed, Rich uses the doorknob to nudge the man's body. As he watches his head limply fall to the side, he sets the knob on the floor. "Let's see who's under there," he says. Leaning over the top of the man, he unbuckles his helmet and slowly pulls it from his head.

His bushy eyebrows, mustache, and sideburns are stark gray and well-manicured; they perfectly accent his leathery tan skin.

Rich drops the helmet from his hands. "M-Mason Samuels ... it can't be," he says, stammering as he tries to speak.

With a heavy gasp, the man's chest lifts and his eyes bulge. In a panic, Rich rushes to unbuckle the seatbelt. "Don't worry, sir, I'm going to get you out of there," he says.

As he nervously fiddles with the metal clasp, Rich feels something tightly grip his forearm, and his heart drops. Frozen with fear, he slowly turns to face the man.

Slowly pulling him closer, his idol stops his shallow breath, and his eyes dilate. "Son, you listen to me. I don't have much time. In the first drawer ... of night... nightstand," he says, whispering. In his hurry, his words blend.

Rich watches the life leave the man's eyes and releases his arm. As the man slumps, Rich carefully exits the driver's seat, his eyes fixated on the pallor of his oxygen-deprived skin. His mouth still droops, hanging open from uttering his last words.

Taking another step back, Rich watches with horror as Mason's face undergoes a disturbing transformation, appearing as if roaches are crawling beneath his skin. "Not you ... too," he says, stunned.

A flash of lightning reflects off the tips of his elongated facial features and pointed ears.

Rich jumps, and as he remains focused on the corpse's twisted features, he reflects on his last words. "The ... nightstand?" he asks; he can't figure out what he was trying to say.

Mid-thought, thunder roars, shaking the room. He flinches at the sound of a honking horn accompanying it and shifts his attention to the open door.

A car is slowly coming down the driveway.

After taking one last look at the lifeless body, Rich steps outside. Closing his eyes, he enjoys the warmth of the approaching headlights and the soothing rain on his scalp, imagining it washing away his guilt.

With his chin raised, he takes a deep breath, savoring the refreshing scent of pine in the air and relishing in the clock's silence.

16

DON'T TELL

F ocusing on the rain's rhythm, he enjoys the soothing touch of each droplet, warming his skin. Each drop creates a soft pitter-patter as it hits the ground, creating a symphony of tiny echoes.

"Are you almost done in there?" Roy yells, killing the peaceful ambiance.

Enjoying the cleansing aspect of the water, Rich isn't ready to open his eyes. "Eh," he mumbles, not fully listening.

The creak of a door's hinges fills the air, followed by the sound of his uncle snapping his fingers.

Roy races closer; his quick, heavy footsteps clack against the marble tile floor. "Come on, boy, time's up. You got to get a move on," he says.

Still trying to ignore him, Rich leaves his eyes closed until the sound of a plastic curtain sliding open sparks his adrenaline, and he feels something slap his bare chest. Gasping in surprise, he inhales a nose full of water and feels the trickle stop against his skin.

"Hate to break it to you, but you have to take a shorter shower today," Roy says. Stepping away from the faucet's handle, he continues, "You got to get a move on and get dressed."

"Huh?" Rich asks in a state of confusion. As his heart races and he struggles to catch his breath, his eyes land on a fluffy green towel waded near his feet, and he immediately grabs it to cover himself. "Where ... where am I?" His eyes flutter, scanning the tiled walling.

Roy chuckles. "What do you think? You are in a bathroom," he says, motioning to the porcelain bidet in the room's corner.

Even though he doesn't recognize the toilet, he swiftly wraps the towel around his waist and rolls his eyes. "I can see that," he says.

"Then why did you ask the question?" his uncle asks.

Noticing Roy's skepticism, Rich hurries to exit the shower and, analyzing the surrounding area, tries to play it cool. The room is massive, and the architecture is ornate. His stomach churns as he recognizes the white marble with speckles of gray swirls. It matches the details of the entryway of the mansion on the lake.

Although he finds Rich's behavior odd and can't pinpoint where his head is, Roy knows they have things to do. After allowing a brief pause, he slowly starts walking toward his nephew.

Rich's eyes are glued to his approach, and he becomes nervous. Watching his uncle get closer, he smirks to hide his confusion and chuckles. "I was messing with you," he jokes, playfully jabbing his chest.

Abruptly, his uncle matches his laughter. "Good," he says, shifting speed; he walks behind Rich and nudges his back. "Now, let's go. We got to get a move on."

Rich listens, and as he takes his first step, his mind becomes scattered. Although he can recall bits of his encounter, he finds some details fuzzy and can't help wondering how much time has elapsed.

His uncle pushes harder to speed up his pace.

The silence makes Rich uncomfortable, and he stumbles over his words as he works to validate his memory. "Is this ... uh... um... is... are we?"

He stops stammering as his attention drifts to the carved stone double sinks. Hanging from the wall above them is a monogrammed white cotton towel embroidered with the initials M.S.

The thought of Mason Samuels makes Rich nauseous.

Roy takes a deep breath as they cross the threshold from the master bath into the main bedroom; his smile extends from ear to ear. With another inhale, he sighs. "Take it in. That is the smell of new beginnings."

Abruptly, Rich opens his eyes, startled by the ice-cold sensation of marble under his feet. The thought of being in the bedroom of a man he watched die forms knots in his stomach.

Ignoring his squirming, Roy ramps up excitedly and, giving a vast laugh, thinks back to the garage. "Oh, boy, you should have seen your face with that plot twist at the end. I never would have guessed the man would off himself right at the finish line, but hey, I can't control free will. He knew what was coming since his contract was up," he says, hitting Rich's back, trying to get him to laugh. "Honestly, I wasn't sure if you would make it at one point. But, hey—you proved me wrong. You earned this." He grandly motions as each of his words becomes faster than the last. "You earned all this, buddy. You earned it fair and square."

Rich breaks into a sweat and, becoming internally paralyzed, forces a chuckle. Panning the bedroom's perimeter, he only thinks about his idol's corpse in the car. The image of his lifeless eyes and slumping body makes him shudder, and he tries to change the subject. "Did we win?" he asks.

With a quiet sneer, his face becomes stiff. "What do you think?" he asks.

Hearing Roy's sarcasm, Rich anxiously chuckles. "Should have known," he says; his attention shifts forward.

Across from a white ornate marble fireplace is an exquisite king bed. As he stares at it, he notices a stark black outfit perfectly laid out on the turned-down white sheets. It oddly matches the one on his uncle's body.

Finding his behavior suspicious, Roy gives his back a heavier nudge.

The closer they get, the more Rich can feel his irritation, and he eyes the slacks, button-up shirt, and cowboy boots. "Why is it all black?" he asks, clearing his throat.

With a heavy grunt to fight back his laughter, Roy pats his back and says, "Well, son, we got a funeral to attend."

Fixating on the outfit, Rich gulps. "Who ... who died?"

Rich's reaction is better than Roy expected. "That's a good one," he says. Stepping back, he leaves his nephew at the foot of the bed.

Rich doesn't notice his uncle getting further away as his colossal laugh echoing through the room masks his footsteps.

Roy's lips curl into a devilish grin as he walks faster to the exit. He stops just before the door and snaps his fingers for his nephew to listen. "Oh, Rich, one last minor detail," he says. After pausing, he talks faster. "I would think of a story if I were you."

As Rich fixates on the mourning apparel, the distance of his uncle's voice catches him off-guard. "What—what do you mean? A story for what?" he asks, stammering.

Roy's smile grows devious; he has been waiting to drop some news, and, bursting at the seams, he swiftly says, "You are at the top of the brackets right now, and with us getting further into the season, the press will want to ask you some questions about your relationship with him."

Rich interjects, gazing at his uncle's back. "But—"

His uncle's boisterous voice drowns him out. "Nope. Before I hear any complaining, you should know that I took the reins for the entire week after he died so that you could get your shit together. So, I don't want to hear any excuses. This is your time to shine," Roy says, his words escalating in energy.

Immediately, Rich feels violated, and rather than relieved, the pause makes him panic. "But ... I... I didn't know him," he says, finishing his thought.

Roy gives a casual shrug. "That's not what everyone else thinks after the man left you his entire estate, so I would start thinking of a better story than that."

Facing the bed, Rich is haunted by the sight of the funeral clothes.

"Honestly, boy, I would be surprised if they didn't ask you to speak," Roy says, waiting for his nephew's reaction.

At a loss for words, Rich gulps; he feels trapped in someone else's narrative.

Smirking, Roy takes a quick look at him. "Oh, cheer up, kid. There is always the option not to attend and play the role of the winning villain … Just to be clear, I'm all for that choice. But we both know you have a soft side, so that's unrealistic. I mean, you barely could kill a man who was old enough to die from a broken hip," he says.

The longer he stares at the clothes, the more distraught Rich becomes over potential questions that may be asked. Still in denial, he shakes his head. "I don't get it. None of this makes any sense. Wh … why would he leave me this house?"

Tired of his nephew stalling, Roy returns to the door and says, "It's simple. He didn't have a choice … Anyhow, you're the one who chose this house. Not me. How else do you think we'd get this place after he kicked the bucket? People who have money have a thing called a will, and you can't just take their shit. It took some careful planning to put this deal together, especially with his greedy brood," he says.

Consumed by guilt, Rich's heart races, and he attempts to justify his actions. "Maybe they never liked the guy, and maybe they'll be happy he's gone," he says, thinking of the Samuels family's reactions to him showing up at the funeral.

Roy rolls his eyes. "Yeah, I'm sure everyone will be cheering at the news that another legend has offed himself and screwed his family out of their inheritance," he says. His voice turns serious as he lifts his hand, motioning for Rich to hurry. "Just get yourself dressed. You have nothing to worry about. The family won't give you any trouble. Ben was your biggest threat, and I've already taken care of him."

As the door slams shut, Rich cringes, looking at the clothes. The thought of losing his only racing friend eats at his conscience. "Shit," he says. "I didn't think about Ben. I bet he's gonna hate me. I mean ... if I were him, I would hate me right now." As he puts on the outfit, he shudders at the possibility of the interaction.

The outfit's perfect fit boosts his confidence as he settles into his new reality. Giving the room one last scan, he shifts his attention to the only window. He pictures the morning sun streaming through the parted gold velvet curtains hanging to the floor from the curtain rod with intricate golden artichoke finials. "I can't believe this is all mine," he says, sighing. "I bet you have a perfect view of the lake from here."

The draped fabric moves with a subtle sway. It is accompanied by a sound that disrupts the blissful moment. "Rich," a voice whispers. "Rich."

Frozen in place, he listens intently to the strangely rhythmic sounds, feeling his body tense up. "Nah, it's nothing," he says, forcing the last button through the hole of his sleeve. "I'm all done with my task. I'm in the real world now, not the other one, so no need to worry."

The curtain gently moves once more.

With a nervous chuckle, Rich steps toward the exit. "The only thing this outfit is missing is a watch," he says, glancing at his wrist and picturing a gold designer band around it.

"All that fame, but at what cost? Is it worth the blood on your hands?" the voice asks.

With his eyes fixed on his wrist, Rich can't escape the haunting image of blood dripping from his fingers. His heart races. Quickly spinning in a circle, his attention lands on the window.

The hiss of the voice lingers behind the curtains.

Rich confidently plants his feet on the marble flooring. "I busted my ass for this," he says, gritting his teeth, practically spitting. "You got that?! I got nothing handed to me; I had to work for everything I got."

Taking a moment to cool off, he keeps his eyes on the velvet panels. "Just as I thought, nobody's there," he says, watching the curtains hang lifelessly.

A wave of anxiety washes over him, prompting him to divert his gaze toward the gleaming silver toes of his black alligator-skin cowboy boots. Distracted, he remains unaware as the left side of the curtains silently lifts away from the wall, exposing a hint of the hidden body lurking behind the fabric.

While he continues analyzing the details of his boots, Rich can't shake the eerie feeling that he is being watched. One by one, finger impressions form on the crushed velvet surfaces as invisible hands stealthily retract the curtain. Sparks of daylight creep through the glass, and the material gathers as it comes to a stop.

Out of the corner of his eye, Rich notices a man standing in the center of the large window, perfectly framed by the velvet. The heaviness of the man's stare makes his stomach churn; he watches sweat drip from his hairline onto the floor.

The sound of leather pant legs rubbing together cuts through the quiet as the man takes his first step. His movement is accompanied by childlike laughter from each corner of the room.

As he steps further away from the harsh daylight, the red hue of the man's clothing and helmet becomes more apparent. A glistening light reflects off his head.

Rich glances at the matching red racing attire and falls quiet. "No way. That's impossible! It can't be Mason Samuels," he says, eyeing him from head to toe.

The man takes another step closer. Rich feels his reality blur as the man's footsteps fill the room. He swiftly scans his surroundings, expecting to see the ticking clock. "No, this can't happen here. No way. Not here," he says, questioning everything he knows. "This can't be happening right now. Can it?" The heavy thuds of his beating heart accompany profuse sweating, and he pulls his shirt collar from his neck for ventilation.

As Mason's corpse staggers closer, his stiff limbs warm up, making his walk less rigid. The sight of him returning to life brings Rich flashbacks of his body lying in the car. "What the fuck is going on?" he says, "How ... but you—you died." As he stumbles over his words, he glances at the sponsorship patches on his chest and peers through the plastic shield, noticing his bushy white eyebrows and bloodshot eyes. Every detail confirms that it is indeed his idol.

As Rich watches him continue forward, he nervously takes a step back. Mason lifts his hand, and his raspy voice whistles for air. "Don't," he says, "move."

The command gives Rich chills; he wasn't prepared for a showdown. "I swear, I didn't mean to take your house. Honestly, I had no idea it was yours. Uh, well … once I realized I had no other option. It was too late. I understand this is a shitty situation, but I hope you can understand. It was you or me," he says.

Realizing the explanation isn't going smoothly, he turns to make a run for it, only to find himself face-to-face with the man, his shield no longer covering his face. Startled by, he jumps. "What the—" he says. Hyperventilating, he struggles to catch his breath as he glimpses Mason's pointed chin protruding from the base of his helmet.

Mason tightly latches onto Rich's shoulders, pulling him closer. Forced to meet the man's gaze, he discovers an unknown horror in each pupil. They serve as a portal to hell, projecting his future, and he is terrified of what he sees. He tries to look away, but his body convulses, and he can't speak.

With Rich's undivided attention, Mason whispers, "Listen to me, son, and listen close. The whole fame thing will screw you over; no matter how much you try to escape the price of it, it will own you. He will own you. That damn Devil will never let you go. Shit, he won't even let you sleep. Please take this as your warning, my boy. It's gonna get worse. Way worse. You gotta find a way out if you can."

A forceful knock reverberates against the door, rattling Rich's nerves. He snaps his head away to look, and his mouth gapes open like he is going to scream.

Mason aggressively cups his gloved hand over his mouth to silence him and frantically whispers in his ear. "The drawer," he says.

The door bursts open, and adrenaline floods Rich's body. Between his heavy breaths, he hears Roy's voice echo through the room and anxiously looks at him standing in the open doorframe, his face harboring a look of confusion.

Taking a moment, Roy looks his nephew up and down and bursts out in laughter. "What the hell happened to you? If I didn't know better, I'd say your clothes won the fight."

His uncle's hilarity strikes a nerve, causing his eyes to bulge from his pallid face. "Uh ... um...." he stammers, his eyes darting from side to side, ready to point out his ghostly companion.

But Mason is nowhere in sight.

Not entertained by Rich's charade, Roy's chuckles turn to silence. "If this is too much for your little human heart to handle, we can just make a deal, and I—"

With a burst of anger, Rich cuts him off. "No! No more fucking deals!" he shouts, shifting his attention to the curtains.

Everything appears normal.

Rich's mind swirls as he works to pull it together. He follows his uncle's disapproving gaze to his shirt; sweat pools under his armpits. He swiftly adjusts his outfit, straightening his shirt and neatly tucking it into his pants. With a worried laugh, he shrugs. "I'm just feeling a little nervous about the whole funeral thing. That's all. I've never been to one before," he says.

Roy looks him in the eyes and clears his throat. "Well," he says, shifting his attention to his nephew's forced grin and smiling, "better get used to it."

The foreshadowing comment brings an ominous cloud over their conversation as they stare at one another uncomfortably.

Suddenly, Roy breaks the silence with a laugh and motions for his nephew to follow.

Rich's face loses its expression as his anxiety grows. Mason's last words repeatedly play in his head as he follows his uncle. Wanting to distract himself, he takes a final scan of the room before exiting.

There is something odd about the white nightstand near the bed. The style does not match the rest of the bedroom set, and the drawer has been left ajar.

Something about it sparks familiarity, propelling Rich to the last moments with Mason in the garage and his warning in the bedroom. Realizing he may have solved the riddle; his eyes grow wide. "The nightstand. The drawer," he says under his breath. "That has to be what he was talking about."

The sound of his nephew's muffled excitement piques Roy's curiosity, and without turning, he shouts over his shoulder, "Did you say something?"

Rich scrambles to craft an excuse, knowing he can't disclose the truth. "Oh, it's no big deal, Uncle Roy," he nervously says. "I was just taking in the sights. You know, after living in the trailer park all my life, sometimes it's hard believing this is my new home."

The sound of naivete in his nephew's voice makes Roy giddy with excitement. "This is just the beginning. Trust me. It will only get better from here," he says with a grin.

Rich watches a skip enter his uncle's step as they pick up their pace. Not used to this side of Roy, he follows the cue and feeds into what he wants: someone malleable. Playing up his small-town innocence, he tests the waters. "Oh, boy, I can't even imagine anything nicer than this," he says.

As Roy listens to the awe in his voice, his smile turns devilish. "Just wait," he says, snickering. "Just you wait." The hiss in his voice continues to resonate.

Rather than wincing, Rich feels cocky. He knows that, just like racing a car, the Devil has blind spots, and with winning never having been an issue, he is sure he can beat him at his own game with a bit of practice.

17

BEAUTIFUL DAY FOR A FUNERAL

Walking down the stairway, Rich visualizes Mason Samuel's corpse in the garage, and, keeping his eyes on the adjacent wall, his subconscious searches for the door. The fragments of his memory haunt him.

Only a few steps ahead, his uncle switches gears and picks up his pace.

Rich matches him, hurrying to catch up, and they dismount off the last step onto the ground floor. His heart races as their heeled cowboy boots click against the marble. The cadence is reminiscent of the torturous clock.

Feeling on edge, Rich clears his throat; he needs a distraction. "So ... are we taking the truck today?"

Roy quickly answers. "Not this time. I knew we needed to show up in style, so I had them send a car for us," he says.

Rich spots the garage door out of the corner of his eye. "Okay," he says. "I guess that makes sense."

The damage to the door has been repaired, seamlessly integrating it with the architectural design. Its renewed appearance provides relief, allowing Rich to brush over his trauma.

Returning to the conversation, he looks at his uncle opening the front door. "Wait... 'them?'" he asks.

"I thought it was the least they could do since you are the estate's heir," Roy says.

Even though it doesn't settle well with him, Rich shrugs. "I guess that makes sense," he says.

As Roy watches his nephew step over the threshold, he points into the distance. "By late morning, the fog will be gone from the lake, and the sun will shine through the clouds," he says.

Outside, an SUV's engine runs quietly amid birds' chirping and insects' clamor. The red glow of the rear taillights grabs Rich's attention, as does the polished shine of the black paint. "Damn, that looks official," he says proudly. He has never seen one up close, much less been inside one before. The closest he's gotten is watching politicians on TV riding in them.

Roy slams the home's front door shut. "Exactly. That's the point," he says. As he rushes past his nephew, he brushes his shoulder, motioning for him to follow.

Rich is startled by the sound of the driver's door opening, and he sees a man dressed in a black suit and tie quickly race around the car, opening the back door. He wears a derby-style hat to mask his buzzed brown haircut and receding hairline. As Roy climbs inside, the driver gives a smile. Rich looks at the pair of wire-rimmed glasses sitting on the bridge of his nose with a hint of skepticism. Then, noticing a gleam from the driver's dress shoes, his stomach churns.

The way the sun hits the polished leather matches the reflection cast by the headlights on the garage floor.

As he struggles to resist being pulled back into the terrifying memory, Rich is torn from his daze by his uncle's fingers snapping loudly, and he quickly makes his way to the car.

The driver closely watches his approach and, straightening his posture, nervously smiles. "Uh, beautiful day, isn't it, sir?" he asks.

In front of him, Rich stops; he feels someone watching him. He glances over his shoulder and notices the curtain swaying in one of the home's upper windows. Thoughts of the warning fill his head and send his heart racing.

Interpreting his distraction and silence as a sign of offense, the driver hastily apologizes. "God, I am such an idiot. I'm so sorry. I shouldn't have used the word beautiful, especially under the circumstances. It's, um ... it's just... I'm a huge fan of yours," he says. "I didn't mean any offense."

Only catching bits of his rambling, Rich selectively hears the words of praise and feels his fear fade away. "What's your name?" he asks with a smile.

The driver breaks eye contact, looks at the ground, and wipes away a droplet of sweat from his temple as he answers. "Jonathon. Johnny, for short. That's what everyone calls me."

Watching him squirm makes Rich feel important, and the man's embarrassment feeds his ego. "It's always nice to meet a fan," he says, extending his hand toward him; he glances at his uncle.

With a smirk, Roy gives him a nod. Rich returns his attention to the driver and shakes his hand. "My name is Rich," he says.

Johnny stutters. "Oh ... there is no need to introduce yourself, Mr. Richardson. Everyone knows who you are," he says, his face beet-red with embarrassment as he nervously grips his hand.

Rich releases his grasp and grins. "Remember, I'm a normal guy, just like you," he says.

Seeing his idol climb into the backseat renders Johnny speechless, and after shutting the door, he can't help but fixate on his star-graced hand.

Roy hops in from the other side and looks over at Rich. "How did that feel?" he asks.

Rich watches the driver through the window's tint as he rushes around the vehicle.

"You keep that up, and they will be eating from the palm of your hand," Roy says with a grin.

While savoring the moment, Rich's attention is drawn to the sound of the driver's door opening and the man quickly getting behind the wheel. They make eye contact through the rearview mirror. "Johnny, you are right. It is a beautiful day for a funeral," Rich says.

Intimidated by his confidence, Johnny nervously nods and begins to drive.

Unable to stop his grin, Roy glances outside and chimes in. "Sure is ... I bet dear old Mason would have loved it," he says, lowering his chin to appear sad. "May he rest in peace."

As Rich listens to his uncle's performance, he casually looks out the window and notices a truck parked in the driveway - the same one he saw in his dream. The sight makes him feel uneasy. However, realizing it's the least of his worries, he dismisses it and shifts his focus to the day ahead.

All three remain silent for the rest of the car ride, allowing Rich a moment of peace to prepare for what's to come.

After thirty minutes of passing countless trees and fields of green, the vehicle decelerates. The click click ... click click of the turn signal pulls Rich's gaze to the front seat; he fixates on Johnny's tightening grip around the wheel.

As he wonders what is causing his nervousness, he notices the arched entrance of the cemetery. Standing below a large picture of Mason Samuels is a man wearing a black suit. He flags for them to stop while juggling a pile of black t-shirts.

Johnny anxiously rolls down the window and motions to the back, unable to read the man's expression through his sunglasses. "I ... um, I'm here to drop off," he says.

With an expressionless pause, the man approaches and shoves a wad of shirts through the window. "Straight ahead," he says.

Johnny hesitantly nods, rolls up the window, and quietly passes the shirts to the back. Roy grabs them, and holding one up to examine, shields his face to hide his excitement.

On the front of the shirt is a large black-and-white picture of Mason Samuels giving a thumbs-up. He is wearing a large gold medal that reads Race you to Heaven.

Staring at the image, Roy fights back a snicker. "Here we go," he says under his breath.

As they make their way down the cemetery's gravel drive, Rich keeps his gaze fixed on what's ahead.

In the distance, a large crowd wearing all black is gathered behind rows of white folding chairs. While some individuals sport sunglasses, others have come prepared with umbrellas, ready for any sudden shifts in the weather.

A long row of signs, painted with vibrant red race cars, juts out of the ground, guiding vehicles to the parking area. While keeping a watchful eye on the road and its many potholes, the driver carefully navigates and parks in a spot labeled Rich Richardson.

As Roy forces his smirk to fade, he sets the shirt in a pile on the backseat and redirects his attention to the window. The cluster of onlookers stares in their direction; their arrival has drawn everyone's attention.

Rich clears his throat to mask his nerves. "What a turnout," he says.

Johnny anxiously reaches for the door. "I'm going to step outside and give you a moment," he says. He takes a brief pause, then continues. "Um ... just tap the window when you're ready, and I'll open the door for you to get out." He exits quickly, and the slam of the car door rattles the interior.

Rich gives a delayed nod.

Pushing the shirts aside, Roy scoots closer and, taking a deep breath, lets out a sigh. "Isn't it just glorious?" he says.

"Uh ... what do you mean?" Rich asks, surveying the crowd outside the window.

Roy chuckles. "Look at all those people. Most of them probably never spoke to the guy. They only come to these things because it makes them feel important, like they matter in the world. In that short moment, as they sit in those uncomfortable chairs, they're not thinking about the man's life, but rather the chance to brag to their friends about where they've been, and through their friends' starstruck eyes, they get a taste of someone else's fame. It gives them a sense of importance they've never experienced, as if they finally matter in their otherwise miserable lives."

Feeling a pat on his shoulder, Rich glances at his uncle, who chuckles. "When you die someday, it'll be the same. As I always say, the more mourners at the funeral, the lonelier the deceased. Even when you're dead, people still want something from you."

The car falls quiet.

"Now that we've had our little pep talk..." Roy says. Tapping the window, he ramps up his excitement. "We have a funeral to attend."

Rich flinches at the sound of the driver opening the door beside him. As light floods the vehicle, Roy pulls a pair of aviator sunglasses from his pocket. "Oh, almost forgot," he says, extending them in his nephew's direction.

Rich snatches them from his hand, and glancing at the driver, puts them on. Still feeling guilty about his earlier comment, Johnny nervously digs his toe into the soil as Rich steps out of the car. "I sure am sorry for your loss, Mr. Richardson, and again, I apologize again for earlier ... I... I..."

Wanting more, Rich lets him go on, and with each passing moment, he can feel the groveling restoring his self-assurance; it makes him feel in control.

Johnny continues, "I'll be waiting right here until the service is over. That way, you know where to find me."

Rich acknowledges him with a nod and steps aside, creating room for Roy to join them. "Thank you, Johnny. I appreciate all you have done for us today," he says.

"He is right. You've been a great sport," Roy adds. Stepping forward, he places his hand on Johnny's shoulder and, glaring directly into his eyes, says, "With that said, we will see you after the service."

Taking the hint, the driver nods and quickly scurries around the vehicle, settling into the driver's seat before closing the door.

Together, Rich and Roy turn to face the waiting crowd.

18

THINK FAST

Feeling a surge of confidence, Rich turns to Roy and gives him a thorough once-over. "Why aren't you wearing a pair?" he asks.

Roy watches him play with his sunglasses and leans closer, not wanting to make a scene. He turns his shoulder away from the crowd and whispers, "Because that would look suspicious."

The matter-of-fact response irritates Rich. Speaking through his teeth, he removes them from his head. "Well, why am I wearing them, then? I'm not gonna be set up," he says.

Roy quickly intervenes, forcing them back up the bridge of his nose. "Remember, this isn't my first rodeo, kid. I've been through this before, so I know I can keep it together. You, on the other hand, are a wild card," he says, speaking from the side of his mouth. He gives the crowd a sad look and acts like he's wiping a tear from his cheek, covering up their disagreement. Rich reluctantly listens and rolls his eyes.

His uncle abruptly lowers his voice and speaks faster. "Tell you what—I'll make you a deal: you do well today, and I won't make you wear them at the next one," he says.

As Rich watches Roy lift his hand for a handshake, he briefly glances at the gathering area for the service. The crowd of onlookers has doubled in size. Worried they are making a scene, he folds. "Fine," he says as he walks toward the crowd.

Roy matches his pace, staying beside his nephew, and, on alert, he spots something approaching in the distance.

He clears his throat as a subtle warning, making Rich nervously look around until he spots the woman rushing toward them. Her heavily sprayed bleached blond hair accentuates her vibrant choice of makeup, and her determined expression makes it obvious she is on a mission. Unable to run in her tight black dress, she gallops to gain speed, her kitten heels disappearing in the soil.

Rich's attention locks on a cameraman following close behind her. As she closes in on him, he glances at her distasteful attire. He sees the microphone and, in a panic, accidentally looks her in the eyes. "Shit," he says, adjusting his sunglasses.

Roy notices his jaw clench and, without so much as flinching, monitors him from his peripheral vision.

Desperate for the story, the woman speaks into the microphone while running, hoping Rich won't escape. "My name is Kirsty. I'm with Channel Twelve News, and I have just a few brief questions to ask you," she says, sliding to a stop right in front of him. Without inhaling, she rapidly fires her agenda; the pace of her words is reminiscent of that of an auctioneer. "How are you feeling? I know your next race is only a few days away. Do you think this tragedy will affect your performance?"

Rich attempts to dodge the microphone shoved in his face and, unable to avoid it, gets pegged in the jaw. He squeezes his fists to keep himself composed and reminds himself that to win, he must play the game.

The reporter eagerly watches him take a deep breath, waiting for him to speak.

"Well, Kirsty, thanks for asking. It's been a tough week, and going back will be hard after such a terrible tragedy," he says. A flicker of sadness crosses his face, but he quickly recovers, maintaining his gaze on the camera's lens. "But I know Mason would want me to keep going. So that's exactly what I will do. I'm gonna give this next race everything I've got. I'm gonna win it for him."

The reporter hangs on his every word; his energy is magnetic. He snaps his fingers, and when she looks, he points his finger toward the sky. She stands, her mouth agape, completely transfixed by the sight of the number one.

He fights a smirk as he walks away.

Kirsty notices the cameraman twirling his finger, signaling that time is up. With an anxious chuckle, she awkwardly retracts the microphone to her lips. "You heard him, folks," she says. "His grief will not stop him from competing. It will only add fuel to the fire of his winning streak. He is here to win it for Mason."

The cameraman zooms past her shoulder to film Rich walking away.

"To all you folks tuning in at home," she says, motioning for the camera to focus on her and fixing her posture, "this is Kirsty from Channel Twelve, reporting live from Mason Samuel's funeral."

Rich feels a rush of excitement as he gets closer to the gravesite and sees the sea of reporters. "Time to shine," Roy says with a smirk. Glancing at the mob, he snickers. "Let's see what you got."

Their whispers build, and they swarm in mass chaos, racing each other for the story. Desperate for their segment, they all want to be the first to get answers. The closer they get, the more they clamor for Rich's attention, shouting over one another. As he watches them throwing elbows, he clenches his jaw and confronts them head-on.

They circle around him like a pack of hungry vultures, their shouts growing louder. "Is it true that he gave you his entire estate?"

The question surprises Rich; it is much more contentious than what he had experienced with the previous reporter. "Well—" he says but is quickly cut off by a reporter shouting over him.

"How long have you known him? Were you and Mason close?"

Trying to pinpoint who is asking the question, Rich shifts his attention to the right.

"Rich ... Rich, over here! Can you comment on the rumors about you being Mason Samuels's hidden love child?" a female voice shouts.

The sound of each question coming from a different direction overwhelms Rich. He finds it difficult to know where to look and who to respond to first.

Before he can catch his breath, the next reporter asks, "What are your thoughts? Was it a suicide or murder?"

Rich tries to stay focused and composed, facing straight ahead as the questions get tougher.

The next person interjects, "I just found out from someone on the inside that the family had no clue about you. How does it feel to be kept a secret?"

Rich flinches.

"Is it true you are speaking at the service?!" a man shouts from the crowd.

Upon hearing the boisterous voice, Rich loudly clears his throat. Immediately, they fall quiet. Knowing they are waiting for him to speak gives him power, and he watches as they eagerly extend their microphones toward him.

Then, with a sigh, he calmly addresses the crowd. "Out of respect for Mason and the entire Samuels family, I ask you to join me in a moment of silence."

Roy notices as Rich bows his head; the others follow. Playing along, he faces his nephew and puts a hand on his back.

Rich glances at him from the corner of his eye. "I understand you've got questions, but this day isn't about me. It's about Mason and us celebrating his life." Lifting his gaze, he scans the crowd and, looking at each of their faces, continues, "So, if you'll excuse me, it has been a hard day, and I am gonna take my seat to pay my respects."

In an instant, the reporters are overcome with emotions—a mix of confusion and guilt. Unsure of when to break the silence, they wait awkwardly.

As they glance at one another, a man in the back of the group can't stand the stagnation; he is ready to burst. "We are sorry for your loss, man," he says. His interjection creates a ripple effect, and the swarm of reporters parts, creating a pathway.

Rich makes his way forward and gives a pursed grin and a nod to thank them. A slow clap resonates from behind him.

Caught in up the moment, Roy scans the group and, hearing the applause grow, hurries to catch up.

They reach the seating area and stop at the back row of chairs. Rich takes a deep breath, and looking at the rows, begins counting the seats. As his attention lands on the last chair, his eyebrow develops a subtle twitch, and he mutters, "Sixty-six. There are sixty-six." An image of the red car door flashes into his mind.

Roy leans closer. "Pretty clever, if you ask me," he says, scanning the seats.

Each chair is elegantly draped in a black linen chair cover with fabric gathered at the legs and tied with a quaint red-and-white burlap bow.

The colors trigger another flashback—this time, not of Mason's car, but his jumpsuit. As the image of the man's dead body haunts Rich, he directs his attention to the center aisle.

Black flower petals scatter the grass, leading to a freshly dug hole at the front. Next to it stands a life-sized cardboard cutout of Mason Samuels from a soda company sponsorship ad.

Upon glimpsing the figure's thumbs-up, Rich anxiously glances at the back row. "This looks like a good spot," he says, but as he is about to sit down, his uncle grips his shoulder.

"What's gotten into you?" Roy asks. Pointing to the front, he continues, "Family sits up there."

Rich takes a nervous gulp and reluctantly looks at where he's pointing, locking eyes with the cardboard figure. His heart races as his eyes slowly pan to the adjacent seating. Before now, he hasn't noticed the mix of people in the first few rows.

Rich clenches his jaw and whispers, "How was I supposed to know? I've never been to one of these before. Remember?" His attention is immediately drawn to the last two open seats, which are situated right in the first row, front and center.

Roy pauses. There are troves of footsteps approaching from behind, sounding like a herd of stampeding cattle. Adjusting his expression, he changes his tone. "Sounds like the ceremony is about to start, so we better take our seats," he says, placing his palm on Rich's back. With a gentle push, he cues him to lead the way.

Rich quickly steps back into the aisle, his eyes locked on the two empty chairs, knowing there is little room for error as he scans the family's backs, preparing to start his approach. The commotion behind him makes his posture stiffen as they reach the front.

Amid the chaos, the crowd's buzzing whispers build, sounding like a hornet's nest.

19

BURIED SECRETS

As the crowd takes their seats, Rich feels their stare on his back; they are waiting for him to make his move. Surveying the empty chairs, he realizes he's nearly the last one standing. While he decides which of the two seats to take, a golden glow from the third seat grabs his attention; it's coming from Ben's blond hair.

With his arms tightly crossed, he slumps in his seat. As rays of sun reflect off each glistening lock, he looks down at the mound of dirt, his eyes red from crying.

Rich nervously shifts his body while glancing at the wrinkles forming in his black suit, and, not wanting that moment to be their first interaction, he makes a quick decision to take the aisle seat.

Before he can sit down, though, Roy takes it from under him and sits first.

Cringing, Rich reluctantly directs his attention to the empty seat next to his friend. He knows he must say something, but as he takes a deep breath to speak, a man's voice projects through the microphone, stopping him. "Family and friends, I welcome you to this gathering and ask you now to take your seats," the man says. His charismatic tone makes everyone fall silent.

As Rich anxiously sits, he notices the crowd directing their attention toward a man slowly making his way down the aisle. He is wearing one of the memorial shirts handed out at the entrance, layered over a white dress shirt. The collar sticking out from the neckline has a dark orange streak that appears to have been unsuccessfully scrubbed with water.

Rich looks at his khaki pants, then his voluminous white hair and the thick sideburns that contrast his sun-tinted skin.

As the man reaches the head of the aisle, he feels the Lord running through him, adding a skip to his step; he waves to some individuals he thinks he should know. "Now, I see a lot of familiar faces out there, but for those who don't know me, my name is Earl Farris. I am the pastor of the Southern Baptist Church located right here on Church Street. You might ask yourself, 'Why does this man standing here look so much like someone from my television?' Well, don't go getting your eyes checked because you are not mistaken. I am on television, leading you in prayer every Sunday," he says, his voice booming with excitement.

Everyone watches him, scooting to the edges of their seats.

"But today is not about me. I am here for only one reason: to lead you through this time of worshipping ... I mean honoring the life of our dear friend," he says. "Praise God, Hallelujah." Shifting his tone, he makes it sound more sorrowful.

On cue, the crowd responds, "Praise the Lord."

Suddenly, the pastor takes off running down the aisle, all fired up, waving his hands in glory. As the man runs by, filled with the spirit, Rich fixates on his mouth, spewing praise. He can't take his eyes off his glistening veneers. Something about their oversized shape and pearly white shade is mesmerizing.

Winded, Earl slows his pace as he makes his way back to the front, and, with his back to the crowd, he lifts his hands to the sky. "Together with our dear Holy Spirit above, all your love and friendship that you bring today makes this sacred gathering mighty special, and on behalf of Samuel's family, I would like to extend their thankfulness," he says. His booming voice echoes through the trees as he smoothly pivots to face the congregation.

The onlookers stare at him in awe.

Noticing them hanging off his every word, he dramatically lowers his gaze. "They are truly grateful for each and every one of you. You all meant something special to this great man, and it means so much to the family that you chose to be with them on this important day to honor the one and only Mason Samuels."

The crowd remains silent.

With a deep sigh, Earl turns and addresses the family. "Let us pray," he says, bowing his head.

In unison, everyone follows, looking to the ground; sniffles scatter the air.

Rich joins in and, lowering his head, glances at Ben from the corner of his eye. He's still fixated on the dirt, staring in the same spot.

Suddenly, the pastor begins again, his low tone rattling the ground. "Dear Father," he says, starting the prayer; he weaves around the chairs to keep everyone engaged.

Rich can't stand the thought of Ben being mad, and he seizes the moment of distraction to break the ice. He shifts closer toward his friend and quickly whispers, "Hey, man, I'm sorry for your loss. I know things may look bad, but I can explain everything when we have time to talk."

As Ben listens, his eyes narrow.

Finding hope in his movement, Rich talks faster. "I didn't mean for things to end up like this. I swear."

Each of his words fills Ben with anger; holding his breath, his face turns red. "You ... you took everything," he says; barely able to keep it together, he starts to shake.

Before he can say another word, Rich interjects, stumbling over his words. "I didn't mean to," he says. "We're friends. I would never do anything like that if I didn't have to."

"'Have to?' He left you his car," Ben says, running out of air. "I'm sure that blows."

Rich is caught by surprise. He didn't know he had gotten the car, and, fighting a wave of excitement, his eyes grow wide. He stares at the piled-up dirt surrounding the hole and thinks about what to say.

Ben has no interest in giving Rich a chance to defend himself and abruptly continues through clenched teeth. "Save it, asshole. We aren't friends," he says. Running out of breath, his seething words become quieter. "You are dead to me. Dead ... to... me!"

Rich, determined not to give up, contemplates his response.

As the pastor finishes the prayer, he lifts his hands. "Amen," he says.

The rest of the congregation joins in. "Amen," they reply.

Both Rich and Ben remain silent.

Lowering his hands, the pastor prepares to tell the crowd a story. "Over his time on earth, Mason has touched many lives with his integrity and honor. For as long as I've known him, his generosity has known no bounds. He gave many donations to our church, offering youth an opportunity to succeed," he says. Stopping, he takes a moment of pause.

Rich feels guilty as he listens to the long list of Mason's charitable acts. While watching the pastor wipe away a tear, he nervously pinches the leg of his pants, attempting to suppress his own emotions.

Rather than being empathetic, Roy finds the man's theatrics entertaining. Swiftly fighting off a devious smirk from forming on his lips, he leans closer to Rich, nudging him with his elbow. In a quiet mumble, he rapidly speaks. "If I knew good old Earl was here to lead the service, maybe I would have been the one wearing the shades."

Paying little attention, Rich struggles to make sense of his uncle's remark and instead fixates on the pastor's finger, fascinated by its gestures. He sees something odd in his mechanical movement; it doesn't seem natural.

Without warning, the pastor's focus shifts, and he cups his eyes and averts his gaze as if concealing something. "Sorry—if you would excuse me for a moment. Going into this, I thought I could stay strong, but I'm only human, and my emotions are getting the best of me," he says. Then, with a sniffling chuckle, he jokes, "Or allergy season is among us."

As he turns away slightly, the audience responds with warm laughs and exchanges sympathetic glances.

From Rich's angle, he can still see Earl's finger, which is now jabbing at the skin of his under-eye. Something about it is disturbing and makes him wince. And though he can't get a full view, it's clear that the motion holds no similarity to wiping away a tear.

Earle pokes and prods, trying to stop his under-eye skin from sagging and revealing what lies underneath. As he fights to push the flesh back in place, he reaches into his pocket, pulling out an eyedropper filled with quick, dry glue. "Sorry, my eyes are a bit irritated by all that crying. I'll just be a minute more," he says, squirting some drops in his eye before applying pressure to the skin.

Initially, Rich paid little attention to the man, but now, he carefully examines him and notices that his features, concealed by his long sleeves and pants, appear to have slight points at the joints. "No fucking way," he mutters. "That can't be."

Able to assume what he's thinking, his uncle notices his body tense. "Yup," he whispers, then shifts closer. "How else would he get his service broadcasted on a network? At first, I took him on as a joke, but that man was onto something. Don't let his presentation fool you—his business is a gold mine. It's the only reason I let him stay beyond his contract."

Rich cringes as the pastor, now sporting aviators, turns to face the audience again. Giving a grand gesture, he looks at the clouds in the sky. "Praise the Lord for lifting my sorrow. I am good as new," he says, then smirks at Roy. Then, shifting to a sad expression, he scans the audience. "With his strength, I know I can hold it together for the rest of our service."

Rich's heart races; he doesn't know who to trust.

As the pastor shouts louder, his broadening stare narrows down, locking on to the first row. "Typically, this is the part of the service where the closest family and friends of the deceased would come up to share their memories of their dearly missed loved one," he says. Catching eye contact with Rich, he can taste his turmoil. "But in typical Mason fashion, he left behind specific instructions on how he wanted this day to go."

Suddenly, the Samuels family glares at the mound of dirt and shakes their heads in disagreement.

Refusing to look away from the pastor's stare, Rich fights his nausea and, clenching his jaw nods. Despite the emotional toll on others, he remains focused on the bigger picture—where he can shape his own story.

The pastor starts with a joke to ease the tension. "I feel like this boy's ears have been burning lately. He has been the talk of the town not only for his success on the track but his closeness to a hero," he says, and continuing, he lifts his hand for the grand reveal, pointing toward Rich's seat.

"Remember, ladies and gentlemen, everyone deserves a shot at redemption. So, without further ado, I invite the other man of the hour, Rich Richardson, up to the stage to share his story," Earl says, motioning for him to approach.

Gasps and chatter erupt in the audience.

Rich stands and takes a deep breath; something about everyone talking about him fills him with angst and importance. It feeds his ego and boosts his confidence. He quickly removes his sunglasses and puts them in his pocket.

Roy maintains his silence, clenching his teeth. Even though he feels disrespected by the off-script action, he understands that causing a scene is not an option. He eyes Rich with skepticism as he heads to the front.

Rich smoothly pivots and scans the crowd. He brushes off the family's boycott in the first row and directs his attention to the other attendees, who are eagerly waiting for him to speak.

Sensing the tension, the pastor proves his loyalty with an embrace. "You only got one shot, kid. Don't blow it," he whispers. Then, breaking the hug, he claps while leaving center stage. Abruptly, the audience's chatter stops, and they join in the applause.

Rich subtly tips his chin and lifts his hands, silencing them. Reveling in his control, he glances at the pastor and, motioning toward him, brings him back into the conversation. "I just wanna say, Pastor Earl, I have been watching your sermons on the television ever since I can remember. So, I gotta admit, I'm a little Starstruck sharing the stage with you right now," he says. After taking a pause, he continues, "We were too poor to have our own TV, but when my mama, God rest her soul, fell into a coma when I was real young, I'd go every Sunday to visit her and watch your service on the hospital TV. You got me through a real dark time in my life. God bless you for that."

Sounds of sniffles flood through the seats, setting an empathetic scene.

With a brief pause, the pastor focuses on Rich, attempting to analyze his next move. Unable to get a good read on him, he tentatively plays along and remains in character. "Praise God," he says. Directing his attention to the audience, he lifts his hands to the sky. "He is wondrous and full of miracles."

Whispers circulate through the crowd. Rich quickly motions to the front row. "That man sitting in the aisle seat over there is my uncle. For most of my life, he's been the closest thing I had to a dad," he says, forcing a sniffle. "He stepped in when my mama couldn't raise me."

Loving the praise, Roy proudly places his hand on his chest and, seizing the spotlight, turns to give a wave to the audience.

To retain control, Rich clears his throat. "Now, I know what y'all are thinking." He points his finger to himself, talking faster. "Why is this guy the one talking instead of the family? And, well, I'm about to get to that. I know my standing up here has ruffled some feathers, so I want to clear the air."

Everyone eagerly scoots to the edge of their seat.

Waiting for them to settle, he sniffles. "Sorry, folks. This is tough for me to talk about. I've had to keep it a secret for so long. But ever since I can remember, Mason Samuels has been my idol," he says. Pretending to have a memory come back, he forces a smile. "When I was a kid, I used to play with this old tin toy car and imagine I could be half as good a racer as him someday."

Unable to hide their curiosity, the family lifts their gazes to watch him mimic rolling it through the air.

Suddenly, Rich's mind drifts into a dark place as he envisions the toy room of the house, and a chilling howl, resembling a child's laughter, grabs his focus. Panicked, he quickly glances at the family.

They are nowhere to be found, and sitting in their place are the dead, decaying boys.

As he scans the rest of the audience, their once-radiant faces now appear ashen and lifeless, resembling corpses. The grass beneath their feet is brown, and scents of death waft through the air.

The young children sit with their mutilated arms crossed and their heads hanging limply, tilted toward the dirt floor. As their pupils snap in unison to focus on him, their blood-covered grins stretch from ear to ear.

The terrifying movements make Rich wince. Despite the frightening scene, Rich resists the impulse to run.

One by one, they open their mouths and release hideous snarls, showing their teeth. He watches with horror as their fangs sharpen and their skin glows red. Before his eyes, they are transforming into the very demons they are.

The dirt wedged in their gruesome wounds makes it clear they have crawled straight from hell. "Vroom, vroom," they say. "Vroom ... vroom."

Listening to their gnashing teeth imitate a starting engine, he winces again, this time noticing the color of the sky. As a storm approaches, dark clouds roll overhead, perching above, casting darkness over the scene. Looking up, he wonders if it will rain.

Then, hearing a series of harsh cracking noises accompanying the progression of darkness, his attention is pulled to a disturbing scene. As the children's mutilated throats produce wet cackles, they project drops of red spit that sprinkle the freshly dug dirt, turning it the color of tar.

Every heavy thud of his beating heart urges Rich to flee.

"Rich ... Rich...Rich..." they say. Their hellish chorus lingers as their bodies contort, slinking to the grassy floor.

Staring in horror, he watches their butchered limbs fuse into rigid angles, and they climb onto one another. They form together as they rearrange their broken bones, smashed cartilage, and dislocated arms and legs. "You're next..." they say, growling as their heads swivel toward him.

Feeling their glares, he analyzes their attempt to create the shape of a car, and his heartbeat grows louder. The sight mirrors the aftermath of a horrific wreck, and he fights to suppress his scream.

As they hiss, they disconnect from one another. He watches their bodies, now more mangled than before, tumble, dispersing on the ground. They slink like slugs, leaving thick sludge as they crawl toward him. The look in their eyes appears cannibalistic. "He will devour you alive if that's what it takes," they say; their animalistic snarls are threatening.

Getting closer, Rich watches in panic as they writhe before him, their crimson liquid spattering his face, while he desperately tries to move his uncooperative limbs. He closes his eyes, anticipating his last breath, but when he's met with nothing more than the spray growing in abundance, he slowly reopens his eyes to look.

Droplets of rain are sprinkling from the sky.

"It's okay, Rich!" a man's voice shouts. "We support you!"

A woman chimes in. "Stay strong! Speak your truth!"

He flinches, his eyes quickly scanning the faces of the family and the rest of the audience. Unlike before, everything appears back to normal; the corpses are gone.

Frustrated with himself for losing control, he quickly takes a card from the pastor's book and pretends to wipe a few tears from his cheek. "Sorry, folks ... I am just having a tough time talking about this," he says.

The rain increases, turning into a moderate shower. As raindrops cascade onto Rich's hair, the crowd swiftly opens their umbrellas, and the popping sound of their expansion shatters his peace.

"You'll never beat the clock," a demonic voice hisses from the open grave.

Convinced that the Devil is trying to make him fail, Rich clenches his jaw to channel his anger and continues. "It wasn't until my mama took her last breath that I discovered why I felt so close to him," he says, and, trying to drown out the howling voices in his head, he talks faster. "On my mama's deathbed, she told me something that would change my life forever," he says. "'Rich, being a racecar driver isn't just a dream; it's in your blood.' And that's when I found out Mason Samuels was my dad."

The crowd loudly gasps.

He hesitates, standing next to the life-size cutout, before turning his attention back to the audience. "I know this news may come as a shock to many. Heck, when I found out, it shocked me," he says. Making eye contact with Ben, he notices the demonic heckling fall silent, and, internally rejoicing, he softens his voice. "Man, you know, you were the first friend I made in the pros, and I really hope we can make amends because it sucks having you all angry with me."

Ben smiles, acknowledging his apology.

As they share a moment, Rich finds the longer he looks at him, the more the mangled boy comes to mind, and the image of him in Ben's place rattles his nerves. "Honestly, it's been eating me alive," he says, clearing his throat.

The wobble in his voice moves the audience. A man rushes forward to hand him a tissue. He takes it and blots his eyes. "If I upset any of you, I didn't mean it. It wasn't until my first race with Ben that I found out. Then, when my mother died, I fell into a slump," he says, glancing at the family. "I never intended for anyone to find out like this. I ... I didn't know what else to do."

Having never had a great relationship with his grandfather, Ben has always suspected he was full of secrets; he wouldn't be surprised if the man told Rich not to tell anyone.

As they exchange a warm grin, Rich's tense demeanor lifts. He broadens his attention to the remaining family members. "I didn't see any of this coming. He talked about feeling guilty for missing me growing up and all, but I never imagined he would leave me with a bunch of his things. I wanna make it right. So, if you want the stuff, he left me ... I... I..."

A group of reporters sitting in the back scrambles to turn their microphones on, preparing to record the family's response.

Their clicking buttons cause Ben's mother to panic, and her posture stiffens. Worried about adverse publicity, she anxiously straightens her modest black pencil skirt and Angora sweater neckline. Brushing a piece of hair from her face, she clears her throat. "That's all right, Hun. There's plenty to go around," she says, lifting her finger. "I think I can speak for all the Samuels by extending you a warm welcome to our family."

Rich watches her glance over her shoulder to ensure the reporters are listening, and her pinched smile makes it evident to him she is in pain—not over the loss of her father, but the dollar signs slipping away.

Clearing her throat, she rises to her feet and speaks loud enough for all to hear. "It is such a blessing that you found your way home to us." She reaches for Ben's hand to give the impression of solidarity, but he flinches and swats her hand away, unaccustomed to her display of affection.

Swiftly, Rich places his hand on his chest. "Thank you from the bottom of my heart," he says, and, ramping up his theatrics, he raises his voice. "I'm so grateful to Mrs. Samuels and the rest of the family for their kind words. For the first time in my life, I feel like I belong somewhere."

The crowd shows their support with a collective sigh.

Rich shifts his attention to the audience. "Before I hand the stage back to our prominent pastor, I just wanna thank everyone for coming," he says. Dramatically pausing, he looks up to the sky as the sun emerges from the clouds, declaring, "I know Mason is up in Heaven right now, already best friends with our dear savior, Jesus Christ, standing side by side and looking down on us with proud eyes."

The air fills with applause and the clicking sound of camera shutters.

Watching the crowd's responses, the pastor is left speechless, having seen no one other than himself command an audience with that level of power.

He can't stand the sight of Rich getting all the glory, and, unable to remain on the sidelines any longer, he rushes forward. "Let's hear it for Rich!" he shouts, while pulling him in for a hug. Mid-embrace, he quietly whispers in his ear, "You are a natural kid. If you get tired of the car thing, you know where to find me." He releases him with a wink, then twirls his finger in the air. "All right, folks, the time has come! Lower him down!"

Rich puts on his sunglasses, returns to his seat, and joins the crowd. The crane's engine roars, hoisting the casket high as shrill beeps signal the beginning of its descent into the earth.

As the box disappears, the pastor motions for the family to step forward. Funneling into a line, they each grab a handful of dirt, stand next to one another, and momentarily pause to bid their goodbyes. The reporters dash to the front to film them standing side by side. With the flash of the camera, the family members throw their handfuls of soil into the hole, then spin in unison to pose for a group photo.

As the reporters disperse to give them privacy, Rich cringes at the sight of Roy, who's still in his seat, sitting behind them.

The family awkwardly falls silent, waiting for the remaining crowd to disperse.

Ben's mother uncomfortably clears her throat to break the silence, unsure how to act without the media. "So ... are you planning on changing your last name?" she asks. "Or..."

The sound of her question makes Ben's face turn bright red. "Jesus, Mom," he says, rolling his eyes; he looks at his friend. "I'm sorry, bro ... just ignore her like I do."

She nudges him with her elbow, and they return to their painful silence as they wait for more of the crowd to clear.

Thinking it's good enough, Ben is ready to escape his embarrassment. "Okay, bro, will I see you at the upcoming race?" he asks.

Rich nods with a smile. "May the best man win," he says.

20

LEFT BEHIND

As they settle back into the car, everyone is quiet. As Rich reflects on the interaction with the family, he can't help thinking about his uncle's earlier absence, and, keeping his voice low, he breaks the silence. "So, why didn't you join the photo?" he asks.

The car hits a bump.

Not wanting to interrupt their conversation, the driver nervously looks in the rearview mirror to ensure they aren't upset and tentatively apologizes. "Sorry," he says, then swiftly returns his gaze forward. The men are too engrossed in their conversation to notice him.

Roy laughs. "I'm not a Rich Samuels," he says. "They don't want a picture of me."

Rich narrows his eyes and stares at him, sensing something is off.

"That would be weird," Roy says.

The car picks up speed as it enters the highway, but quickly slows. "Looks like we may hit some traffic," the driver says as he spots a wall of brake lights ahead.

Rich gives a quick nod while staying focused on his uncle. "I never thought of that," he says. Then he turns his attention to the window, watching the colors of trees passing by.

The rainfall picks up again, sprinkling onto the glass. "It's gotta be because of the rain. I swear, people can't drive in this weather, you know?" The driver chuckles nervously as he makes small talk.

The sound of light taps from the water hitting the vehicle's top creates a sense of peacefulness, especially when paired with the black tires' quiet ride on the smooth pavement; it's almost hypnotic.

As Rich feels his eyes become heavy, he rests his head against the upholstery of the side wall.

The driver reaches for the temperature control of the car. "I hope you don't mind if I adjust the heat," he says, turning the knob. "With this storm settling in, I want to ensure the ride stays comfortable while we're stuck in this horrible traffic."

A warm burst of air exits through the vents and filters throughout the car.

Feeling coziness surround him, Rich's body relaxes further. In his dozing state, he hears the eerie murmur behind his headrest.

"Don't..." it says, gasping. "Don't ... close your eyes."

Rich is already too far gone; it's not enough to stop him from entering a deep sleep.

Roy grins while watching his nephew drift off from the corner of his eye. Then, he directs his gaze to the driver. "That's all right. We have no other plans for the day. I know our boy, Rich, needs the sleep anyway," he says.

The car slows as it follows the sea of lights, and the driver chuckles at Rich's light snoring. "I'd say so," he says.

Rich succumbs to his exhaustion, falling into a deeper sleep. Met with the dark abyss of his mind, everything becomes quiet except for the tap ... tap...tap of the rain.

The car abruptly stops as the driver responds to the vehicle ahead. The shift in momentum jolts Rich awake. His surroundings appear hazy. Wincing to clear his grogginess, he yawns. "What's going on?" he asks.

The rain has picked up substantially, and the downpour makes it impossible to see anything beyond a few feet ahead. Noticing the outline of red taillights, he squints, trying to make sense of things. "Why isn't anyone moving?" he asks, and, feeling himself sweat, he unbuttons his shirt. "Also, man, would you mind turning the heat down a notch? It's hotter than hell in here."

Though the temperature setting remains consistent, the heat continues to climb. "Come on..." he says. Unable to hide his irritation, he directs his attention to the driver's seat.

Even though the car is running, the seat is empty.

"Hey ... man?" he asks, and scanning the car, he finds his uncle is nowhere to be found.

There is an unusual dreariness to the ambiance, triggering concern.

"No," he says; his heart races. "I ... um... I just closed my eyes for two seconds." Trying to understand what's happening, he glances at the seat beside him and spots the Mason Samuels's t-shirts that were handed out at the funeral.

He sighs with relief. "Never thought I'd be so happy to see that face," he says, touching the material with his hands. He picks up the shirt and, unfolding it, stops.

The Mason Samuels shirt no longer displays the original iconic image; instead, it features a discolored picture resembling his postmortem appearance in the garage.

As Rich looks into his lifeless eyes, an unsettling wave of fear washes over him. "I'm sure there's gotta be a simple explanation for this," he says.

Nervously throwing the shirt to the floor, he redirects his attention to the window. Through the dark tints and heavy mist, he can see the glow of brake lights.

As he presses his face against the glass, a loud static blare from the car's stereo startles him, and a wave of cold air brushes the back of his neck.

"Hello, Rich," Roy whispers faintly through the static.

Confused about what's going on, Rich cannot keep his composure; he feels blindsided. "How ... how long have I been out?" he asks in a panic.

Rather than an answer, the static builds.

Fueled by rage, he strikes the back seat with his fists. "Roy, answer me!" he says, pounding harder. "Answer me!"

A laugh slowly weaves through the static, taunting him. "No need to explain the rules again, so let's get down to business," Roy says. "You've got until the clock runs out to finish your task."

The sound of his unwavering tone makes Rich wince. "But I just finished the last one," he says, shutting his eyes to think as his frustration builds. "You can't keep doing this ... you—"

But before he can finish his sentence, Roy cuts him off. "Oh, yes, I can," he says. "In case you forgot, I own you."

Rich feels powerless, his body tensing as a gentle breeze brushes his closed eyelids. "How can I enjoy what I earn if you don't let me live my life? Huh?" he asks; each word comes out faster than the last.

As he waits for a response, the electric static fades, and crickets chirp, setting a new scene. He focuses on the sound of the rain pelting the roof. "No, no, no," he says. Reluctantly opening his eyes, he's met with darkness.

He's no longer in the car, and the pungent odors of sulfur and lumber waft through the drafty air.

He leans forward in his seat to get comfortable. It is now wood rather than leather. "Where the hell am I?" he asks. The rustle of his synthetic pants and the sound of his racing boots tapping against the concrete incites panic in him over the unknown tasks he'll face.

A myriad of voices whisper from the darkness. "Tick, tock, tick, tock, tick, tock."

Remaining seated, Rich glances from left to right and finds himself in what appears to be a shed. "Show yourself!" he shouts.

A demonic laugh pierces the air, followed by a slight movement in the shadowy distance.

Rich's eyes dart to specks of fluorescent green light dripping down the wall. Little by little, they create the numbers of the countdown clock.

"Shit," he says. "Shit!" In a panic, he jumps to his feet and feels his helmet forcefully shoved onto his head. He swings his fists at the darkness but is met with nothing but air and the sound of footsteps running away.

The tin siding of the small building rattles as the door slides open. He moves his visor to the top of his helmet to get a better view. Slivers of moonlight trickle inside, illuminating a row of garden tools mounted to the wall.

Paranoid of the dwindling time, he snatches a shovel hanging by its handle. He sighs heavily. "All right, we've got two hours left. I can handle whatever it is in that time."

As he takes his first step forward, a set of heavy footsteps races across the concrete floor.

Rich nervously tightens his grip on the tool's wooden handle and sprints toward the open door. With each stride, high-pitched giggles follow close behind, and little fingers grab at the material of his uniform. "Stop it!" he shouts, swatting the air with the shovel while quickening his pace.

"Never close your eyes ... never close your eyes," a voice whispers, starting soft, then turning into a demonic screech that rings between the tin walls.

"Ignore it," Rich says, shaking his head. "You gotta keep going."

"Don't close your eyes!" the voice interjects again, getting closer.

He jumps through the doorway and tumbles to the ground, dropping the shovel. Taking a quick scan of his surroundings, he swiftly grabs the implement again before shifting his attention to the moonlight. The way it casts a sheen on the lake holds an incomparable beauty.

Standing up, he gazes at it while brushing away the grass from the knees of his race suit. Thinking the view looks familiar, he glances over his shoulder to see what's behind him. As he analyzes the backside of the large home, sweat drips from his forehead to his cheeks beneath his helmet.

It's Mason Samuels's estate.

He anxiously jabs his fingers into the opening of his visor and uses his glove to dry his brows.

A splash resonates from the lake, followed by a heavy mist rolling onto the grass and quietly creeping closer.

Ignoring it, he seeks solace in the familiar thick curtains while staring at the upper window of the master bedroom. "None of this makes sense," he says. "Why am I here? This shit only happens on race day, and that's still a few days out."

A louder splash emerges from the lake.

As he turns to look for the cause, unbeknownst to him, the lamp in the upper window flickers, illuminating the silhouette of a man watching him.

Rich heads toward the water to investigate, only to discover the noise is coming from the direction of the wooden dock. While changing his course, he squints to get a clearer view through the darkness and notices a person sitting at the end of the pier. Fog wraps each hunched vertebra of their spine as they dangle their feet into the murky water, splashing it with their toes. He observes the rigid movement of the individual; there is something unhuman about how the individual's ribcage expands and contracts with each breath.

Continuing his slow approach, he cautiously clears his throat. "Hello?" he asks in a barely audible whisper.

The swish-swashing of the water becomes more aggressive.

With a tight grip on the shovel, Rich cautiously steps onto the first wooden plank of the dock. A shrill creak escapes the board under his foot. In a state of panic, he shifts his weight and anxiously looks at the wooden slat beneath his boot.

Abruptly, the figure's movement and accompanying splashes stop.

Rich's eyes stay fixed on the person at the end of the dock as the dense fog muffles their sinister laugh.

The being disturbingly arches backward into a handless bridge, revealing that it is a man.

As Rich stares, he analyzes the deep burns on the man's face and notices that his charred lips have the hue and texture of a seared marshmallow. The injuries make his identity unrecognizable.

"So, you're the replacement," he says. Rich watches in shock as the man's eyes bulge and protrude from their sockets while he coughs up water, moss, and a toad from his lungs.

Unaware of the amphibian's projection from his throat, the man becomes animalistic upon hearing its croaking, quickly grabbing it and stuffing it back in his mouth. Its squirming triggers his pupils to dilate, and he instinctively closes his eyes and chews. As he swallows the dissected flesh and bone, his esophagus expands like a snake to accommodate the size.

Rich stands in stunned silence, his mouth hanging open as he clenches the shovel tightly.

Continuing to twist, the man's head reaches the dock, and he then slides onto his belly like a snake as maggots pour out of his rotten nose.

Noticing something different, Rich fixates on the fluorescent green tone of his irises; they match the viper on the hood of his racecar.

"You must be his shiny new plaything—fresh young blood," the man says, while moving into a crouching position to continue. "I was just like you once: young and eager. I thought I was at the top of the world. That was until the Victor Cup of 1972." A thick southern accent lingers through his hiss.

Rich cringes at the sight of his abrupt frown, which reveals muscle and bone beneath the deep burns. Confused about why he's mentioning that race, he anxiously laughs, taking a step back. "Are you a race fan or something?" he asks, unsure of where he's going with it.

With a slight tilt of his head, the man observes him intently. Rich nervously continues, "Most people wouldn't remember, but that race made Mason Samuels legendary."

The man taps his fingers against the dock. "What else?" he asks.

Rich feels like he is being tested. "Uh...." As he starts to speak, the image of the famous crash that put his idol in the lead makes him cringe. "Well ... I know there was a fatal accident. I can't recall all the details, but I think number thirteen caused the crash, and the driver's name was Kyle ... Beck. I don't know for sure; he was a newcomer and did little after that, but when he tapped Cody Mill's bumper,

I heard it sent his car into a deadly tailspin. It was a terrible tragedy. Cody was an absolute legend. He wasn't quite on the level of Mason Samuels, but he was a true leader of his time."

The man's face turns sour.

Rich talks faster, imagining the car engulfed in flames. "It might have been the worst crash in the history of racing. The car must have flipped a dozen times before catching fire." Slowing his speech, he looks at the man's open wounds. "Say ... are those burn marks?" He gulps.

Angered, the man spews spit and talks over the top of him. "Nothing like Mason Samuels? Ha! I was unstoppable. I was greater than him," he says.

Embarrassed not to have recognized him sooner, Rich freezes. "Wait ... Cody Mills?"

Answering him with a sneer, Cody slinks forward. His growl makes Rich stammer. "W-wait. Are you blaming Mason for what happened?" Not getting a response, the sight of Cody still approaching makes him panic. "If this is some beef you have with him ... he wasn't even near you. He was in the pit getting his tires switched ... that's how racing goes. Shit happens."

Cody curls his lips. "Come on. You gotta be smarter than that. There's a reason you don't remember the racer that was pitting my car. He never existed. It was all a big cover-up. They took that story and ran with it," he says, baring his teeth.

As he crawls closer, Rich fixates on the bits of the blue material from his race suit that are melted to his skin. "But—but I saw..." he stammers, shaking his head.

"The smoke coming from the car?" Cody asks with a laugh. "What about the collision? Did you see the crash?"

"They said the other footage was too graphic for television," Rich says, second-guessing himself; he tries to think of any other details he can remember. "The news people said that's why they couldn't show it or interview the other driver. He was traumatized and ended up in a loony bin or something."

As Cody nears the grass, the moonlight highlights his elongated features. "Just wait and see. You are disposable, just like me. It's only a matter of time before he discards you," he says with a cackle.

Rich flinches at the sight of his pointed attributes. "No, I'm nothing like you," he says, stepping back; he shakes his head. "I'm something special. He won't get rid of me. He said it himself."

Suddenly, Cody stops, and his body flatlines on the grass. Convulsing, he slowly morphs into the demon lurking beneath his skin. "Tick, tock, tick, tock," it says. The sound echoes in Rich's ears as its eyes glow red with a renewed intensity.

Rich's gaze jumps between the demon and the sound of tiny clusters of air bubbles bursting in the lake water. Pushing through the ripples, bodies wrapped in dingy linens float to the top.

He looks at the filthy bindings wrapped around their head, torso, and feet as they drift through the fog. Upon reaching the muddy bank, they roll onto the grass ledge and wriggle like earthworms fresh out of a hole. The sound of their moans triggers Rich to run.

With a laugh, Cody motions to the corpses covered in sheets, summoning them to join him. "It's only a matter of time before you become someone's task and die like us," he says. "You can't avoid it! You're only delaying the inevitable! Soon, he will dispose of you, and you'll be trapped in this never-ending hell!"

Rich quickens his pace for the house, shifting to a sprint. He is out of breath as he reaches the back of the home. Hisses echo off the trees behind him; the haunting sounds are closing in.

Tugging hard on the door, he realizes it's locked. "I'm nothing like you! You'll see," he says, his voice filled with panic.

He notices a welcome mat at his feet and flips it over with his shovel. Specks of moonlight illuminate a piece of metal; it's a key.

As he hastily picks it up, the snarls grow louder from behind, jolting him and causing him to fumble. "Shit ... shit," he mutters, his hands trembling as he struggles to align the key with the lock. Realizing the key doesn't fit, he turns around.

A monstrous growl escapes the demon, now perched just a few feet away.

Rich attempts to retreat, but his back is met with the door's wooden surface.

The gnashing teeth bite at his ankles, trying to taste his flesh.

"Get back!" Rich yells, swinging the shovel. "Get back, damn it!" He screams as he repeatedly bludgeons the creature over the head with the sharp side of the spade.

With a thud, its body lies sprawled out on the ground.

Quickly hopping over it, Rich takes off in a dead sprint around the side of the house. Along the path, his motion triggers the home's security lights.

The strobe effect from their blinding flashes illuminates the nearby landscape. The number of bodies has tripled in size; they fill the lawn.

Using the light as a guide, Rich rounds the corner of the home. Knocks pierce through the air; they sound like they are coming from the front door.

Worried about triggering more lights, he stops.

The front porch's overhead lamp is on; a woman is standing at the entrance.

Rich's eyes widen; he finds her modest black skirt and sweater familiar. "What is Ben's mom doing here?" he quietly asks under his breath while nervously gripping the shovel's handle tighter. Usually, when he sees people in his dreams, their complexions are altered from reality, but from the side, her skin tone appears rosy and alive.

As she continues to knock, something about the sequence feels odd; typically, Rich knows his purpose by now, but his mission doesn't seem clear. "But why would she be here?" he asks himself. Panicked, he glances at the terrain, trying to find a fluke, and notices her black sports car sitting in the driveway.

The license plate spells out her maiden name: Samuels.

Rich feels his heart's heavy beats in his chest. "Shit. Is she the one I'm supposed to kill?" he asks, looking back at her standing at the door.

As she impatiently stomps her feet, she kicks the entrance, making a ruckus. "Come on, open up," she says. "I know you are in there, you son of a bitch!"

Rich hears tiny snorts echo from the back of the home between her rambunctious thwacks. Caught at a crossroads of where to focus his attention, he anxiously looks to the side of the house, sweat pooling beneath his helmet.

The demon, regaining consciousness, is slowly returning to life.

"Goddamn," Rich says.

As he tightens his grip on the shovel, Ben's mother shouts louder. "You may have fooled everyone else, but I know who you and your so-called uncle are," she says. Huffing heavy breaths, she exudes desperation.

Waiting for her to finish her sentence, Rich can't avoid her threat. "What's wrong with her?" he asks. Reluctantly returning his attention to the front door, he clenches his jaw and, knowing what he must do, takes a step forward.

"I'm not the villain here! You are the liar! My father had a vasectomy," she says with a grin. "So, unless you two moochers want me to call the cops or disclose that secret to the rest of the family, you'd better open the door now!"

Rich freezes in place. "Wait ... what?" he asks, muttering under his breath as her words make him panic. "Shit. I hadn't thought of that being a thing." Filled with pressure, he tries to think of ways to combat the narrative.

Coming up empty-handed, she pounds harder. "I'll give you until the count of three to let me in," she says. "One..."

With no other option, Rich knows the most straightforward solution: she must die.

Before she can continue her count, the front door sounds a creak as it starts to open, masking his footsteps against the concrete.

She plants her feet on the porch and puts her hands on her hips. "I knew you would come to your senses," she says, watching it open to a crack. Then, she uses her toe to nudge it further; her complexion turns stark white. "Wait ... Dad?"

"Mason?" Rich says. Then, silently, he finishes his approach toward the porch's sizable brick steps.

Overwhelmed, Ben's mother stutters on in disbelief. "What ... um... what... what are you doing here? I told you I would take care of this," she says, nervously playing with the material of her skirt.

As Rich watches, he finds her behavior off.

Rather than a joyful reunion, Mason coldly stares into his daughter's eyes. "I told you what to do, and you didn't listen," he says.

Creeping closer, Rich remains out of sight as he eavesdrops on their conversation.

Mason's eyes appear deranged; they twinkle fluorescent green. The way his daughter watches his zombie-like corpse is indifferent, like nothing has changed, and even though his words sound like mumbles, she nods at every syllable.

"You know I can't wait the full week," she says, rolling her eyes. "I have a family to feed and bills to pay. Anyway, you should be dead ... you died. It would be best if you weren't even here. That wasn't part of the plan."

Mason slowly removes the helmet from his head. She witnesses his skin sag, accentuating his callused and pointed features. "All you had to do was listen to me for once in your entitled fucking life!" he says.

His aggressive tone rattles her. "What ... well... I..." she stutters, glancing from left to right. "What happened to you?"

He moves forward, positioning himself within the doorway. "I can't save you," he says.

Convinced the whole thing is a joke, she anxiously laughs. "That's a good one," she says. Thinking he's wearing a mask, she leans forward and grabs his chin.

Each of her aggressive tugs makes his grin deepen.

The interaction sends a wave of cold chills through Rich's body; Mason's behavior reminds him of his uncle.

Ben's mother releases her grasp. "There's nothing I can do. You didn't listen," Mason says. With no emotion in his words, his speech resembles a business transaction.

"Wait ... you... can't be serious," she says. Scrambling, she reaches for the back of her waistband.

Knowing now is the time to prove his loyalty, Rich notices the imprint of a revolver and hurries, sneaking up behind her. Ready to step in, he shifts his grip on the shovel.

She hears the shovel's edge scraping against the brick, and in a swift motion, she spins to face Rich and gives a cocky smirk. "Well, if it isn't the man of the hour," she says.

The grin deepens on Mason's face.

With a laugh, Ben's mother looks at the racing suit on Rich's body. "Is there somewhere you are trying to speed off to?" she asks.

Rich doesn't know where to focus. "Uh..." he says, glancing at Mason's unblinking eyes.

She relentlessly edges forward. "Silly me. Do you not understand what I'm saying? Oh, that's right—maybe I should speak slower. I nearly forgot you came from the trailer park. I'd be more than happy to dumb it down for you," she says as she pulls the revolver out of her waistband.

Rich shifts his attention from her sarcastic laughter and looks past her.

As Mason's stare fixates on the back of her head, his demeanor stiffens, and his black fingernails sprout through the ends of his gloves. Each rip in the leather makes room for his elongating fingers to extend, hooking through the open visor of his helmet and removing it. The porch light reflects off the object's vibrant red color as it dangles by his side.

Distracted by the luster, Rich becomes complacent and doesn't notice Mason's skin molting to a crimson hue. As his purging hair falls out in clumps onto the floor, a wave of whispers comes from the front doorway. "Tick, tick, tick, tick, tick, tick, tick, tick, tick, tick, tick, tick," they say.

Convinced it's just wind circling the porch, Ben's mother chuckles at the terror in Rich's eyes. Wanting to exacerbate his fear, she waves the gun, pointing it at his head. "So, do we have a deal?" she asks. "Or what?"

Her threat startles him, and as he closes his eyes to take her out with a swing, she screams and the front door slams shut.

Not knowing what's happening, Rich opens his eyes and is shocked to see she has vanished. The sight of fresh blood splatters on his helmet shield causes him to hyperventilate.

The entire porch is painted red.

Frenziedly wiping the thick liquid off his visor with his sleeve, Rich realizes the streaks are making it impossible to see, and in frustration, he raises his helmet's shield, dropping the shovel. "Dammit," he says as it lands in a pool of blood.

Anxiously, he looks to the bottom of the closed front door and realizes the stream of red is still pouring out from inside the home. "Did I? But ... if... I didn't," he says, squinting at the entry. He can see the white coliseum-like pillars out of his peripheral vision; not spared, they, too, are splashed with gore.

The image of Mason's devilish face and long, bony fingers haunts Rich. Feeling like he's losing his mind, he closes his eyes to regain composure.

The sudden sound of metal rattling shatters the silence, causing him to look. The realization that it's Roy unlocking the door throws him off. Quickly turning, he spots the rear taillights of the black suburban as it leaves the driveway.

It's now evening, and the sun has gone down.

Returning his attention to his uncle, Rich takes a deep breath. The shovel and gore have disappeared. "The great thing about car crashes is that there is no traffic on the other side," Roy remarks. "You should feel rejuvenated after that long nap. You were dead asleep, snoring the entire ride home."

Rich is taken aback as he struggles to make sense of his reality after the funeral.

"Yep, you got a real nice snooze," Roy says as he finishes opening the door.

As he glances at the shirts from the funeral wedged under his uncle's arm, Rich questions the validity of his dream and wonders if the dark tasks only happen during his races. With a nervous laugh, he forces a smile. "Sure did. I feel more rested than ever," he says. "I probably won't have to sleep again for a week."

Before Roy can open the door, Rich pushes past him to get inside. The more he attempts to remember the horrifying events, the more he doubts the accuracy of his hazy recollections. Regardless of what's true, he fears being discarded like Cody, so he holds his cards close.

Roy grants him a head start and watches him ascend the stairs. "Oh, by the way, Rich..." he says.

Upon hearing his uncle's voice, Rich stops and slowly faces him. "Yeah, Uncle Roy?"

After a moment of hesitation, Roy continues. "Thought you should know—I got a call that Ben's mother got into a crash on her way home from the service."

Rich intentionally avoids looking at him and redirects his sight to the top of the stairs. "Oh?" he asks. "Is she okay?"

"It was fatal," Roy says.

As he hears the words, a wave of fear washes over Rich. He tries to hide the waver in his voice as he asks, "What about Ben?"

His uncle smirks. "Critical condition."

Rich's eyes grow wide at the unexpected response. Thinking back through the blurred chunks of reality, he remembers the license plate and then the tinted windows of the black sports car. Irritated with himself at not having thought of Ben being in the vehicle, he wonders how much he saw. "Geez. I suppose they're right about tragedies coming in threes," he says, shaking his head.

"Guess all we can do is wish him a speedy recovery," Roy says. "I can drive you up to the hospital to visit him if you like."

Rich is done with the charade and wants to get to his room. "Man, it's been a long day. You go ahead without me. I don't know if I can take seeing him all bandaged up right now," he says with a look of despair on his face.

Roy matches his expression and replies, "I understand…"

Before his uncle can finish, Rich sprints up the remaining steps.

Waiting for him to shut the door to his room, Roy smirks and tosses the memorial shirts onto the floor. He feels something caught in his throat and fishes out the blockage with his nail.

It's a tattered piece of black cashmere.

With a devilish chuckle, he walks onto the porch, shuts the door, and swallows it.

21

NO SLEEP

Rich paces in his bedroom and hears the truck's engine start outside. Pulling aside the curtain, he gazes through the window. "Thank God. I never get any time alone," he says, releasing the velvet and turning back to the room.

The material's bright golden hue and the memory of Mason hiding behind the panels are distracting. Anxious, he takes a deep breath, attempting to level himself out, and mutters, "I just need some time to figure this shit out."

There is a slight sway in the curtains.

"M-Mason?" he asks. He dashes to the bed and takes a seat. His eyes are fixated on the window, refusing to blink.

As the sounds of the truck fade into the distance, the heavy velvet panels settle to a stop.

Rich falls to his back on the mattress and stares at the ceiling, contemplating the earlier events. Struggling to focus, he counts the flaws in the texture and shuts his eyes. "All right, so what if Ben was in the car when his mom showed up at the house?" he asks, and, trying to downplay the severity of the situation, he shrugs. "Maybe he didn't have a good enough view to see anything. Or, better yet ... maybe he didn't recognize me."

As the image of the black sports car comes to mind, he visualizes Ben's eyes peering through the window's tint. He shakes his head to clear his thoughts, bringing him back to reality. "I'm so stupid! What am I even talking about?" he asks. With a grunt, he reaches over his head and grabs a pillow. Needing a release, he shoves it over his face and screams. "I was wearing my racing uniform. There's no chance he didn't know it was me."

As the feather stuffing dampens his words, the room returns to silence. The ambiance brings him peace, and as he leaves the pillow draped over his face, his mind drifts into a non-REM state, ignorant of his surroundings.

Something stirs in the room, whispering. "Don't close your eyes ... he's watching you."

Trying to ignore it, he buries his face deeper into the billowy material. The more the voices persist, the more his annoyance turns into rage. "I know, I know ... don't shut your eyes, Rich, blah, blah, blah," he says, mocking their tone. "Jesus Christ, can't you all think of something different? I just wanted a moment to think. That's all! I'm tired of hearing that shit. It's driving me up the wall. Why don't you tell me something I don't know? It's making me feel like I'm living on some fucked-up Groundhog Day!"

Instead of stopping, more voices join in. "Little by little, he will devour your soul until there is room for him to live under your skin," they say. "Don't close your eyes."

The grim twist only adds to his fury, turning his face red. He can't take any more. He chucks the pillow toward the noise. "Stop it!" he shouts. "Shut the hell up!"

The voices abruptly stop. He pauses and, heavily breathing, looks at the ceiling; a shift in the light causes his heart to race.

The room embodies a sudden darkness that feels like déjà vu.

He frantically feels the top of his head, and gripping his hair, he glances at his chest. "I ... I knew it. I'm still awake," he says with a sigh of relief and a nervous chuckle. "I'd remember if I closed my eyes."

A drop of liquid hits his forehead and trickles to his lips. He hears a raspy voice as he frantically spits to eliminate the sour, metallic taste creeping into his mouth. It's coming from the direction of the drip overhead.

Another droplet of liquid falls, this time on his chest. Holding his breath, he refuses to look up, watching the spot darken to a burgundy hue as it soaks into his shirt. "Who ... who are you?" he asks, gulping nervously.

With a wheezing inhale, a man coughs. Rich's eyes widen as he hears it directly above his head.

"Richie boy ... Rich. Richie. Rich," the man says, emphasizing each word with an explosive hiss.

Quickly, Rich lifts his shoulders to his ears to block out the noise.

The man takes a deep breath, grimacing as he feeds off Rich's heartbeats. "You look terrified. Are you afraid?"

Rich clenches his jaw to combat his fear. "I know I'm awake, and you can't do anything to me. I know because I'm not wearing my race gear, so I'm definitely not asleep," he says.

Disregarding him, the man above stirs and, letting out a raspy exhale, projects the anxiety of the gathered heartbeats.

A jolt of electricity surges through Rich's body as a finger jabs the side of his neck, causing his muscles to spasm and his head to shake uncontrollably.

Abruptly, the voice strikes again, talking more quickly with conviction. "You know who I am," he says.

Rich's throat tightens as panic sets in. "I don't ... know who the hell you..." he says, his voice strained as he clenches his teeth, forcing out each word, "are."

The man's words gradually transform into a sinister, demonic laugh. "You sure about that? Think harder," he says, "Tick, tock, Tick, tock, Tick, tock."

The ticking sound infuriates Rich. "Leave! Now, get out!" he screams. Spit flies as he tries to catch his breath.

Everything falls quiet.

The silence restores his confidence. "Nothing but a coward," he says.

Chuckling, he rises to his feet, but his laughter abruptly stops as he is immediately knocked back down.

A man wearing an identical black race suit and helmet to his own is silently hovering above, watching him. His intense stare triggers Rich's heart to race and paralyzes him with fear. He glances at the green number eight embroidered on the man's sleeve, then reluctantly at his face.

A pair of snake-like eyes, glowing with fluorescent green, peek through the blood-speckled shield of the man's helmet. Rich analyzes the red, callused skin surrounding them and feels a drop of liquid hit his chest. Quickly, he shifts his attention to find where it has fallen from.

Each sponsorship emblem on the man's torso oozes fresh gore.

The sight of blood saturating the cloth brings back memories of the gruesome scene on the porch and the taste of the drip on his lips. Nausea overtakes him. "Who the hell are you?" he asks.

With a smirk, the man slithers his tongue around in his mouth. "I'm you," he replies.

The room spins with anxiety. "Wait, what? No, that's impossible," Rich says, his voice trembling as he sees the man inching closer. "You can't be me. I'm me."

As the man looms overhead, his mouth opens wide. Rich watches in horror as his serpent-like tongue slithers between his sharp, black teeth. "I'm the side you hide," He sneers. "I'm the sin within."

Unable to escape the man's breath, which smells of rotten eggs and decay, Rich nervously glances at the sharply pointed chin jutting from beneath the helmet strap.

With a menacing growl, the man continues, "Have you looked at your reflection lately?"

Something about how his voice resonates feels odd, like an internal dialogue in his head. Confused, he looks everywhere but up.

The dark entity gnaws at his lips with anticipation, causing the black crust around his mouth to crumble with each bite. The sound of each crunch escalates Rich's fear. "I'm nothing like you!" he screams with all his might while frantically shaking his head.

The voice chuckles softly, gradually fading into a whisper.

As the demonic presence dissipates, Rich immediately springs to his feet. The curtains rustle across the room again, and he is convinced that the thing is hiding behind him. "You know what? This is the last time you're gonna torment me!" He charges at the curtains, shouting louder, "Get the hell outta here!"

The room spins around him as he sprints across the space, causing him to stumble. He yanks the material away from the window. "Your time is up. Not mine!" he says with an air of vengeance, but there is nothing there, and the emptiness causes his thoughts to spiral out of control.

Footsteps scurry behind him.

Hearing laughter resonating from the bathroom, he turns around, fists clenched. "Where the hell are you?" he says. With a crazed look in his eye and a maniacal cackle, he rushes forward to follow the noise. As he approaches the arched doorway, he smirks.

Alluring whispers call from inside, enticing him through the entrance. "In here," the voices say. "In here."

With an irrevocable step, Rich thrusts himself into the darkness. The thud of his boots on the marble creates a loud echo, assaulting his ears.

Suddenly, the voices stop.

He takes a deep breath and scans the room. The door slams shut behind him, making him jump. "I know you're hiding in here," he says, scanning wildly, searching for any sign of movement.

A puff of air brushes his cheek as the whispers begin again.

He glimpses the white porcelain sink from the corner of his eye and grins, convinced that he has spotted something. "Gotcha," he says, sprinting through the dark and accidentally running his hip into the counter. "Shit," he says, kneeling in pain; he rests his hands on the cold stone. His frustration fills him with anger.

From the darkness, a man's voice whispers, "Richie, Rich, Rich."

The sound of his name sends chills down his spine; he presses his hands into the marble to stop his trembling. "Stop being a coward and show yourself," he says.

In response, a cold, callused hand wraps around his throat, constricting his airway. The fingers tighten, creeping up his neck, forcing his head to look at a pair of glowing green eyes directly in front of him. He's mesmerized, unaware of the cold, slimy sensation slinking over his fingers.

With a quick rattle, the man's voice hisses.

The room undergoes a disturbing transformation, with unsettling sounds growing in intensity as rattlers and vipers drop from the ceiling and crawl through the cracks, covering the floor and countertops. They are everywhere.

Rich hears his name and, glancing back to the mirror, notices the eyes are no longer there.

The chaos escalates, growing louder. Desperate to make it stop, he claws at his ears till blood streams down his neck, and the pain's severity makes him shake uncontrollably.

The voice persists. "Rich, Richie, Rich."

He screams, and forgetting about the snakes, slams his palms into the counter.

With a hiss, the snakes' teeth latch ahold of his skin, and their venom enters his veins.

As his flesh melts off the bone, Rich hears his name again. This time, it's clear the voice lives inside his head. His eyes widen, and the poison weakens his knees, forcing him to collapse into the pit of serpents.

Feeling each agonizing strike penetrate his skin, he closes his eyes.

22

GET WELL SOON

Walking through the hospital's parking lot, Roy passes by a patch of grass. He angrily pulls a handful of wild dandelions from the dirt. "Ungrateful brat," he says. Slapping the earth from the roots, he enters the double glass doors.

Across the stale entryway is a nursing station. On a mission, he approaches, wearing a forced grin.

A woman in light-blue medical scrubs sits behind the desk, her eyes fixed on the computer screen. Almost done with her double shift, she pulls her blond-brown hair into a low bun; the caffeine is wearing off.

Roy taps on the counter to get her attention.

Startled, she smiles as she regroups. "Hello there! Is there something I can help you with?"

He glances at her badge. "Yes, Karen, there is something you can help me with. I am here to see a kid by the name of Ben Samuels. Do you know what room he is in?" he asks.

Since she's been dealing with reporters all day, the sound of his name strikes a nerve. "I'm sorry, but he's not taking visitors right now," she says.

"Well, you see, Karen, that answer doesn't work for me," Roy says. Leaning closer, he motions to the wildflowers in his hand. "I have something I need to give him."

Her attention shifts to the wilted bouquet. As one of the yellow petals tumbles to the counter, she frowns. "Isn't that thoughtful?" she says. "I am sure they will last until tomorrow."

Roy angrily tightens his grip around the stems, milking their moisture.

With a sense of unease, Karen watches as the pale drops of life drip onto the mauve Formica surface in front of her.

"Okay, Karen," Roy says with a scowl. "I'm gonna do something I rarely do for anyone, but I will do it for you. Here it is ... I'm gonna be honest."

The nurse breathes in, preparing to speak, and he leans closer. Casually resting his elbows on the counter, he lifts his hand to silence her. "Look, Karen, I've already had one hell of a day, and to be quite frank, it looks like you have, too." After a momentary pause, he looks at the bags under her eyes and casually shrugs. "Plus ... I just had a heavy meal and am slightly more sluggish than usual. If I were to kill you now, your death would be slow and, considering my mood, probably more painful than necessary."

She stares at his smile; it doesn't match his morbid words. Convinced she is mishearing him, she tries to clarify. "I'm ... um, sorry, I'm running off very little sleep right now," she says nervously, giggling. "Can you repeat that?"

With a grunt, Roy waves his hand, clutching the flowers. "The last thing I need for you to do is complicate things," he says. Then, warming his tone, he adds, "Plain and simple—I need to see the boy."

Karen catches sight of the time on the computer, and a surge of relief washes over her; there are only ten minutes left before she can clock out. "Wait, your boy? As in your son?" she asks.

Pondering his response, Roy squints to discern her expression. "Yes?"

She immediately begins scribbling on a sheet of blank name tags.

Swiftly, she retrieves the one she has filled out and holds it toward him. "If you had started with that information, we could have saved ourselves a lot of trouble," she says.

Roy looks at the nametag with an inscription in black marker that reads Ben's Dad.

Reaching the last minutes of her shift, she's ready to wrap up their interaction. "It's a way to let the staff know you're not one of those pesky reporters," she explains, waving more vigorously, urging him to take it. "Here ... just put this on your shirt. We've had to deal with so many of them today. Only his immediate family is allowed back to see him."

Grabbing it with a smile, Roy puts it on and steps away from the desk. "Perfect, thanks," he says.

As she packs up her things, Karen shouts after him, "Oh, room six! He is in room number six!"

Roy gives a thumbs-up and rushes down the hall. Fluorescent lights brighten his path. It's relatively quiet except for a small cleaning crew mopping the floors.

He looks down the hallway, quickly scanning the room numbers, and notices a staff member exiting one of the doors. While attempting to read the name tag on his chest, he notices the prominent mustache. It's the same male nurse who was assigned to Rich's mother's room.

As he moves closer, the nurse locks eyes with Roy, recognizing a sense of familiarity, but struggles to remember where he has seen him before.

"Shit," Roy says under his breath. Convinced the gig is up, he smiles to acknowledge the nurse and holds up his flowers. "Just here to see my boy," he says.

Abruptly, a beep comes from a pager on the nurse's hip, and, appearing stressed, he gives up trying to place Roy's face. He quickly nods to acknowledge him as he passes. "Great kid. Better hurry before he gets too tired. I just left his room, and I'd say you have about ten minutes before his pain meds kick in. Enjoy your visit," he says, then continues down the corridor until reaching the end and exiting the hall.

Roy walks to the door he saw the nurse exit from and stops in front of the brass plate screwed to the wall; he smiles. "Number ... six," he says. "How lovely." Hiding the drooping flowers behind his back, he slowly opens the door.

In the center of the room, Ben lays in his hospital bed, comfortable, his body carefully tucked into the cotton sheets. Roy looks at the heavy white gauze wrapped around his temples and carefully shuts the door.

Already knowing who it is, Ben ignores the handle's click and continues staring at the wall.

With an enormous grin, Roy whips the drooping bouquet behind his back. "Surprise," he says. Ben's eyes roll as he approaches the end of the bed. "Hey, there, Ben ... Benny Boy. I got to say, you are in better shape than I thought you'd be."

As he listens, Ben clenches his teeth. "Yup, they cleared me. I am good to race this week," he says.

The sound of his emotionless response causes Roy to be dramatically enthusiastic. "That's fantastic," he says, setting the flowers on the small table near the bed.

Refusing to look, Ben notices their sad state from the corner of his eyes. "What do you want? Why are you here, Dad?" he asks.

"Whoa there, son," Roy says, grinning and giving a little shoulder nudge to lighten the mood. "Is that any way to treat your old man?"

"You've never once followed through on your promises my whole life. And then, guess what? I find out at Pop's funeral you're working with the guy he left everything to," he says. "I saw how you tried to avoid the family photo at the end."

"You know the agreement your mother and I had. We opted to keep our lives out of the public eye," Roy says. "It makes things a lot less complicated."

Growing angry, Ben quickly changes the subject. "I got it when we talked about pops having to go, but why did she have to die?" he asks. Refusing to look at Roy, he stares at his sheets. "She was all I had left, and you knew that."

Having assumed the question would arise, Roy clears his throat in preparation to respond. "You know how she could get when money was involved," he says. Settling at the end of the bed, he crosses his legs with a shrug. "She left me no choice. She got in my way."

"Why would she do that?" Ben asks.

Roy knows it's related to Mason, but he has no clue how they hid their plan from him. Not wanting to get into it, he tries to smooth things over. "What do you think? You know your mother," he says, sparing Mason the details. "Ever since I've known her, she's maintained the conviction that there was never enough."

Ben directs his attention back to the sheets, deep in thought.

Noticing his shift, Roy talks faster. "Your mother could be such a wildcard. I had to act fast, and I didn't mean for you to get caught in the crossfire."

"Why didn't I find out until Pops's funeral you're playing daddy to that Rich kid? The one who is beating me. You told me this was my season. I was supposed to be the untouchable one. Not him," Ben says, glaring at his father with seething anger. "You even gave him Pop's car. That was supposed to be mine!"

While Roy listens, he nods and says, "I can see how that might appear a certain way and make you—"

Abruptly, Ben talks louder. "I'm not interested in hearing your bullshit. If you don't follow through, there will be consequences."

"It's all part of a bigger plan," Roy says, trying to maintain his composure.

Having heard that response before, Ben sarcastically chuckles. "Sure."

Roy, unable to control his temper any longer, stands. His frustration consumes him, sharpening his features and filling the room with his demonic voice. "You ungrateful, spoiled brat."

Pretending to be unbothered, Ben keeps a straight expression.

"I've done everything for you and that goddamned thankless mother of yours," Roy says, pacing the room. "I'd be careful if I were you. You might suffer her fate if you don't change your attitude." With his fists clenched, he storms toward the door.

Ben briefly drops his guard and gulps.

As Roy reaches the door, he stops. Realizing how harsh he came off, he takes a deep breath, and his pointed features slowly return to normal. "Just focus on getting well, kid. I've got the rest under control," he says.

The sense of relief Ben feels when the door closes is short-lived, as a chair in the corner moves. As it scrapes against the tile, he can feel annoyance welling up inside him, causing his body to tense. "You know I have a minor concussion," he says.

Suddenly, the light flickers and starts pulsating rhythmically overhead.

"Jesus Christ, Mother, what the fuck do you want from me? I already told you I would get your revenge!" he shouts.

As each strobe brings the severely mangled body of a woman to life, blood oozes from her gashed flesh, and with a fluid-filled breath, she attempts to speak, but all that's left of her jaw is her flailing tongue, making it impossible.

Disgusted by her wounds, Ben refuses to look at her face, which is lacerated past the point of recognition, or the dangling shoulder meat where her arms used to be. "Well, I'll be damned ... look at that. You can make friends after all," he says, a hint of amusement in his tone. He chuckles upon seeing a faint outline of a female figure standing beside her. "All it took was for you to stop talking for people to like you."

A sudden blinding flash comes from the woman, diverting his attention from his mother to her. The room fills with an uncomfortable static as the entity becomes clearly visible, her hospital nightgown drenched in blood and a broken television resting on her shoulders.

"Who the fuck are you?!" Ben asks.

The disjointed image of a mangled smile plays across the fractured pieces of glass, and as it speaks, the projection of her lips moves to follow her words. "I want Rich dead," she says. Her speech causes the static to heighten.

As he listens, Ben feels the corners of his lips twitch. "I take it you know him," he says.

She gives a grimacing nod.

"Perfect," he says, returning his attention to his mother. "You really nailed it in finding this one. Who would've thought you gotta be dead to be useful?"

A wet, gurgling noise emerges from her esophagus.

Quickly, he returns his attention to the fractured grin on the television. "I want to hear everything you know ...

and don't skimp on any details," he says. "I need to know him like the back of my hand."

Loretta's skin wrinkles into a joyful smirk as she listens from within her unconventional enclosure.

23

PULL THE TRIGGER

Night has fallen, and the lights are off; a man's whimper builds to a scream, filling Rich's head.

He wakes to the image of vipers playing through his mind. Hyperventilating, he listens for their hisses, trying to remain calm by keeping his eyes shut. His head throbs, and his body aches.

As he shifts to get comfortable, the sound of a plastic sheet crinkling beneath him makes him open his eyes. "What the..." he says, staring at the ceiling. His stomach drops. There are speckles of blood skewing his view.

With a loud tick-tock, the haunting rhythm of the clock suddenly fills his mind. Echoing through the drafty space, reverberating like a pendulum from hell, while tiny fluorescent fragments of the green light swirl around Rich.

He shudders at the noise, and in an instant, it all clicks as he realizes he is dressed to kill. Panic overwhelms him when he sees the green lighting becoming the timer and senses the tightness of his uniform.

Suddenly, a vent above blows hot air that smells of cleaning supplies and latex gloves. Recognizing the familiar scent, he slams his fists against the mattress. The bed's metal frame beneath him releases a squeal with each brutal whack. "No, no, no," he says.

With a loud beep, the countdown begins.

In a hurry, Rich sits up, and feeling the bed move, he realizes it's on wheels. "Shit," he says, spotting a nurse's desk toward the end of the long hallway. As he shifts his focus to the gurney beneath him, a wave of crackling static comes from inside his helmet.

Abruptly, a man's voice cuts through the chaos. "Bet you didn't see that coming, did you?" he asks; a cynical cackle follows.

Rich's eyes widen; his uncle's familiar tone sends chills through his bones. "Wh-why am I here at the hospital?" he asks.

Roy snickers at the tremble in Rich's voice. "You seemed a bit unnerved over the tragedy last week," he says. "So I thought it was best for me to attend the race this week. Think of it as a reward for your hard work. You asked for a break, and here it is. Take this as my gift to you."

Rich clenches the sheets, his anger mounting at the thought of someone taking away the only thing he loves, racing. "Tragedy? We both know I didn't even know the guy. This wasn't what I meant," he says, scanning his surroundings.

His uncle's laugh creates a squeal in the static, making him wince. "Cheer up, buttercup," Roy says.

The foreboding sound of the clock makes Rich grip the bedding more tightly. "You still haven't answered my question. Why am I here? I can guarantee you that the clock isn't counting down to no damn vacation."

"You're a sharp kid, Rich. So, while I was at the hospital visiting Ben," he says, "I encountered a tiny issue that I thought was only fitting you took care of." With a snicker, he takes a moment of pause.

The sound of dead silence escalates Rich's anxiety, and, unable to take it, he tries to fill in the blanks. His mind races as his attention wanders to the doors lining the long corridor, and he wonders if Ben is hiding behind one.

Cutting through the static, Roy mumbles, his words inaudible. The unfamiliar darkness in his voice catches Rich off-guard as he hears it resonating through the gibberish. Even though he fears the answer, he knows he's running out of time. "C'mon, just hurry up and tell me who you want me to get rid of." His complexion turns pale as he nervously listens to a rush of static.

Roy's voice blares through the helmet, as clear as day, asking, "Do you remember that male nurse you bumped into at the hospital the night you killed your mama?"

Taken by surprise, Rich stammers as he tries to clarify. "Are—are you serious? You're talking about that guy who claimed he knew me when I was a baby?"

"Yup, that's the one. The guy with the mustache," Roy says.

Although he is happy not to hear his friend's name, Rich can't help but remember the man's pleasant demeanor. "Why him? What did he do?"

Roy clears his throat while concocting a lie. "He knows you killed her," he says.

Rich's mind is racing as he plays back the moment in his head, trying to remember how he would know. "He ... what?" he asks, his heart fluttering.

Without a pause, his uncle's voice deepens with a vicious undertone. "He threatened to tell everyone that you offed your mama," he says.

The wobble in Rich's voice dissipates; he knows what he must do. "Okay. I will take care of it," he says.

As Roy's presence fades away, his words linger in the air, hauntingly echoing in his wake. "Tick ... tock...tick...tock." As the static overtakes each word, the heavy sounds of the clock resonate down the long corridor.

Rich quickly glances up at the ceiling to analyze the bold glowing timer, then shifts his attention to his surroundings. "No problem," he says. "Three hours." He squints, thinking he sees something up ahead. The dim lighting creates an illusion, making the hallway appear never-ending. As he sits for a moment, staring into the abyss, he can't shake thoughts of the nurse tearing away all his hard-earned success.

The gurney's wheels screech as he shifts his weight, amplifying the tension as he swings his legs to the edge of the bed with a vindictive laugh. "I mean, who does he think he is, anyway?" he says. "The idiot doesn't know who he's fucking with. He doesn't know what I've been through to get to where I am. One thing is for damn sure: he's going to learn today."

Swiftly dismounting, he hears his boots click against the tile, and, inhaling the musty air, he smiles. The gloomy scenery hasn't changed.

Inadvertently mirroring the rhythm of his footsteps to the beat, the clock's ticking intensifies with each quick stride while he searches the surroundings for clues. His eyes narrow as he follows the movement of a shadow sweeping through the darkness ahead.

The sound of a child's laugh prompts his chest to tighten, but he continues without pausing, fixating on the loud ticks of the clock, veering right at the hallway junction.

It leads him to the hospital lobby. Not seeing any sign of the target, he stops in the middle of the large room. Besides the sound of the clock, everything is quiet.

As his breaths weigh heavy on his lungs, he catches sight of a shadow out of the corner of his eye near the reception desk, and he is convinced it may be the nurse with the mustache; he shifts his attention toward it.

A resounding stomp shakes the tile floor, followed by the unmistakable sound of the double glass entry doors swinging open and closed. Realizing it's coming from behind him, Rich quickly spins toward the room's entrance.

On the other side of the dirty glass, a few tall lamp posts are scattered across the parking lot. Sparsely placed, they cast a dim light on the back of a man's light-blue scrubs; he's walking away.

The sight of him makes Rich's blood boil. "No chance in hell. You aren't getting away that easy," he says. Worried about the man's quickening pace, he swiftly pushes the doors open to exit.

The sound of the clock falls quiet. Startled by the silence, Rich quickly steps outside and snatches his hand away from the glass.

Without resistance, the door gains momentum, slamming shut behind him.

The sound makes the man in the distance slowly turn around.

Rich slides the shield of his helmet up to get a better look, and, seeing the stubble on his face, his stomach drops.

The stranger releases a carnal grunt. Then, with a primal twinkle in his eye, he locks his gaze on Rich.

As the man approaches, Rich watches each light he passes flicker, revealing fragments of an unrecognizable face and causing him to take a step back. "Who ... are you?" he asks.

The man's crooked smile reveals his anticipation of his moment to speak. "Well, well, well. Look who's here. If it isn't the little bastard child in the flesh," Rut says. "The one who thought he was too good to take my last name."

Rich's eyes widen, and he quickly takes another step back.

Pinching his shirt sleeve, Rut chuckles. "You like my outfit? I stole it from a man nurse."

Rich frantically looks from left to right. "Crap," he mutters. All he can think about is the time remaining on the clock and how this interruption is delaying him from finishing his task.

With a kick of his foot, Rut throws up his hands, pointing at Rich; he sarcastically laughs. "Hell, I bet you don't even recognize your old man," he says, gritting his teeth and angrily spitting his words.

Rich fixates on the top of the dirty white shirt poking out the V-neck of the scrubs.

"What a sad … sad day," Rut says, shouting with excitement. His steps become stomps. "You may think you're better than me, but I got news for you: you are nothing but a talentless loser who sold his soul for his success."

As Rut passes another flickering light, Rich cringes at the gory wound on the frontal portion of his skull. Shards of bone mushroom out from a heavy mound of bloody flesh surrounding a gaping hole dead-centered between his eyes. "Get a good look, boy! You're the reason she put a bullet in my head," Rut says; picking up his speed, he charges forward.

Rich's heart races as he sees him barreling toward him, and he quickly reaches for the door and sprints inside. He is immediately greeted by the relentless ticking of the clock, its sound tormenting him as he anxiously watches Rut getting closer through the glass. "Come on … get it together," he says, fumbling near the handle to find the lock.

"You can run, but you can't hide!" Rut shouts. "You and your mama are gonna reap what you sow! You'll pay for what you've done. Like a father, like a son. I'm gonna put a bullet in your skull!"

Unable to find a latch, Rich glances down at his hands and panics.

There is only a keyhole.

Quickly glancing up, he sees Rut is almost at the door. "Shit," he says. Not having time to secure it, he spins around and takes off in a dead sprint for the hallway. He scrambles with each step, pushing against the walls for momentum.

The hospital doors slam open, shattering their glass. Now inside the lobby, Rut screams at the top of his lungs. "Tick, tock, tick, tock!" he says, mimicking the clock.

Gasping for breath, Rich gets to the crossroad in the hall and, hearing a gunshot pierce through the air, makes a quick decision to go left. As he heads down the way he came, he glances up at the ceiling.

The fluorescent green numbers strobe and, with a glitch, skip to show only one hour remaining. Children's laughter and crackling sounds play through the intercom system.

Shocked by the lapse in time, Rich lowers his head and pushes on; the blood-spattered shield of his helmet falls over his eyes, skewing his view. He moves faster, unsure where to go.

In the distance, he notices the dim light of an open door through the speckles of blood. Focusing on the glow, Rich clenches his fists and, darting toward it, shifts his attention to the brass plate. The six etched into the metal gives him an eerie feeling; it mirrors the one he had remembered projecting through the static of the television screen.

As his déjà vu brings him to a halt at the door, another gunshot echoes from the lobby. Desperate to hide, he rushes inside, and as he pushes in the lock, he hears Rut's muffled footsteps and whistling coming down the hallway. "Where are you hiding, my boy?" his father asks.

Rich remains motionless, staring at the entrance, scared to budge, while hearing him pound on each door, starting with the first one at the end of the hall. "Are you in here?" he asks. Kicking in the door, he fires a shot.

The harsh pop makes Rich flinch. "Fuck," he says.

Rut quickly moves on to the next room in line. With a loud knock, he shouts, "Anyone home?"

Rich listens as another shot is fired, and sweat drips down his brow. Hearing Rut getting closer, he scans the worn wood, and he remembers staring at the exact spot after entering his mother's hospital room before killing her.

Three loud knocks sound from a few doors down. "Am I hot or cold?" Rut asks, and, with a demonic cackle, he kicks it in.

Overwhelmed by his fear, Rich can't control his watering eyes and sniffles. Needing to breathe, he pushes up the shield of his helmet, and as he's wiping the tears away, he hears an agonized moan.

Rut moves to the next door and knocks.

Listening, Rich holds his breath and, noticing the groans getting louder, turns to look. The sight of wadded sheets on the unmade bed prompts panic, and he carefully steps closer, unveiling a gruesome detail: the cotton has been strategically placed to hide fresh blood splatters that stain the mattress.

Another round of desperate cries accompanies the gunfire.

Rich carefully examines the signs of a struggle. Then, his eyes are drawn to the space on the other side of the bed.

As loud banging comes from the fifth door, the moans blend with the chaos of the ticking clock.

Upon hearing the muffled plea once more, he becomes increasingly convinced that it could be the nurse he has been looking for. He takes a step closer. "It's him or me. I got no choice," he says. "I got to get the fuck out of here." The sound of Rut shooting his gun makes him quicken his pace, and, turning the corner of the bed, he freezes. "Holy shit."

It's worse than he expected. The man left only in his underwear, has had his limbs bound by medical tape and his mouth wrapped in thick layers of gauze to silence him. He's been severely beaten, and blood streams from his ears and nostrils.

Rich watches the man's eyes bulge as he frantically tries to speak, pleading for help. Glancing at the mustache sticking out above the tight cotton wrapping, a glimmer of metal catches his eye.

A necklace is caught in the winding bits of the man's burgundy chest hair.

Swiftly kneeling on the floor, Rich lifts the object from his skin to examine what is hanging from the chain. Hanging behind a gold-colored cross is a pendant featuring a silver number eight with the name Rich Richardson prominently displayed on the front.

Surprised, he struggles to find his words. "My ... my race number," he says, shifting his attention to the man's face. He looks at the terror in his eyes. "You don't wanna ruin everything for me, do you?"

Overcome with guilt for his sinister thoughts about the man, he briefly drifts away into his mind until loud knocks on the wooden door jolt him back.

Each thrashing rattles the walls, accompanied by Rut's screams. "Tick, tick, tick, tock. It's about time you suffer like me and rot."

With tears in his eyes, Rich watches the pendant drop from his shaking palm. "I'm ... so... sorry," he whispers.

Then he lowers his visor to cover his eyes.

The sound of Rut kicking in the entrance pierces the air.

Snatching the man's hair in his gloved hands, Rich slams his head repeatedly against the tile, smashing his skull. Amid the brutal attack, he flinches as a loud gunshot reverberates through the room, and liquid drips from his head to his body.

24

DON'T SPILL

Another loud pop cracks through the air.

As Rich hyperventilates and covers his head, he is greeted by the smell of gasoline and freshly cut grass. He is oblivious to the crowd scattered around him and the man drenching him in champagne.

Roy slows as he weaves through the bodies, trying to sneak up behind him. "Hey there!" he shouts. "How's our first-place champ doing?" he asks, fighting back a snicker.

Reluctant to open his eyes, Rich feels his uncle's hand touch his back and jumps, straightening his posture.

Roy talks faster as he continues, "Sorry about disappearing. I had a few odds and ends to sort out."

Rich nervously laughs, and glancing at his racing jumpsuit, spots a gold medallion around his neck. The way it dangles reminds him of the nurse's necklace. Overcome by guilt, he tries to redirect his mind and, with a nervous chuckle, awkwardly fixes his hair.

A series of crackles reverberates above. Roy grins from ear to ear. "How are you enjoying the fireworks?" he asks.

Feeling an oncoming wave of emotion, Rich shifts his attention to the spectacle in the night sky. "Yup, it's great ... never seen anything like it," he says. Just as a tear is about to escape his eye, he slaps the side of his neck, pretending to squish a bug. "I wish there weren't so many damn mosquitos, though." He chuckles to hide his pain.

Just in time, another giant boom sounds from above. Breaking off into tiny crackles, it distributes bright colors like a lightning strike covering the sky. The spectacle, much more extravagant than before, commences the grand finale. The crowd roars, sending claps and cheers echoing across the grandstands.

While scanning the cheering fans, Rich observes the other race teams dispersed across the track. The drivers are surrounded by their pit crews, creating their cloistered cliques, distinguished by their matching colors and numbers.

A fit of laughter catches Rich off-guard. Quickly, turning to look, he spots a group of men in forest-green shirts; each has the number twelve embroidered on their sleeves.

"Is ... um... uh..." Rich stammers, struggling with his words.

As Roy notices where he is looking, he takes a moment and clears his throat. With a casual shrug, he leans closer, his voice dropping to a whisper. "Yeah ... so, about that... it turns out I got some misinformation. Ben was never in critical condition. He was fine. I guess he was only slightly banged up, so they cleared him to race," he says. "By the time I got to the hospital, they were already sending him home."

As Rich listens to his uncle, he frantically analyzes each face, searching for his friend. Expecting a different response, his uncle rolls his eyes. "Don't bother; you're wasting your time," he says.

Confused, Rich swiftly pivots to face him. "Wait ... what?" he asks. "Why?"

Roy redirects his gaze to the colors fizzling above, and his demeanor turns cold. "The kid already left. He's a bit of a sore loser if you ask me," he says.

Rich looks to the ground. "Shit," he says, kicking a rock. "I was gonna talk to him after everything that went down at the funeral and stuff."

Upon hearing his nephew's disappointment, Roy responds angrily, believing that Ben's spoiled behavior does not deserve any concern. "What for?" he asks. Noticing his tone may come across as harsh, he adjusts it to be more pleasant. With a forced smile, he calmly continues, "I mean ... no need to worry. I already talked to him before the race to smooth things over."

Rich sighs with relief. "Oh, great," he says. "How did he seem?"

"Seemed fine to me," Roy replies.

Happy something is going right, Rich grins.

Roy lowers his voice, trying to preserve the mood. "We just let him win a race, and things will be as good as new," he says. "Easy as cake. No more drama."

Rich pauses momentarily, processing his uncle's words, and his eyes widen. "What did you say?" he asks.

Not wanting a scene, Roy talks faster. "Think about it. The whole thing is a win-win for everyone involved. He gets to be first for a race, and then we are even," he says. "Plus, it breaks your streak, making everything appear less suspicious. I mean, usually, newcomers don't just come in and win everything."

Unable to look past his uncle's first statement, the thought of willingly losing makes Rich cringe. "But ... I don't want to be second," he says, his emotions spiraling as he clenches his fists. "I ... I earned being the best. Not the second best ... the best."

"Whoa, champ. One race isn't a biggie. Think of it as a long play," Roy says. Then, seeing the reactions of others nearby, he lowers his voice to a whisper. "We let him win one, and we don't have to deal with any bullshit. To me, that's a bigger win than crossing the finish line first. Remember, we are in this for the long haul."

Rich is finding it difficult to focus on his uncle's words. The image of the male nurse won't leave his mind, and he is haunted by the sensation of the man's hair twisted in his grip. He shakes his head to break his thoughts. "No! Uncle Roy, that doesn't work for me. You gotta think of another deal," he says with conviction, his voice growing louder. "I went through a lot of crap to earn my spot, and there's no way he's gonna take it from me."

A handful of people notice the disturbance and casually glance over. Smiling at them, Roy tries not to look suspicious. "You need to cool it," he says through clenched teeth.

Rich angrily stomps his foot, his eyes fixated on the ground. With a laugh, Roy turns his full attention to the onlookers. "He's just ramped up about winning!" he says. "That's all! No need to be concerned."

As the crowd redirects their attention back to their groups, Rich releases a heavy sigh. Roy aggressively grabs his arm, pulling him closer, and tightens his grip. Rich winces in pain as his uncle's fingers leave a black-and-blue imprint on his skin. "Look, kid, you are making a scene. We can continue this conversation in the truck," Roy says.

Holding back his rage, Rich reluctantly complies, "Yeah, Sure ... Roy," he says, forcing a smile.

Roy yanks him away. "Come on. Let's go," he says. Out of patience for Rich's act of rebellion, he pulls harder and grunts under his breath, "Now damn it."

Hearing his uncle's shift in tone, Rich quickly follows. As they silently walk across the track, they hide their true feelings behind fake smiles while waving to the people they pass.

Once they're out of view, their toothy grins turn to scowls as they quicken their pace toward the parking lot.

Roy quickens his pace as they near the car. "I'll drive," he says. Releasing his nephew's arm, he hops into the truck's cab. The slamming door sends a shiver down Rich's spine as he climbs into the passenger seat.

All is quiet, aside from the sound of the starting engine. Both are too angry to talk as they silently gaze out their respective windows, avoiding eye contact and watching the highway scenery go by.

Reluctantly, Rich clears his throat, knowing he must discuss their interaction despite his reservations. "So, what race?" he asks. "Which one did you tell him I was supposed to lose?"

Roy lays his foot on the gas.

The silence fills Rich with anxiety. "Uncle Roy," he says; his voice shakes. "Which one is it?"

With his attention fixed forward, he listens to the waver in his voice and shrugs.

"Well, there's only one left," he says.

Rich freezes. He knows that significant periods of time have passed without his notice. Yet, in the year-long season of twenty-six races, he can't remember taking part in any except for a single lap in the first race, indicating that Roy has likely possessed his body more often than he's let on.

Sensing his misgiving, Roy responds by pushing down harder on the gas pedal, causing their speed to surge. "Why else did you think they had that fireworks show?" he asks, annoyed.

In a panic, Rich sits on his trembling hands to conceal signs of his paranoia. His heart quickens as he confronts the reality that he is merely a pawn in his own existence. Apart from the horrific acts he is conscious of, he is even more terrified of the possibilities of the atrocities he's unwittingly taken part in.

Roy glances at him from the corner of his eye and, with a sarcastic chuckle, wants to stir a reaction. "Honestly, I thought you were smarter than that. Perhaps I got it wrong, thinking you were cut out for a life of luxury," he says.

Each of his uncle's words strikes a nerve, as Rich fears becoming disposable; with a laugh, he switches gears, still noticing Roy watching in his peripheral vision. "Come on,

Uncle Roy, you know me!" he says. Cracking a smile, he snickers. "I'm just fucking with you."

Skeptical of his sudden confidence, Roy waits to see where he's going with the conversation.

Rich laughs loudly. "You got to learn how to shoot the shit," he says. Reaching over the seat, he gives his uncle a nudge. "So, you want me to throw the championship? That's cool," he says, winking and leaning back in his seat. "Like you said, we're in it for the long haul, so one race doesn't mean much. It's really not that big of a deal in the grand scheme of things."

As Roy lets up on the gas pedal, he grimaces as he allows his nephew's words to marinate. "I'm glad we see eye to eye," he says. "Matter of fact—gotta say, you might be my favorite."

Keeping his focus on the house quickly approaching, Rich smiles, feeling back in control.

A moment of silence passes as they pull into the driveway, and Roy parks the car. Rich notices his grip slowly tighten on the leather of the wheel; he can tell his uncle is in the middle of a thought.

As Roy stares at the garage door, he turns off the truck's engine. "You know, I gotta admit..." he says, slapping the wheel while releasing a boisterous round of laughter.

Unsure what's so funny, Rich nervously joins in.

Running himself out of breath, Roy gasps. "You really had me for a moment," he says, barely able to speak. "I was worrying we were having a redo of 1972." The inside joke with himself makes him laugh even louder.

As Rich exits the car, cold air brushes against his skin, and a voice whispers in the night breeze. Each raspy word is coming from the direction of the lake.

The thought of the creature from the dock makes him cringe, and though he tries to ignore it, goosebumps plague his skin.

25

DON'T DREAM

A click pierces the air; it pulls Rich's attention away from the lingering murmurs. Realizing it's the front door unlocking, he rushes to get inside.

With a grin, Roy happily allows him to go first. "What an eventful day! It's time for you to get some well-deserved rest," he says.

As Rich enters, he suddenly feels someone watching him, causing him to stop and glance toward the garage door.

Although the staircase beside it mirrors the one that leads to his room, the carpet runner looks more worn, showing its age. Glancing at the top, he focuses on where it leads. His stay in the house has been brief, and his recollections of it are even briefer. When he initially saw the second staircase, he assumed it was purely decorative, only leading to a bay window with a view of the grounds or a reading nook, but as he looks closer, it appears to go to a separate wing.

Roy leaves the door open so as not to create any noise. Sneaking up behind Rich, he angles his body to see where he is looking and grins. "The splendor never gets old, does it?" he says, snapping Rich out of his daze. Panic washes over him as he realizes he has lost track of how long he has been stagnant. "Uh ... sure doesn't," he says. Nervously clearing his throat, he scrambles toward the staircase leading to his room.

Roy analyzes Rich's nervous demeanor as he follows him up the staircase, and noticing him start to relax, he abruptly breaks the silence. "I gotta say, I'm so damn happy we can be ourselves around each other." He snickers as he watches his nephew trip on the last step.

Rich tightly grips the ornately carved railing to regain his balance, his body tense as an odd static fills the room, adding an air of unpredictability.

Roy wants him exhausted, no matter what he says, and he'll do whatever it takes to keep the conversation going. "It's so liberating not having to suppress what's lingering inside. Wouldn't you say?" The space is filled with unease as he waits for his nephew's reply.

Rich gulps. He can sense Roy's unwavering stare. Feeling pressured, he answers, "Uh-huh ... yeah, sure. I, um ... agree."

Thrilled by his uncertainty, Roy dramatically sighs. "I'm so glad we have put all our differences behind us just in time for the big day."

A soft noise echoes down the hallway. Believing he hears footsteps, Rich nervously scans the darkness and anxiously laughs. "Yeah, yup," he says.

Roy closes his eyes, his lips curling toward his ears as he delights in the pounding of his nephew's racing heart.

The dark continues to captivate Rich. He is too nervous to look away. "This weekend is..." he says. He hesitates and begins to doubt the accuracy of his timeline.

The uncertainty in his voice causes Roy's cheeks to lift into points and his chin to elongate. "The Victor Cup in good old Charlotte," he says, finishing his nephew's sentence.

"So, we still got a few days, right?" he asks, trying to sort out the thoughts running through his head.

Roy cuts in with a snicker. "Yes, but I'm sure it will be here in the blink of an eye," he says.

In an instant, Rich's eyes widen as he realizes time is running out. He needs to come up with a plan swiftly. All he desires is to race, and given his strained relationship with Roy, he knows that the Victor's Cup final might be his sole opportunity.

He knows that beyond that, nothing is guaranteed. Whether he stays for another season depends on the ever-changing whims of the Devil, which can shift at the drop of a hat.

"Can you promise me something?" Rich asks.

Intrigued by the proposition, Roy shifts his pitch, releasing a guttural snarl. "Sure, boy ... tell me what you desire," he says.

As Rich hears the excitement in his uncle's voice, he takes a deep breath to keep himself composed. "Will you let me drive?" he asks, gaining confidence as he asserts himself. "In the championship."

Roy's tongue emerges from his mouth with an eerie hiss, resembling a snake sampling the air. "Let me think ... Oh, why not. It's a deal," he says; his words rumble and rattle the crystal in the grand chandelier.

The clinking and crashing of the dangling glass grabs his attention, causing his heart to race with the fear of it crashing down.

Roy lets out a raspy gasp, his skin reddening like an ember and his teeth morphing into jagged molars resembling porous volcanic rock. "You get some sleep now," he says, his smile extending from jawbone to jawbone. "I have some things I need to catch up on," he says.

Rich feels a puff of air on the back of his neck.

"So ... it's best that you don't come looking for me if you hear any bumps at night," Roy whispers in his ear.

Rich cringes.

As his uncle's voice fades, an eerie quietness engulfs him.

Quickly, he glances down the stairs toward the front door, which is now closed, but he can't recall hearing it shut. He scans his surroundings, searching for any sign that could reveal if he left. "Hello?" he asks.

The electric candlesticks of the chandelier flicker.

Seeing no sign of his uncle, Rich spins to face the hallway, trembling as he squints into its abyss. "Just a few steps," he says. With a gulp, he anxiously picks at one of the sponsor patches on his jumpsuit and, taking a deep breath, races down the hallway.

As he stops to open the bedroom door, he feels someone watching him. The air is thick with an eerie feeling, heightened by the sound of small bursts of laughter.

Slowly, he turns to look behind him, his breaths growing rapid and shallow. Met with the emptiness of the hall, he rushes to get inside, and, flipping on the lights, he locks the door.

Finally alone, he presses his back against the door's cool surface. Flashbacks plague his mind, making it impossible for him to relax as his attention jumps from the bathroom arch to the curtains.

The thick gold velvet hangs motionless. Even though there is no movement, his heart races and sweat drips from his hairline. Feeling his body overheating, he quickly unzips the top of his jumpsuit and pulls at his white tank top, allowing air to circulate against his skin.

As the draftiness of the room cools his chest, he shuts his eyes to focus.

"Don't close your—" a voice whispers.

His eyes spring open. "Everything is all good," he says, wiping away his sweat; he looks to the curtain. The heavy velvet material remains still. "See? We are good. Nothing to worry about."

His attention darts to the bathroom. The open door prompts his memory of the snakes, causing him to dash across the room and close it. As he turns to face the room, a wave of fatigue washes over him.

His race helmet, devoid of blood or gore, rests peacefully on the neatly made bed. Intrigued by its freshly polished shell, he walks toward it. The closer he gets, the more he notices the haunting sound of static.

It's coming from inside the helmet. "Rich, Richie..." a man's voice says, interjecting between the radio crackles.

Rich stops at the foot of the bed to listen, grimacing as he glimpses his reflection in the visor. Even though he knows it's himself, there is something unrecognizable. The shape of his face is slightly different. Its features are harsher. Unable to look away, he imagines the man hovering over the bed.

"When's the last time you've seen your reflection?" he says; his demonic tone haunts Rich's mind.

Rich clenches his jaw and places his hands on the mattress. Drawn to the static, he shifts closer and feels his lids become heavy. "No, you know what happens when you shut your eyes," he says, pushing himself away from the bed.

The radio static produces small popping sounds that resemble muted bursts of laughter.

Listening to the muffled tone, his eyes widen, and everything clicks. "That fucker! You want me to fall asleep," he says, pointing his finger at the helmet. "I got news for you, buddy: You aren't gonna get rid of me that easy. I'm onto your little game. Come hell or high water; I will drive. I, Rich Richardson, am gonna race, and dammit, that's final!"

A slight rattle exits the vent, and the room temperature rises. The warmth makes it harder to stay awake; unzipping more of his jumpsuit, Rich storms around the room. "You're not gonna win. I won't let you," he says, fanning himself to dry his soaked undershirt as he scans the area of the bed.

Abruptly, the nightstand catches his attention. It's no longer pressed against the bed; it's been moved away from the frame.

Immediately, he charges toward it. "First the helmet ... now this? Where are you hiding?" he says, spinning around and scanning the room. With each heavy breath, his imagination runs wild, and his frustration makes him shout, "I know you're here somewhere!"

The lighting bobbles, flashing brighter, accenting the room's emptiness.

Rich turns upon hearing something behind him, only to find the cabinet's top drawer wide open. His heart races, pounding in his chest. "Who's there?"

He notices something sticking out from the drawer and cautiously steps toward it. It's a dingy white envelope marred with grease smudges.

The sight of the postage addressed to him makes his eyes grow wide. "What the hell?" As he grabs it, his hands tremble, his eyes fixated on the dark-red handwriting. Quickly, he turns it over.

On the backside is a stiff red wax seal on the lip's fold, imprinted with sixty-six.

Gently pressing his fingertip on the indented numbers, he lowers his voice to a murmur. "That's Mason's ... um... race... numb—" he starts to say, but he suddenly stops speaking as, from the corner of his eye, he sees the window's curtains lightly sway.

As the motion stops, a dark figure emerges from the velvet. Rich can recognize who it is without seeing their face; the masculine figure is Mason.

The vents rattle, and suddenly, the temperature in the room becomes unbearably hot.

In need of relief, Rich lifts his moist palm off the envelope, and as he reaches for the jumpsuit zipper, sweat drips from his face, streaking his name on the document.

The salty mixture has turned the bold ink into a crimson smear. Finding it oddly reminiscent of the gore on his visor, he looks at the residue of his skin. Then, as he sniffs the tip of his thumb, a waft of iron enters his nostrils. Able to taste a metallic tinge, he panics, wiping his finger on his pants.

Suddenly, Mason moves, shifting his weight from side to side. "Open it!" he screams.

Rich jumps and pushes past his nerves, ripping open the seal. Quickly fetching the paper from the inside, he drops the smeared shell to the floor.

26

WINNER'S PARADISE

Muffled voices scatter through the air, making it hard for Rich to think as they grow louder with the heat.

A jostle in the curtain triggers his nerves, and unable to ignore it, he glances toward the window; the heckling voices abruptly stop. Everything appears normal; the curtains are completely still, and the shadow of the man is gone.

Rich redirects his attention back to the letter. As he unfolds it, a shiver forms under the sweat drenching his skin. "You only have two things you gotta do. That's it. You gotta focus and stay awake," he says. "You can do that."

Finishing opening each fold, he pauses.

There isn't just one piece of paper, but two.

Not wanting to risk smearing the note's handwriting, he sets the letter on the bed for safekeeping and swiftly straightens each crease of the page.

Unlike the letter, this one is quite large, and grid lines fill the space of the slightly transparent material, helping scale the charcoal and lead-toned drawing.

As he looks closer, a sense of eerie familiarity washes over him. It's a diagram of the Samuel's estate. Swiftly, he moves his gaze to a small red circle on the map. "That's definitely my bedroom, and that red mark is on my nightstand," he says, realizing the location is his room.

The outlines of other shapes make sense when he compares them to the surrounding furniture.

As he moves the picture closer, he confirms the accuracy of the items' placement in the room, and the wheels of his brain turn. "So ... if I am here on the map... then that means..." he says, touching the map. He slides his finger, tracing his steps back to the foyer. His curiosity triggers him to talk faster.

"Maybe I can find out what's hiding at the top of the other set of steps," he says, stopping his finger at the bottom of the adjacent staircase. He can't help panning between the two. In person, they appeared similar, but the drawing shows them as very different.

The one nearest to the garage has been colored in a significantly darker shade. "That's weird," he says, trying to make sense of it.

Each bold line detailing the steps is indented, creating divots in the paper—the artist's heavy hand gives it a textured appearance.

His eyes shift to the uninviting nature of the railing. The wooden posts bring to mind the tangled complexity of a thorny briar patch. Though hesitant to journey further, he moves his finger, dragging it against the page to ascend the steps. "Shit," he mutters, realizing he left a trail of smudges halfway up the stairs.

Thinking he had wiped the sweat dry from his hand, he checks his fingers for any signs of moisture causing the smear, but they are perfectly dry.

Upon closer examination, he notices that some sections of the ink have a glossy sheen, as if they were freshly drawn.

"But how in the world..." he begins.

Then, he notices something new on the steps: a stick figure stands at the top, turned sideways; it has the same sheen as the other easily smudged markings.

While analyzing it, he brushes his fingers over its black ink-sketched face. It has no expression.

Then, suddenly, with a jarring motion, the stick figure's legs bend at the knees.

Rich's eyes widen, and he yanks his finger away. "What the hell?" he says as the figure begins a rigid march.

He clutches the page tighter between his fingers as the ominous presence disjointedly steps down the shadowed corridor. As the figure makes its way to the end of the hallway, it disappears into the dark shading of the room's single door.

His heart races. "But ... but... where did it go?" he asks frantically. He scans the page and, struggling to find it, moves it closer to his face.

Even though the wing has an overall darker ambiance than the rest of the blueprint, the room where the figure has vanished is even more ominous, intentionally blacked out.

Determined to see what's behind the opacity, Rich remembers a trick he learned in school, and, holding the paper in the air, he uses the light to dissect what's hidden beneath the fresh ink. Squinting, he thinks he can make out a few letters. As he struggles to piece them together, he stammers, "The ... the De-Devil... play..."

The light flickers.

Laughing nervously, he mutters, "That's ridiculous. That can't be right. I mean, what ... uh, what would that even mean?"

Despite his best efforts, he can't make sense of it. With no pictures to guide him, he can only visualize a child's playroom, which adds to his confusion. Feeling overwhelmed by the endless possibilities, he becomes desperate for a distraction. He scans the map for more places, and his gaze falls on the yard behind the house.

As he looks closer, his eyes are drawn to the outbuilding. On one of its walls, there is a sketch of various garden tools accompanied by three words. "Tools of mayhem?" he asks. Puzzled by its meaning, he scans the page, trying to make sense of the cryptic message. Suddenly, it dawns on him, and he remembers the term "mayhem" from professional wrestling, which is always linked to chaos and violence.

"Maybe it means the tools are used for doing bad things. I mean, I guess I used the shovel as a weapon, but they're totally blowing it out of proportion with all those fancy words," he mutters. The thought makes him shudder.

In an attempt to forget the encounter, he diverts his attention to the lake area, specifically the dock. Everything is just as he remembered, except for one new thing.

The boards have been marked with an inscription. "Noisy, it listens?" he reads in a whisper. Then, he sees a shadowed space drawn in at the end and recalls the loud creak when stepping on the planks, and the phrase makes sense.

Another inscription lies on the opposite side of the darkened spot. "Beware, they hide...," he reads. Feeling a flashback coming on, his eyes dart to the body of water. Small oblong sketches scatter the areas between the waves. Cringing, he remembers the bodies floating in the lake. "Nope, not going there," he says, shaking his head. "We're not gonna go through that again. Once was plenty."

Eager to put it behind him, he hastily skims over the rest of the document. Not confined to his experiences, other tiny phrases and sketches fill the estate blueprint. Rather than standard labels, like those used for rooms and furniture, each hand-drawn addition harbors a warning.

Suddenly, it hits him: It's not just any map; it's been made as a reference key to staying alive. It's meant to alert him of what lurks on the other side.

Horrified, he looks at the number of captions marking the spaces he has never been to. It resembles a nightmarish minefield, lying in wait for its next unsuspecting victim. "Damn, I really could've used this earlier."

A bold title graces the top of the page; the curly ends of each letter add a morbid sense of happiness.

"Winner's Paradise?" With an anxious chuckle, he whispers, "More like a winner's hell if you ask me." His eyes wander to the ominous markers. Overwhelmed, he returns his gaze to the area outlining his bedroom; his complexion turns stark white.

According to the map, the stick figure from the opposite wing is standing at the far end of his hallway.

Gulping, he falls silent, carefully listening, and, thinking he hears footsteps, spins to face the door.

A rattle echoes from the vent, kicking another heat wave into the room. With apprehension, he looks back to the map, and, seeing the figure has shifted, he trembles.

The dark entity is now positioned directly outside the door, its arm outstretched toward the knob.

As sweat drips down his face, each beat of his heart creates a thunderous roar in his eardrums, and he clenches his jaw, trying to keep it together.

Slowly, three steady knocks echo through the room.

He winces with terror, tightly closing his eyes to think. "Come on, Rich," he whispers, "Get it together." Regaining his focus, he hastily retrieves the letter from the bed, hoping it holds the key to his escape.

The doorknob rattles as it rotates one way and then the other. Whatever is outside is trying to get in.

He scans the note, desperately seeking any direction for what to do. Although the letter starts with a formal salutation, the rest is filled with the exact repeating phrase: Don't let him in ... don't let him in...don't let him in.

"Don't let him in?" he says. "That's it? That's all the great Mason Samuels has to say? This ... this is bullshit. Any idiot could figure that out." His anger builds, and, crumpling up the paper, he throws it on the ground. The thought of everything he has been forced to endure makes him shudder. He looks up to the door, channeling his rage.

The movement of the knob grows aggressive, each manic twist releasing a loud rattle. Screams from the lake add to the chaos, effortlessly projecting through the window's glass as if it were made of air.

Rich covers the side of his head with his palms and, trying to think, glances at the window and takes a deep breath. The putrid scent of decaying flesh and bleach permeates the air, invading his lungs and nostrils.

Coughing, he races around the room to locate the origin of the stench and realizes a dense, boggish gas is seeping in from beneath the door. "What's that thing trying to do? Gas me out?"

Feeling like he's losing it, he quickly folds the map and stuffs it in a pocket. As he paces the room, the suffocating vapor thickens, and remembering what occurred in the garage, he knows he can't stay.

He glances back at the bed. Even though the haze impedes it, the light still glistens against the helmet's tough shell, reminding him of what matters most.

"Come hell or high water, I'm gonna make that son of a bitch keep his end of the deal. I'm screwed either way, so I might as well go for broke. One thing's for damn sure, this time, I'm gonna drive," he says, zipping up his jumpsuit.

"And he's gonna learn the hard way that I always keep my promises," he grumbles as he shoves the helmet onto his head and snaps the buckle, charging toward the door with renewed determination.

With a flick of the lock, he throws it open and, preparing to meet the thing from the drawing, flails his fists.

"Woah there, partner!" Roy says, catching his hands and laughing. "Looks like someone is excited about the race."

Rich recoils, shocked to see his face.

Releasing him, Roy looks him up and down. "We still wearing that? It's been days," he says.

Rich flips up the shield of his helmet. "Excuse me?" he asks, convinced he must have misheard him.

His uncle grabs the fabric on his shoulder. "You've been wearing that thing since we got home from the race," Roy says.

Rich pulls away and nervously glances back into the open door of his room.

Slivers of daylight stream through the part in the heavy velvet curtains; it is morning.

Rich is unsure how much time has passed, but he remembers it being nighttime just moments ago.

Fighting back a snicker, Roy leans closer to see what he is looking at.

As he slowly removes the helmet from his head, Rich can feel his uncle's stare. "I'm wearing the outfit to practice for the reporters," he says. Knowing he can't let his uncle see him sweat, he forces a confident chuckle and, turning to face him, he dramatically frowns. "See? Like that." He laughs. "With my winning streak and all, I want to be as believable as possible when I lose. We wouldn't want anyone to think I threw the race, would we?"

Roy squints, his eyes locked on his nephew as he dissects each of his movements. Then with no time to spare, he smirks, "You're quite the good sport," he says.

Rich feels a sense of relief as his uncle exhibits no suspicion.

Roy shifts his attention to the dark circles under his nephew's eyes. "How'd you sleep? Are you good? Did anything keep you awake?" he asks. Excited for the reply, he grins from ear to ear.

"I slept great! Probably the best sleep ever! Slept like a baby," Rich says, talking faster. "It might be the best sleep I've gotten in weeks."

Fighting back a snicker, Roy pats his shoulder. "That's great, bud," he says. Then, tightening his grip, he pulls his nephew closer and glares directly into his eyes. His tone becomes threatening. "You would tell me if you were hiding something, right? You wouldn't keep a secret from me?"

With a nervous gulp, Rich breaks his gaze. "No secrets here," he says. Glancing down at the floor, he notices engine oil on the toe of his uncle's shoe.

Roy snickers. "Good," he says. "That's what I like to hear."

As Rich's mind races, wondering where he has been, his uncle grabs his other shoulder and spins him around to face his room. "We have a busy day today," Roy says, pushing him inside.

As Rich hears his uncle's footsteps trailing closely behind him, he tightens his grip on his helmet and keeps his eyes focused straight ahead. He cringes at the sight of clothing laid out on the bed.

There is a dress shirt with green embellishments and leather pants with stitching to match. Besides the accents, the entire outfit is black.

Anxiously looking away from the embroidered eight on the front pocket, Rich fixates on the black leather belt's golden buckle; it has an engraved image of a hissing viper. Next to it is a chunky chain made from matching gold. As he carefully sets his helmet beside the apparel, he glances at the familiar, freshly polished boots and laughs. "Uh, what's the occasion? Not another funeral, is it?"

Roy's chuckle reverberates through the room. "That's a good one, kid!" he says, clutching his stomach. "But if I were you, I'd save the funny for your interviews. People eat that shit up on press day. They love big personalities. It makes you likable."

The thought of it being the day before the race makes Rich's posture stiffen. He hasn't just missed a day or two, but the entire week. Clearing his throat, he slowly picks the shirt up from the bed. "Time sure flies, doesn't it?"

Roy grins. "I told you it would be here in no time," he says, fighting back a hiss. He twirls his finger, signaling his nephew to hurry. "Don't be shy, now. Go on. Give it a spin! You gotta turn it around and look at the back. Everything is custom made."

With a gulp, Rich uses the crease of his elbow to dry the sweat from his forehead and slowly flips it around. Across the shoulders and going down the spine is a sizable embroidered coiled viper. It not only matches the belt buckle, but also the hood of his car.

As he follows the stitching of green embroidery, he notices a radiant shimmer coming from its eyes. Standing out are two fluorescent emeralds, the sparkle accentuating the mesmerizing hypnotic twinkle they possess. Lost for words, he forces a more extensive smile. The ends of his lips twitch from the strain.

Roy chuckles. "You better believe those stones are real." Motioning to the eyes, his excitement grows. "They may have cost us a pretty penny, but it's well worth it."

Rich breaks his gaze, glancing over his shoulder. "Well, Uncle Roy, I got to hand it to you," he says. Trying to hide his nerves, he talks faster. "It sure is something."

"I knew you would like it," Roy says, grinning from ear to ear.

Rich blinks to break his gaze away from the serpent's eyes. "Gee, you know me so well. It's like you're in my head or something," he says. Turning to face his uncle, he holds the shirt under his chin and shakes it.

Roy stands tall, watching with a grin.

The awkward pause increases Rich's nervousness, and he starts to sweat. "I got to say, you nailed it," he says.

Another moment of silence passes. They smile and hold eye contact as if they're in a staring contest.

Roy's lack of budging makes it clear he is not planning to leave; something has shifted. "All right, then, I'm gonna get ready now," Rich says.

Roy sneers. "Great," he says. He remains rooted to the same spot, unmoving.

Panic takes hold of Rich as he observes Roy's behavior displaying clear signs of distrust. Finding it odd that his uncle is not trying to be discreet, he nervously gulps, and, wondering if he is onto him, he turns to face the opposite direction and starts to change.

"Chop, chop," Roy says, clapping his hands.

Moving faster, Rich quickly zips his pants and buttons his shirt. He turns around and smiles at his uncle while confidently slicking back his hair. "Perfect," Roy says. As his grin twists into a devious smirk, he winks. "Come to hell or high water, we will drive ... that is, if you can get moving so we can be on time," he says. Fighting back a snicker, he turns, facing the door.

Feeling an odd sense of déjà vu, Rich notices a crumpled paper near his feet. Confused about why it's still there, he kicks it under the bed, hoping to avoid the answer, but the haunting crackles of the radio playing in his head, amplifying his unease. "Shit," he says, whispering. He looks at the helmet, wondering how long his uncle has been listening.

Abruptly, Roy pops his head back inside the room and shouts, "Are you sure you're up for this? If not, we can always..." He fades off, taking a deep breath, ready to propose a plan.

Rich charges toward the door. "Nope! Never been better, Uncle Roy ... we have never been better," he says, and staring his uncle in the eyes, he clenches his jaw. "Come hell or high water, I wouldn't miss my big day for the world."

27

SMILE, CAMERA, DELUSION

Prepared for everyone's arrival in Charlotte, North Carolina, a group of men with uniform buzz cuts, matching navy-blue polo shirts, khaki pants, and checkered hats stand in a line. Each one has a huge smile and a clipboard in their hands. Above them, a giant banner drapes the entrance, welcoming everyone to media day.

As Rich and Roy walk toward the entrance, they put on a show, shedding off any tension from the silent car ride.

Rich notices a man toward the center of the line perk up, looking in his direction. Then, without hesitation, he makes his way toward them. "Hey, there! How's it going,

Rich? My name is Cole. I have been assigned to you for the day. My job is to get you from point A to point B with no hiccups," he says, barely able to fit his spiel into one breath. "Apologies for throwing so much at you at once."

Rich extends his hand. "It's nice to meet you, Cole," he says.

Cole happily shakes it, pleasantly surprised by Rich's friendliness. "Likewise," he says. As they take their first step, he glances at Roy. "Sir, I am afraid this is where your journey ends. We aren't allowing any crew or family at the media event this year for security reasons."

Ignoring him, Roy continues to walk.

Cole shifts his body, stops right in front of him, and locks eyes with him. "I'm sorry if I didn't make myself clear. You can either wait in your car or use the waiting area, which has snacks and water available in one of the boxes up top," he says, maintaining his smile.

Roy takes a step back, attempting to avoid causing a scene, and quickly rubs his ear while laughing. "Sometimes I swear the noise from the engines affects my hearing." Directing his attention to Rich, he sarcastically motions to the parking lot. "I'll just wait in the car, then ... unless, of course, you want me to stay?"

Rich smiles, and winking, chuckles. "Don't worry, Uncle Roy, I'll be good ... I won't do anything you wouldn't do." Empowered, he turns his attention to Cole. "I'm ready when you are."

Roy sneers as he watches them get further away and disappear.

As they make their way beneath the stands, Cole ushers Rich onto the track. "Here we are," he says.

Rich gazes at the empty seats in the stadium, picturing the crowd cheering his name, and then redirects his attention toward the finish line, where, already arriving, a crowd of reporters gathers behind a roped-off area.

Cole points to a long table set up in front of them. "That's where you'll be sitting to answer questions. Everyone is seated by their season ranking coming into the race. So, it's you and Ben Samuels in the middle. Then so on and so forth," he says, talking faster.

Rich analyzes the navy-blue tablecloth and the drivers already seated at the table. Only a few chairs, including Ben's, are still empty.

An image of a trophy and the words Victor Cup have been embroidered on the cloth draping over the table in the front center, and each seat is upholstered with a driver's number.

After glancing nervously at the golden trophy for the event, Rich quickly sits down without making eye contact with the other competitors. He hears the loud pop of a flash and has to shield his eyes from a blinding light.

Cole races from the table toward the media. "Hey ... hey! No pictures before it starts! You know the rules," he says, pointing his finger at the culprit.

The other drivers remain silent, keeping to themselves to stay in the zone.

Rich glances at the empty seat beside him and notices movement in the distance. A uniformed man is leading a large group of the remaining drivers. Ben is front and center.

As they get closer, Rich notices a disdainful look on his face, as if Ben is staring straight through him. Then, his outfit catches his attention.

His clothing resembles Rich's, except he's wearing white leather pants and a white dress shirt instead of black. Rather than being embroidered on his pocket, his sleeve displays the number twelve in a vibrant forest green. It's almost like they got their attire from the same place.

Rich scans from the silver chain around Ben's neck to his belt buckle engraved with a twelve, then looks at the shoes on his feet. Aside from the stark color contrast, they are identical. He clenches his fists. "That bastard," he says, whispering under his breath. He knows the only way Ben could have planned that is if he had communicated with Roy.

As everyone else arrives at the table, they pull out chairs and begin settling into their seats. Immediately, Rich shifts his focus to the track, trying to control his anger.

Spotting his tense expression, Cole rushes over and squats in front of him to get his attention. "You need anything before we get started ... maybe water... or..."

Rich hears the chair slide out beside him. "I'm fine," he says through his clenched teeth.

"Well, go get them! Good luck! I'm rooting for you," Cole says and then moves out of the way.

With a snicker, Ben leans a little closer. "Looks like great minds think alike," he says.

His words make Rich cringe. "Let's just cut the bullshit, Ben," he says, looking over at his shirt. Unsure who to trust, he knows he must appear confident to secure the upper hand. "I know all about you and Roy," he says.

Immediately, Ben panics. "Wait, what? You gotta be shitting me. He told you I'm his kid?" he asks.

Rich's eyes widen, and, trying to keep it together, he coughs to mask his reaction.

In a stroke of perfect timing, Ben's gaze is swiftly diverted by a man wearing a headset and shouting. He waves his arms as he runs in front of the table, signaling everyone to be quiet. "All right!" he shouts, his voice filled with excitement. "Let's get this show on the road!" Stepping aside, he continues to flail his hands. "We are going live in three.... two ... one..."

A camera operator moves to the front of the crowd, trailing a man in a dark navy checkered suit. He makes his way to the middle of the table, turns around slowly, and holds a microphone under his freshly shaved chin. "Hello to everyone tuning in today. The moment we've all been waiting for is here. The Victor Cup press day has just begun. Behind me are our sixteen finalists. Each will drive tomorrow, competing in the year's most important race. Whether you're here at the track or watching our live broadcast, I guarantee it will be an unforgettable event." Rich stares at the man's over-hair sprayed chestnut-brown hair; no matter how much he bobbles, the swoop doesn't move.

Slowly, the man turns to face the drivers. "Before I open the floor for questions, I know our viewers are dying to know if you planned your coordinating outfits," he says. With a smile, he extends the microphone toward Rich and Ben.

Ben, with his mind stuck on his last interaction with Rich, stumbles over his words. "Well ... um...um..."

Rich watches Ben floundering and, seizing the chance to win over the audience, he wraps his arm around the other driver's shoulder. "I think what he's trying to say is that we sure did plan this," he says, and, smiling, he pulls Ben closer. "We have become so darn close this season that we wanted to show our support for one another. Isn't that right, brother?"

Ben realizes what he is doing and glares at him, forcing a smile. "Sure is, Rich," he says.

As the camera pulls away to interview another driver, they cut the act. Ben quickly leans toward Rich and whispers, "I know what you're doing. Your act isn't fooling anyone. You better watch yourself."

Trying to keep his reaction to a minimum, Rich calmly replies, "Guess what? The deal is off tomorrow. I'm winning."

Suddenly, the crowd bursts into applause while the reporter carries on with the interviews.

Using the noise as a cushion, Ben takes another jab. "Oh, and by the way, your mother told me she wants you dead."

The thought of her makes Rich shudder. "Um … what…" he says, stammering. He goes silent, at a loss for words.

"I know what you did," Ben says. "She told me everything."

Rich's stomach drops.

Noticing him squirming, Ben leans a little closer. "What if I told everyone right now?" he asks with a smirk.

Abruptly, a reporter shouts a question. "This one is for Rich!"

Unsure of where the voice is coming from the sea of people, Rich smiles, shaking off his nerves. "Sure! Lay it on me!" he says.

"You currently hold the number one spot in the rankings. How do you feel going into the race tomorrow?"

Rich watches a man in a checkered polo run toward him with a mike. After taking it from the man's hand, he nods with a smile. "Who asked that question?" he asks, addressing the sea of reporters.

A hand sticks up from the center of the crowd.

"Great," Rich says, chuckling. "How are you doing? I always like to know who I'm talking to." Then, pausing, he brings the microphone closer to his lips. "To be honest, I've never felt more confident. I am going into this thing number one, and I plan to come out as number one."

The reporters snicker.

It's evident in Rich's smile that he's loving the attention. "I don't want to come across as cocky. I'm just an honest man. So, I gotta tell it like it is," he says. With a swoon-worthy smolder, he adds, "Thanks for the question." Then, with a shrug, he returns the microphone.

Slowly turning, Rich meets with Ben's glare and mutters, "And that's how it's done. Guess Roy forgot to teach you that."

The microphone produces a heavy reverb as the next reporter is about to speak. Everyone covers their ears.

Wincing, Rich shuts his eyes, and everything falls silent.

28

NO TIME

The clamor of the reporters is gone; a dull beep takes their place.

There isn't so much as a breath coming from beside Rich. Sensing something is wrong, he immediately feels a knot forming in his stomach.

The muffled sound of crickets chirping surrounds him. It reminds him of the lake, and, cringing, he opens his eyes to look. He's no longer at the media table. His gaze is met with his truck's windshield; he is sitting in the passenger seat of his car.

The inside of the cab is hazy, making it hard to tell the time of day; everything is dark gray.

As his eyes dilate to adjust, he glances at the window and sees a glowing reflection in his peripheral vision. The light bounces off the protective shield covering his face, and he realizes he is wearing his helmet. He stares straight ahead.

The dim headlights illuminate the large white pillars of the estate's front porch.

In a fit of rage, he forcefully drives his knees into the dashboard and kicks the floor mat. "Fuck!" he screams.

The car's radio turns on.

He listens to the sound of the ticking clock coming from the speakers. "This is bullshit! I'm human, and people blink," he grunts, reflecting on the event. "That doesn't mean you can take advantage of that. You can't do this. This ... um... this is..." His words trail off as he continues glaring ahead.

Specks of green light trickle into the warmth of the headlights and project onto the garage door, forming the numbers of a digital clock; it shows four hours remaining.

Rich spins the dial on the radio. "No, no, no, no," he says, desperately trying to stop the progression.

As he scans the channels, the radio stations produce a hiss. With another spin, the static is interrupted by the revving of the car's engines. It's the familiar sound of the racetrack. He turns up the volume.

A masculine voice blares over the chaos. "Already in full swing here at the Victor Cup, number twelve is taking the lead. Ben Samuels is giving Rich Richardson a run for his money. They are neck-and-neck."

Rich slams the dial to mute the station.

Rather than stopping, the man's enthusiastic voice grows louder. "We may have an upset today, folks, but only time will tell how this unfolds."

Rich pounds his fists against the dash. "Shit!" he says. Enraged, his face turns a fiery red. He punches the dial, cracking the radio facing.

The voice distorts and fades on impact.

He hyperventilates as he listens to the radio's demonic hiss, and pressing his back into the seat, he frantically flips up the shield of his helmet to breathe. "Okay, it's okay. You need to think. It's not all lost. You can't make assumptions yet. I mean you … you still have time," he says, glancing at the dwindling numbers.

A wave of static echoes inside his helmet. The anticipation of the voice prompts his heart to race. He can't wait any longer. "Roy?!" he shouts, trying to make himself heard over the crackle. "What the hell happened to our deal, huh? How come I'm not on the track?"

With a gust, warm air blasts through the dash vents. Reaching forward, he fumbles to flip the louvers shut.

A glitch in the power causes the clock numbers to bobble.

In a state of panic, Rich frantically wipes the sweat away from his brow, his heart racing as he leans back in his seat.

"I thought it would be best if you sat this one out. So, there's been a change of plans…" Roy says.

Rich's anger builds. "But we had a deal. We both agreed I'd race at the Victor Cup this year," he says.

"This is for your own good," Roy says.

Pounding his fist on the dash, Rich screams, "For my own good? You mean for your own good? There is nothing about this bullshit that benefits me!" The thought of Ben's earlier threat makes him shift gears, and, taking matters into his own hands, he slides into the driver's seat. "Guess what? You can't stop me. Yeah, that's right! I'm gonna drive whether you like it or not, and once I get there, I'm gonna kick your ass."

Roy's laughter intertwines with the radio static. "Where are the keys, Rich?" he asks with a sneer.

"Well, Roy, if they weren't in the ignition, the headlights wouldn't be on," Rich replies. He starts doubting himself and checks the steering column, only to realize the keys are missing.

Roy erupts into a cackle, and the clock's ticks fall silent.

Rich hesitantly turns his gaze toward the windshield. The headlights are no longer illuminated, and the clock is nowhere in sight. His voice trembles as he looks out the window. "What ... what happened to the time? How am I supposed to know how long I've got?"

With a commanding howl, Roy takes control. "I thought you might be getting bored with our arrangement. So, today, we are gonna spice things up a bit with a new game. It's called Can You Stay Alive?" he says, snickering. "The concept is quite simple, really straightforward."

Rich's heart races. "What is that fuck is that supposed to mean?"

Excited, Roy talks faster. "I realize I have done you a disservice by making you feel entitled. You need to know your place, and that little display at the media event showed that you don't. As your uncle and the sole male role model in your life, it's my job to take control and fix this. We gotta bring you down a peg—humble you a bit. Being a fair man, I'll give you a choice on how to best correct the situation: you can either wait and see what unfolds next, or take your chances playing a game with those killed at your hands and at the hands of your victims. Option one is a bit of a Crapshoot. Who knows what's in store? Option two is less of a surprise, and you can take comfort in the familiar faces of some of the people you'll be facing. As a little bonus, if you go with the second one and make it, you'll have a chance to live your best life. The choice is yours."

"What about the agreement we had? You said I'd get to race," Rich asks.

Roy's twist of enthusiasm becomes grim. "Well, consider yourself lucky. The agreement was far more binding; if you make it through this, you won't have to answer me. I will let you drive your life and control your destiny. If you hurry, there's a chance you might even get back to the race before it ends. I understand your burning desire to hit that track and win. Hell, I should know better than anyone. I raised you to be a winner. In the end, the option that suits your life best is your responsibility to choose, given free will and all."

Rich stammers, "I—I won't have to do this anymore? I'll be free ... and get to race, right?"

As Roy's voice dissipates into the static, he snarls, "Yes to all three. Now you must decide, are you a winner or a loser?"

Wincing, Rich slams his fist against the steering wheel. "I'm a winner, goddammit!" he says. "I'll be free from your bullshit, and I'll race and win come hell or high water."

The static inside the helmet falls silent. The choice has been made.

Left alone with his thoughts, he absorbs the quiet while his head hangs and gaze fixates on the dashboard.

With each deep breath, the vivid images of the nurse's bloodied face flood his mind, accompanied by a faint stirring from outside.

Suddenly, a door slams shut with a loud bang, startling him.

Rich's pocket makes a crinkling sound as he reaches to lock the door. Unsure of what it is, he shoves his hand inside. His fingers are met with cold metal and paper. Remembering it's the key from before, he pushes it aside and retrieves the folded page. It is the drawing of the house.

The darkness inside the truck makes it nearly impossible to read. He squints, scanning for the dark stick figure to check if it's still present, and, unable to interpret the shapes, glances at the porch light across the way. Warm and inviting, it gives three subtle blinks.

Seeing no other option, he takes a deep breath and, unlocking the car, opens the door and steps outside. As he fixates on the front entrance, he takes a moment of pause, listening for movement.

The muffled sound of the crickets' chirps echo from the stillness of the lake. As he takes off his helmet, the noises grow louder. Setting the helmet on the driver's seat, he carefully shuts the door. He knows if there is any hope of him surviving, he can't risk his uncle finding out his plan.

Large splashes in the lake cause waves to clash against the wooden dock.

Clutching tightly onto the map, Rich rushes toward the porch.

Whispers penetrate the darkness in every direction. "Tick, tock, tick, tock," they say.

He moves underneath the light. Frantically scanning the blueprints, his eyes dart across the page, searching for any pitfalls that await him, particularly the presence of the lurking dark entity. "Where are you?" he says. His attention lands on the wing of the home with the scribbled pitch-black room. "Are you in there?"

With a moan, the voices grow louder. "The Devil's playroom," they say.

Rich recalls opening his room door and expecting to see the entity, only to be greeted by his uncle's face, making him suspect they are one and the same. Stranded in a nightmarish predicament, he believes that unraveling the truth may be his only way out. He widens his eyes, lifting the map to the light, trying to see into the heavily shaded area. "There gotta be something in there he doesn't want me to see," he says.

The light flickers, illuminating something staggering in the distance.

"Shit," he says. Fighting his urge to look, he fixates on the map, memorizing the safest routes; he can feel it watching him.

"Tick, tock. Your time is running out," a voice screams.

Rich's hands shake uncontrollably as he slowly lowers the map, folds it, and tucks it back into his pocket while bellowing moans resound from all directions. He is careful to avoid sudden movements, and, raising his gaze, he scans the surroundings and sees many unclear shapes crawling toward him.

Amid their movement, they freeze, holding their inchworm positions. Perfectly still, they resemble trees and shrubs in the dark.

Holding his breath, Rich darts his attention to each of the shapes. He didn't notice any new additions to the landscaping when getting out of the truck.

With no time for investigation, he shifts his attention to the door. As he quickly reaches for the knob, he hears a small rock skip across the pavement and land beside his foot on the wooden porch.

A high-pitched screech follows, sending an icy shiver down his spine. "Tick, tick, tick," it says.

Rich turns to look and notices the shadowy shapes are closer than before. "What the fuck!" he says, squinting to see more clearly.

With an electric buzz, the light flickers, ushering in a slow, sporadic strobe effect.

Unable to see amid the moments of darkness, Rich hears the clamor of bare feet against the pavement. The light flashes again, illuminating the contorted shapes now closer than before.

Darkness descends upon him again, accompanied by more scurrying sounds.

Suddenly, the air crackles with an electric buzz and a blinding burst of light illuminates dozens of figures, one standing just inches away, wrapped in a damp and dirty sheet. Flooded with horror, Rich whirls around to face the door, desperately scrambling to get inside.

A scream leaves each cadaver's decayed lungs, alerting the others that he is trying to run. They join in, now rushing toward him. There are so many, and for the first time, something dawns on him: the lake was the dumping ground for the secret to Mason's success.

The sound of the door lock clicking startles him, but he swiftly enters and locks the deadbolt behind him. He takes a moment to catch his breath, leaning against the entrance and wiping sweat from his hairline.

The sheet-bound bodies thud against the wooden porch with each crawl and step. The heavy oak plank of the door rattles as they relentlessly beat their skulls against its surface, desperate to get in.

His heart pounding, Rich retreats slowly, his eyes fixed on the door. "Leave me alone. I didn't do a damn thing to you. Find Mason. He's the guy you're looking for!" he yells.

Suddenly, he hears a woman's voice behind him. "Hello, Rich," she says.

Not knowing whether to look forward or behind, he backs up until he collides with something cold and stiff.

The crackling of television static fills his ears.

"You can't escape your mama, little boy. You're gonna pay for what you did." The tone of her whisper shifts higher. A smell of rotten flesh accompanies her voice's demonic ringing.

Rich slowly pivots and, glimpsing the broken screen, stops. Skewed shapes of cars play across the jagged glass. The sight of the race causes his pupils to dilate, and through serrated shards, he notices her contorted grin.

"Come to Mama," Loretta says with a sneer.

Dodging her swinging arms, he glances in terror at the screen. Suddenly, he notices something he hadn't seen before—a shard at the bottom shows a countdown timer.

He can make out a skewed three, and the idea of an hour already slipping away rattles his nerves.

Letting out a wailing scream, Loretta charges toward him, her bare feet making a suction noise as they slap against the marble.

His heart races. "Just because you birthed me into this world doesn't make you my mama!" he says, dodging her grasp. While fending off her attack, he catches sight of the television chord dragging behind her.

He lunges and snatches it from the floor. "Go to hell," he says, giving it a hard yank. Loretta's limbs flail wildly as the force of the momentum propels her to the floor.

As he gives another heave, the chandelier sparks. Each flicker sheds a hint of brightness onto an electrical outlet.

"You've had your say. Now it's time for you to go," he says with a smirk, dragging his mother toward the wall.

The closer he gets to the wall socket, the more the air is filled with the harsh scent of bleach. Paying no mind to the sting and her flailing limbs, he grits his teeth and increases his effort, pulling harder, his eyes locked on his target.

"You think you're so special, but we're the same!" she shrieks.

Her squealing words leave a bitter taste in his mouth. "Shut the fuck up!" he shouts.

Then, without giving it a second thought, he shoves the plug into the wall. The scent of Loretta's seared flesh and burning hair fills the air as the screen sparks.

She remains motionless and silent.

A child's laughter echoes against the marble, followed by a thud near the steps. The muffled growls and snarls of the voracious creatures outside divert Rich's attention, causing him to glance at the door before shifting his focus to the staircase that leads to his room. As he looks up, he sees a woman's mutilated body slowly creeping toward him, already halfway down the stairs.

A horrified expression washes over his face as he looks at her. It is Ben's mother. "Why ... why are you here? I ... I didn't do shit to you."

She pauses, her fluorescent green pupils staring at him through the railing. There are no words, only the sound of her hissing breaths in response.

The shocking sight causes Rich to recoil and take a step back. Having a straight view of the back of the home, he notices the back door has been left open. As he looks closer, he spots a tall, shadowy figure lingering at the edge of the doorway.

It's the man from the dock. "Tick, tick, tick, tick, tick, tick, tick," he repeats, his body swaying back and forth. He ominously warns Rich, "No one can save you now."

Rich knows it's only a matter of time before the rest of the creatures find their way inside, and he doesn't want to tempt fate with Ben's mother, prompting him to bolt up the nearest staircase without thinking of its peril.

The man's demonic laughter rattles the crystal pendalogues of the chandelier. "Go ahead and run, but we'll hunt you down!" he says.

Rich runs faster, his heart pounding as the steps crumble behind him. As he springs off the last step, he feels the jolt of the carpet runner catching his foot, saving him from falling through a patch of rotten wood.

The entire staircase collapses, leaving a pile of ruins in its wake. There is no turning back.

He bends over, hyperventilating, struggling to catch his breath. Casting a glance at the dust cloud behind him, he rushes forward with a slight limp.

29

WHERE THE DEVIL HIDES

The more Rich distances himself from the staircase, the less chaotic things appear.

As he starts to relax, the delayed ache from his previous encounter with the carpet and faulty floorboards proves impossible to ignore. With no light, he finds it impossible to evaluate the injury on his foot or to determine how far he must go to reach a safe hiding place.

He continues onward without an end in sight, growing more exhausted with each struggling step, until a noise breaks through his slightly delirious state.

It is the rumble of a racecar's engine.

The vibration of the floor under his feet fully immerses him in a flashback. "Come on, Rich, focus," he says, shaking his head. "You don't have time for the bullshit. He's trying to throw you off. He wants you to fail."

A dim light emerges in the distance, luring him closer. He notices that the brightness is stronger near the ground and faintly spreads out in a rectangular form along its edges. "That's gotta be a door," he says, taking a deep breath. He forces himself to walk forward. A vibrant sound joins in as he gets nearer, causing him to quicken his pace.

The door's frame is chipped and covered in heavy scratch marks. It looks like someone has tried to cover-up the damage with more layers of paint, but they were unsuccessful.

As he stares at the botched repair job, he second-guesses going inside. "You wanna be free, don't you?" he asks himself; a prickling sensation makes the hair on his neck stand.

Static brushes against the air as a whisper fills the hall. "Tick ... tock." Disjointed; each heckling word has no rhythm, coming from different directions.

He rushes to grab the knob, his hand trembling with urgency, and with a swift turn, he opens the door; all goes silent. As a pungent stench of rot greets his nostrils, the sight of sheer darkness leaves him stunned. The disappearance of the light has transformed the space into a replica of the grim room in the drawing. "But ... it was just... the light was on," he says, thinking about the light under the door.

A low murmur ruins the silence. "Rich, Richie, Rich..." it says, coming from inside the room; its genderless tone is almost melodic.

"I'm not afraid of you," he says with a gulp. "No one, not even you, can stop me from winning. I'm gonna escape this bullshit and win my freedom and that damn race, no matter what!" Nervously extending his hand into the abyss, he bends his elbow and feels for the switch. Barely able to reach the mounted edge of the plastic striker plate, he stands on his toes and leans his upper body inside.

Out of nowhere, something slimy and callused grazes his cheek. A scream echoes loudly in his ear. "How badly do you wanna win?" it asks.

The demonic tone prompts Rich to move faster, frantically patting the wall until he finds and flips the switch.

The fixtureless bulb crackles and flickers before finally staying on above his head.

Disoriented, he jumps when something dangling touches his hair, prompting him to grab and pull it down. He anxiously laughs as the stickiness of the fresh fly strip clings to his hand. "You scared the crap out of me," he says, tossing it to the floor.

His eyes gradually rise, only to be met with a ceiling covered in insect strips dangling at various heights throughout the space. Each tacky yellow ribbon is covered in flies, both alive and dead.

To avoid another collision, he quickly ducks down while cringing at the sight of the insects, still buzzing and wriggling, as they try to break free. "Shit," he says, covering his head.

With a quick scan of the space, he is startled by the rocking horse in the middle of the room. His gaze drifts past it, landing on blankets and dust concealing what seems to be furniture. He knows this place well because he has been here before. "The kids' room? Wait ... but...how," he says. He vividly remembers the room being on the opposite side of the house earlier, confusing him.

A metallic rattling noise fills the room, immediately catching his attention. Looking down, he sees the black toy car rolling across the floor toward him. Its tiny wheels hit the toe of his shoe. In a panic, he kicks it away, his heart pounding in his ears.

The furniture has been pushed to the walls, creating an open space for a large, dark wooden crate. It is covered by a piece of white fabric that has been partially peeled back.

As Rich steps closer, childlike laughter fills the air. His eyes widen. "I gotcha now," he says, hobbling toward the box. He removes the sheet entirely and discovers that the crate has a tightly secured wooden lid nailed down on all sides.

Thinking he hears a knock coming from inside, he digs his fingers into the seams between the lid and base and pulls with all his might. Unable to pry it open, he turns, grabs the rocking horse, and bludgeons the lid with such force that it decapitates the horse, tearing its head from its body.

The stench in the room worsens, triggering him to cough uncontrollably. Sweat drips from his brow as he stares into the button eyes of the wooden horse's splintered head in his hands.

Quickly, he directs his attention back to the lid. The battering has fractured the top and loosened the nails. There is a cluster of hair sticking out through the smashed pieces.

Swiftly, Rich throws the horse's head to the side and, kneeling, smiles. "You smelly little shits. So you wanna play hide and seek? Well, ready or not, here I come," he says, pulling off the last bits of the top. Then, reaching inside, he quickly snatches the hair, giving it a vigorous yank. In one swift motion, he pulls out a crumpled, lifeless body.

The weight turns out to be much lighter than expected, propelling him to his feet. His head collides with the dangling fly strips. Paying no attention to them clinging to his hair, he holds out the object in front of him to examine it more closely.

A man's sagging face stares back at him. Stripped of his innards and skeletal framework, it takes on the likeness of a full-body latex mask with openings for the eyes, mouth, and ear canals. The color of the skin has been preserved through embalming, and its clothing is meticulously pressed and ready to wear.

Motionless, Rich tightens his grip on the hair and scrutinizes the familiar black ensemble. "Uncle ... Uncle Roy?" he says, gazing at the feet attached to a pair of black cowboy boots still resting in the box. Beneath them appears to be another layer of deflated flesh.

The sight of short brown hair makes his heart race, and he becomes frightened as he grabs a handful, unsure of the identity of the person it could belong to. As he removes it from the box, the smell of death overwhelms him, and he jerks back in terror upon seeing the nurse's familiar face with its thick brown mustache. He swallows back his vomit as he catches sight of another human shell beneath the nurse's, carefully folded and belonging to someone else.

The hair resembles Ben's mother's.

The entire crate is filled with preserved skins, each cut down the spines like a costume, making them easy to slip on.

Rich's mind is flooded with horror as he throws his gruesome discoveries back into the box. Swiftly, he gathers the lid pieces from the floor, accidentally pricking his finger on one of the rusted nails as he tosses them inside the box. "Shit," he says. He cleans the blood from the wound on his pants and hides the crate under the white fabric.

The light flickers.

"Tick, tock, tick, tock," a man's voice whispers. "You are next on the chopping block."

Rich stops, and noticing it coming from the direction of the box, he slowly turns to face it. "You don't know what the hell you're talking about. Things are different for me. Once I make it through this, I'm done."

"You're never free," the man says, hissing. "You belong to him."

The fermented casings join in, moaning, "He'll never let you go."

"But ... but... we made a deal," Rich says, flinching as his eyes nervously dart the room.

"If you didn't sign the deal, it's a lie. His words mean nothing!" they say in unison.

"When your contract expires, or he tires of you, he will strip you of your guts and bones and trap you forever in one of his putrid crates. Your only opportunity to breathe fresh air will arise if he chooses you for a dress-up session. Just like us, to him, you will be nothing more than another disguise to aid him in luring his victims and perpetuating his deceit," they say.

In a state of shock and disbelief, Rich scans his surroundings, his panic growing as he realizes that what he had assumed to be ordinary furniture might hold a far more sinister secret. Filled with a sense of urgency, he frantically rushes to yank off the sheets, desperately searching for evidence proving his assumptions wrong.

As he uncovers each item, he discovers a series of crates of varying sizes, neatly stacked on top of each other, with their lids securely nailed shut. Muffled knocks sound from each box, making them vibrate. Whatever is inside is trying to get out.

From his peripheral vision, Rich detects movement in the sheet covering the open crate.

Roy's skin slowly emerges from beneath the fabric. "Tick, tock," it says.

Rich sprints out of the door and into the hallway.

The corridor is filled with the echoing sound of the ticking clock.

Confused and in pain, he clenches his teeth as he heads toward the demolished stairway.

30

TAKE A SPIN

In a state of panic, Rich rushes down the hall and suddenly comes to a halt.

Out of nowhere, the ticks become louder, and when he covers his ears to concentrate, he finds they're originating from within his mind.

He looks down and sees the steps he climbed are intact, while the opposite side's staircase is destroyed. "What the..." he says. Completely turned around, he glances over his shoulder at where he came from.

The wood and gold accents have completely transformed, appearing fully restored.

His mind spirals. "What if they're right? I mean, I never signed the whole deal for my freedom or anything. What if this is some sort of trick?" he says, his words tumbling out faster as he envisions Roy's skin in the box. All at once, fury overwhelms him as he finally grasps the complete picture, and the weight of reality hits him. "That son of a bitch! That ... that was his plan all along! That's why he took the clock ... He didn't want me to leave... He sent me here to die."

Heavy footsteps sound behind him.

He nervously glances downward and swiftly surveys the foyer. Seeing that his mother is no longer there and having already tackled the other dangers mentioned on the map, he makes a run for it. "I gotta ... I gotta get outta here," he says, bolting down the steps.

Rich turns and sees Mason's silhouette standing on the top step.

"Where do you think you're going?" he shouts.

When Rich sees him in his racing suit, a surge of optimism washes over him as he is reminded of the race car waiting behind the garage door and a means of escape.

The number of doors has doubled; there are now two, one new and one old.

He glances back and forth between them, no longer concealed by the stairwell. The sight of the unrepaired wood brings a smile to his face as he recognizes it and knows it is exactly what he's looking for. "Let's get the hell out of here!" he says, sprinting for the door.

Hearing his movement, the creatures outside bash their skulls harder against the entrance, still trying to break it down.

Abruptly, Mason opens his mouth and releases a demonic scream. Vibrations from the high-octave pitch make the walls tremble, shattering the chandelier and the windows' glass. The creatures outside respond with bellowing howls and a frantic rush toward the new openings. As they squeeze through the frames, the jagged shards pierce the fabric, binding and tearing at them, resulting in a crimson mixture seeping through the cloth and dripping to the floor.

Rich thwacks his head as he rushes through the door and, clutching his temples, stumbles into the garage. "Dammit," he says as he loses traction under his boots and slides.

With a shrilling call, the creature's speed up, slithering over the wooden debris. Each of their howls is filled with a thirst for vengeance; they want blood.

As the sound of their approaching footsteps grows louder, Rich seizes the opportunity and propels himself through the car's open window. Landing inside, he is terrified as he gazes at the keyless ignition. Seeing the hole's shape, he quickly searches his pocket for the key he had come across before. "What do I have to lose?" he says to himself, hastily inserting it into the slot while holding his breath. The creatures slam their bodies against the garage door, causing him to jump with every thud, but he quickly turns his attention to the engine as it roars to life.

Drawn to the loud revving, the creatures tear the door from its hinges and lunge toward the car; their wet bodies produce shrill squeaks as they scurry against the marble.

As he glances in the rearview mirror, Rich shifts the car into reverse and, looking at the white garage door, lays his foot on the gas. He tightly closes his eyes. Ready for impact, he prepares for the noise of the thunderous crash.

Instead, he is met with the sound of the engine roaring and chaotic squealing rubber; he tightly grips the wheel. The sensation of a race helmet snug against his ears makes his heart pound.

As his eyes snap open, he is taken aback to find himself mid-race, no longer at the estate. He's back in control, his hands tightly gripping the wheel as he accelerates down the track's straightaway.

Cars surround him from his left, right, and behind, pushing two hundred miles an hour in a pack.

Filled with a mix of relief and terror, his instincts take over. Quickly glimpsing the oncoming marker, he shifts for the turn as static blares through his helmet's earpiece. "Hey, Rich, your car's handling seems off. We're suggesting you pull into the pit," a voice says. "Your tires might be getting too thin."

Immediately realizing it's not his uncle, he takes a deep breath. "Copy that ... Uh, how many laps to go?" he asks. "What's my time?" Out of the corner of his eye, he sees a car with forest-green paint and the number twelve edging up.

Frustrated by the crew's slow response, he tightens his grip. "How much time?" he asks sternly.

"Time won't mean shit if you blow a tire. You need to pull into the pit ASAP," the Crew chief responds.

Rich clenches his jaw. "I'm the one calling the shots. This is my fucking race, and I'll only ask you one more time. I need a time check ... now!" he says.

The Crew chief talks faster. "About ten minutes ... but before you say no. This isn't something to mess with, Rich. You already refused our last request. You are the one who wanted those damn soft tires. Don't push your luck. If one of them—"

With an irritated grunt, Rich turns onto the straight. "Goddammit, I am not stopping! That would throw the whole fucking race," he says. "I'm here to win this damn thing, not lose."

The Crew chief chimes in, "Yeah, but..."

Mid-sentence, Rich uses one hand to steer, unbuckles his chin strap, and rips his helmet from his head. "I'm done with people telling me what to do." He grumbles and throws the helmet to the side while keeping his eyes on the road. The hard-shell crashes against the cage and lands in the behind his seat, generating a loud clang that melds with the ticking of the countdown clock.

Thinking his mind is deceiving him, Rich readjusts his hold and concentrates solely on the engine's roar. "It's nothing," he says, dismissing the methodic beats, "just my imagination."

As he shifts gears and takes the lead, the helmet gains momentum, rolling across the floor and through a small puddle of murky water at the back of the vehicle, finally stopping on the edge of a white sheet.

Rich notices a slight decrease in handling and, being mindful of the tires, keeps a steady grip on the wheel until he regains control. "Where are you?" he asks, checking his sides for the number twelve.

A forest-green car approaches from his right back corner, matching his speed.

Rich deliberately nudges the wheel to veer a little closer. "Hello, Ben," he says. Smirking, he lightly taps his car. It swerves slightly to the right.

Watching the car recover, he imagines the shock on Ben's face and squeals, "How do you like me now? Huh?"

The clock's ticking grows louder, paralleling the volume of the road noise.

Rich's eyes widen as he takes in the sight of his friend's dented front bumper. "That'll show him who's in charge," he chuckles. The overwhelming joy he feels causes him to become complacent, unaware of what is happening behind him in the backseat.

A hand slowly emerges from beneath the tainted fabric. As its gloved fingers wrap around the cloth, it tugs the sheet out from under the helmet.

Rich bursts into laughter, feeling exhilarated. "I'm coming for ya!" he says, delivering another deliberate blow. The impact makes the cars rattle.

"I make the rules now!" Rich says. Glancing sideways, he notices that Ben's car has sustained more damage, including a noticeable dent on the side.

Rich feels a surge of adrenaline as he tightly grips the wheel, the revving engine igniting a fiery sensation in his stomach.

As the tick ... tock...tick...tock of the countdown clock reverberates louder, the car becomes more challenging to control.

Slowly, a hand in the back reaches out and pulls the sheet off its legs, unveiling a pair of sleek racing boots.

Fighting to regain traction, Rich acknowledges the rhythm with a smile. "Hear that? That sound means your time is up," he says. As he's about to ram Ben's vehicle again, he feels a raspy breath against his ear.

"Tick, tick, tick," a man's voice says; each word projects saliva laced with the stench of rotten eggs.

The whisper causes Rich's neck hairs to stand on end, but he remains focused.

With only minutes remaining in the race, he glimpses the foreboding sky, its dark clouds gathering ominously above. "What the—" he says, stammering.

"Tick, tock. That's the sound of my clock," the man says.

Rich's breath catches in his throat, and his body tenses as he glances in the rearview mirror and sees something stirring in the back of the car. The sight of a wet, dingy sheet covering whatever it is triggers a vivid flashback of the menacing creatures he encountered in the backyard of the Samuel's estate.

As the cloth falls away, it reveals a man dressed in a forest-green racing suit crouching behind him.

Fear grips him as he stumbles over his words at the sight of the uniform. "Be-Ben?" he asks.

Ben's devious smile is hidden behind his helmet while his pointed chin protrudes below the strap.

Rich's eyes dart back and forth, catching the glint of the embroidered number twelve on Ben's sleeve and the reflection of his face through his visor.

His eyes, with their fluorescent green hue and slivered pupils, bear a striking resemblance to a viper's.

The memory of his last conversation with Roy haunts Rich, and he grimaces at the thought of him snatching the clock away. He hid it, but not to protect him. It was because he was no longer the protagonist. It was meant solely for

Ben's eyes, counting down the time for him to complete his assigned task.

"Tick, Tock. Your time is up!" Ben says, and, with a snarl, he wraps his racing gloves around Rich's neck.

Struggling for breath, Rich stiffens his grip on the wheel and looks at the approaching markers on the wall.

They are turning the corner to the final stretch.

He guns it and shifts gears, monitoring his rearview mirror as the forest-green car falls into place right behind him. Fighting for air, he grimaces at the crinkling of the map in his pocket. "No way in hell I'm letting you win," he gasps, his face turning a shade of deep purple as he presses the pedal to the floor.

Then, without warning, his foot slams on the brake, causing Ben's car to crash into the back of his own, resulting in a violent flip of both vehicles and the instant release of the grip around his neck.

With a sudden explosion, Rich's fragile front right tire gives way. The deafening noise reverberates through the grandstands as his car is sent hurtling forward, end over end, with even greater speed.

Amid everything rushing by, he glances into the rearview mirror, finding nothing but emptiness behind his seat, before his gaze shifts to the cloudless, bright blue sky. With each flip, he is propelled closer to the finish line, passing the gasping crowd, and ultimately crossing beneath the checkered banners that hang above the track.

As the car comes to a stop, his body battered beyond recognition, the last thing he hears is the horrified screaming of the crowd, yet a smirk crosses his lips, knowing he's the first to finish.

He has won.

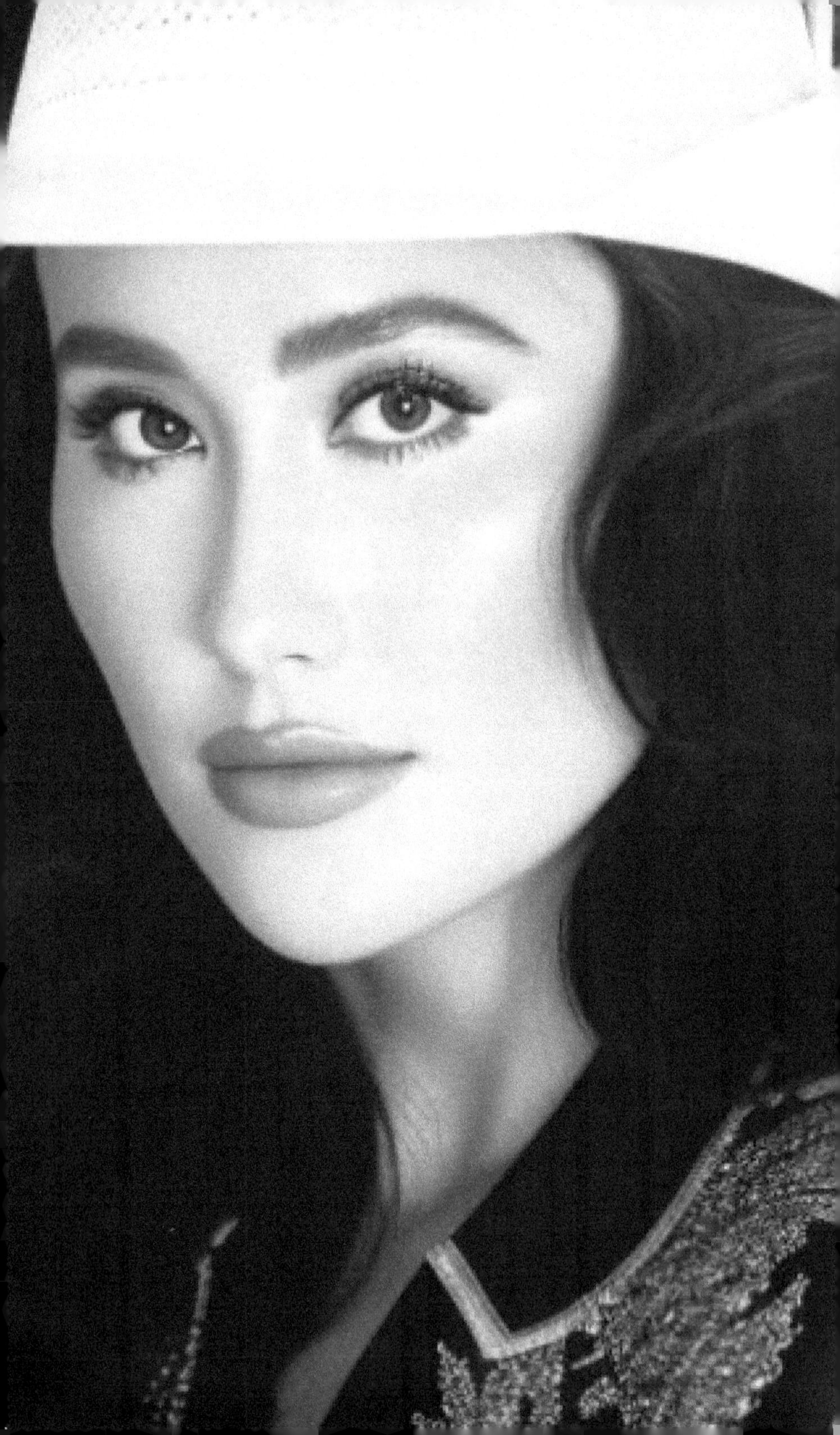

ABOUT AUTHOR

Brigitte, "Gitte," Tamar was born in a small rural Oregon town. Growing up, she was enthralled by scary tales featuring poetic tones and consistently gravitated towards writing darkened narratives. She graduated from Jesuit High School in Portland and attended Texas Christian University in Fort Worth, Texas until she won the title of Miss Oregon USA in 2015.

Once she finished competing in the Miss USA televised program, she received her business degree from Southern New Hampshire University. Then, her MA in Studies of Law from the University of Southern California, followed by graduate certificates in business law and entertainment law and industries.

As an author, she explores the harsh realities of social issues faced by today's generations. This includes the dark outcomes brought on by peer pressure, addiction, homelessness, mental illness, childhood trauma, and abuse. She feels it is essential to share narratives that refrain from sugarcoating the topics society tends to shy away from.

Many of Tamar's published works have been reviewed by critics and production companies, including BroadwayWorld. Her most recent novel, "Hel," released in July 2023, was featured by Mystery Tribune as one of July's best crime and mystery books to watch for.

Also, her most recent children's picture book, "The Lonely Ghost," is a recipient of the prestigious Mom's Choice Award.